ADAM

ADAM

by

DAVID DAVILA

ARPress
ILLUMINATING IDEAS.
EMPOWERING VOICES

ARPress
45 Dan Road Suite 5
Canton MA 02021

Hotline: 1(888) 821-0229
Fax: 1(508) 545-7580

Ordering Information:
Quantity sales. Special discounts are available on quantity purchases by corporations, associations, and others. For details, contact the publisher at the address above.

Printed in the United States of America.

ISBN-13:   Paperback   979-8-89356-289-7
                  eBook   979-8-89356-288-0

Library of Congress Control Number: 2024903338

Table of Contents

CHAPTER I

It sounded like thunder overhead the explosion from the Coast Guard ship echoed out like a huge bomb. The back lash was heard throughout the Metropaleton area of Portland Or. The fear of the end of the world entered people's minds. The world as we've known it was coming to a horrible end at this is what they thought. The end. The end of days revelation was taking place. The fear of or demise? Was the time of the predictions of the world ending taking place now? Was the prediction of World War III upon us? People coward away in their own thoughts letting fear overtake them. Fear shot through us before even getting the information from a dependable source. Panic,fear, setting in like a plague letting one think the worst scenario at hand.

The thought that we had just gone under a terrorist attack. In the Willamette River the fiery inferno of the U.S Coast Guard ship could be seen for miles. It could be seen in all directions. The black, gray plumes of smoke bellowed out like a monster devouring the sky. The smoke took many unimaginable forms. The smoke ascended upward into the sky. Faces of demons, animals, forming as the smoke thickened and bellowed out. Fire trucks, cop cars, and ambulances sirens, cried out their cry of and emergency. Firemen in their yellow fire suits jump out of the fire engines before they had come to a complete stop. They moved rapidly wasting no time. For time was of the essence. They took ladders, fire hoses, axes, then rushed towards the firey inferno. To them it was like walking through hells gates. They worked in unison like ants in an ant farm each men taking care of what their responsibility was. The smoke darkened the rising sun in the sky engulfing the light. Several reporters arrived and hurried to be the first to take a photograph of evil the surrounding the ship. It was Tabloid material. Pictures of the underworld was news and pictures meant money. A lot of money. Catching a face of an evil demon looking out over the city of roses would be front page material. And news is what readers wanted.

CHAPTER 2

Meanwhile back at the shoreline of the Willamette River, Pete, and Johnny rolled over on their backs drench from head to toe with the river water. The earthy fish smell hit their nose.

Johnny moaned as he grabbed his right leg. The pain shot through him like a hot electrical shock. Even with the excitement the pain was still there. He could still smell the strong stench of fish coming from the water. The stench of the fish lingered on him. Pete turn towards Johnny to take a look at his wound. Blood ran out of Johnny's leg to fast for Pete.

"Detective it looks bad," Dr. Robis says as she coils her hair as if to make a ponytail as she strains the water out of it.

"Johnny try and sit up. Give me your shirt." "What the fuck you say."

Pete smiled then said, "Just give me the shirt Johnny."

"It's a thirty dollar shit you mad?"

"Johnny I don't know how bad the wound is but you are losing a lot of blood. It's the thirty-dollar shit or kiss your ass goodbye."

Johnny hesitated for a moment then took off his shirt. He handed it to Pete reluctantly. Pete scrutinized the wound then spoke as he began to tare straps of cloth from the shirt.

"You know I did like the shirt. Blue silk and skeleton print down the shoulders."

Pete wrapped the wound as best that he could making sure that the straps were tied tight.

"Thirty-dollar shirt." "I know it hurts Johnny."

"I've been hurt worse but the shirt," he said then grabbed his leg as he felt a sharp pain.

Johnny moaned then lay back on the ground. He lay silent for several minutes. He looked up at the darken sky. One of the firemen with something in his hand walks up to Pete. He stops handed what appeared to be a journal to Pete.

"I think this is for your eyes-only detective. It seems that they are the doctor's notes. I read some of it then stopped. Too much crazy shit, all mumble, jumble to me. I only deal with fires detective."

"Thanks," Pete says then reaches out for the book.

"You need some help getting up the incline young man."

After a moment of silence Johnny moaned then forced himself to stand. He could hop up the incline he thought to himself. He attempted to walk suddenly he felt a sharp searing pain shoot upward from the ankle to his butt. He stopped moaned out holding his buttock. He sat back down thinking. If the wound was on his calve how did the pain go to his ass. Pete smiled at him thinking the young machismo bull. The fireman saw two of his crew. He yelled out to the two men moving quickly past him.

"You two get a stretcher up here for this man a.s.a.p. Get him immediate attention to his leg."

The fire men turned back around then moved back towards the fire truck. Moments later the firemen returned with the stretcher. They hauled Johnny up to the ambulance. Pete looked out over the river then back at the journal in his hand. He wondered what the fireman had read that had made him stop reading. What did the journal have that he didn't already know? Still he knew there was more he needed to know. The rest of the story. All of it from beginning to the end. There was no debating on whether or not to read what was inside. He was curious. The want to know outweighed anything else. He opened it and began to read. The writing inside started off with an introduction. Dr. Robis scrutinized Pete for a moment but remained silent.

CHAPTER 3

The entry in the journal started off with and introduction.

"My name is Jeffrey E. Mongroll II. Occupation: Geneticist. Date of entry into this log is June 1st two thousand and seventeenth. The time as I look at my watch is 9:45 p.m. I start my story of woe from the very start. From the very beginning of the whole ordeal. I write down all that has happened up to the very end. Psychic no. I just know what I must do. I anticipated the outcome of the end. I write down in these last pages of this journal as I await my own demise. My demise at the hands of my creation. At the hands of my child per say."

Pete stopped reading for a moment looked out over the swirling water of the Willamette River as it moved along. Deep in his thoughts he contemplated what to do with the journal for a few minutes. He turned his gaze back at the pages in the journal. He began to read again. The pages where hard to grasp and to flip over. It was amazing he had not torn a page of as yet. The pages had been soaked at the lower right corner. Pete continued to read.

As humans we fall from grace on occasions. We do what is wrong instead of what is right. As they say we pay for what we sow. I hear Adam approaching now. Its rat claw like feet scrapping along the ships floor. I am scared yes. But I have no other recourse. I must hurry I must prepare for the end. I will explain in as much detail as I can. I begin with myself. Then my colleagues for I want you to know them as I did. I loved and considered life as being good. It was my lost and my hurt that my brain fed on. I want you to know why I was compelled with the ideal of creation. And of the possibility of new life. Of a new kind of human race. Of a race that did not hate or that would get sick from an unknown disease. But a creature that would live through all diversities. I will now begin with who I am. I will divulge all that is needed for one to understand why I was driven to the verge of insanity.

My name is Jeffrey E. Mongroll II. I come from a long line of doctors. Starting with my great grandfather, grandfather, father, mother, and now I Jeffrey E. Mongroll. My father was a prominent doctor in the field of the brain. My mother Janice

T. Mongroll renowned in the medicine field of cancer. I went deeper into medicine. I went to where it all begins. I choose to be a geneticist. I was their only son and they were very proud of me. I studied hard I skipped a couple of grades in elementary. Then a few in high school. I guess one could say I was above average. I guess the word smart or genius will work as well. Conceded not really. The truth is the truth. I am of a medium build somewhat short and chubby. My hair is long down to my shoulders that I tie into a ponytail. My eyes are hazel going more to the green shade. My friends that are the friends that I had teased me. They would say that I looked like Segal. Of course this was during my freshman year in college. I like to agree with them most of the time. But the truth be spoken. I have no real ideal why they even thought that I looked like him. Maybe it was just a joke. Or maybe what brought it on was that I had said that I could wipe the floor up with him. Whatever the reason had been. I am still quite amused by the thought. Now days I only have two people that I call friends true friends.

Mary Gomez and Jacob Lee. The reason for me to document this into the journal is for whom ever finds this journal to understand what occurred. And what drove me to become the monster that I turn into. It was pain, sorrow, and the loss of my beloved father that drove me. I loved my father dearly his lost was as if someone had driven a spike through my heart. My father passed away from cancer. I saw my mother cry literally pulling out her hair with despair. Here she was one of the best doctors having the knowledge to cure cancer.

In her eyes she had fail her husband. She knew and understood the disease. But it still ate away at her soul. With all the knowledge, equipment, at hand with the new meds. Whit the radiation treatments it still took him from her. After my father died my mother followed a few months later. It was love of the purest kind. The kind that kills. Without his love she died of loneliness. This is the simplest way to relate why my mother died.

Mary. Mary was my lover, my colleague, and companion. Mary was a few inches taller than I. She was one of the most beautiful Mexican American that he had ever seen. She had long black hair down to her waist. The color of her hair accented her oval face and her full Latin lips. Lips that where meant to be kissed. She had a beautiful bronze tan. Her eyes a soft brown that could melt butter literally. Mary was born here in Portland. She had lived in the migrant camps. I had been born with a silver spoon in my mouth as they say. It was a hard life for a migrant worker. But somehow, she managed to excel in her studies. Mary was the only one in her family to go to school or college. Whenever there was a teacher parent conference she would have to attend as well. Mary would be her parent's translator. Everything the teacher would tell her she would repeat to her parents in Spanish. For many years after school she would join her father and mother in the fields. Mary did not mind the hard tedious work. What hurt Mary the most was the words from the white kids. She knew it was not the words of children but the words of their parents. She used to say. Children see no color for the world is what God had created for them. It was a world of diversity of color.

Children do not care of one's skin color. To children everyone is equal this is and instinct that humans loose later in life. That is why they say that children are the things that are closer to God. People as they get older become hateful, ignorant, and they begin to lose the understanding. The understanding the meaning to the words of God. Funny she would say if my heart fails give me one from a Black man or Hispanic. I don't care if it is from an alien. If the heart is compatible I would say.

"Just give me the fucking heart I want to live."

I used to laugh out loud when she explained the world through her eye to me. In a way she hit it dead on the head of a nail. Once she had heard a kid talking how Mexican people were taking the jobs away from Portlander's. I guess she could not take it any longer. She exploded this is of course what she had related to me. She wanted me to understand her.

"If you want the jobs in the fields then why in the hell haven't you done so?" In all the years you've been here you could have gone out to work in the fields. Sweated from the hard work for a lousy penny. Mexican people take jobs that most people are too proud to take. These are jobs nobody wants. American's do not lower themselves to slavery. People here want high paying jobs right off. It is just the need with in themselves to attack one for their own selfishness. For the satisfaction of their own egos. The thirst for it is greater that the need to take the jobs."

I loved to hear her explain things for I could see the passion and the anger in her words. The way we met was as well a fairy tale in its own. I can recall the day as if it were just yesterday. I went in to one of the corner stores to get coffee before class. I walked down one of the isles down to the far right corner of the store. I stopped in front of the soda cooler that hummed away softly. I turned walked up to the coffee dispenser. I placed a cup into position I pressed one of the buttons for chocolate. I filled the cup half-way then went to the coffee side and filled the rest of the cup. I grabbed the cup into my hand. I walked a few steps then stopped. I turned and grabbed a back of chips of the rack. I then turned back around. I began to walk to the cashier. I was not looking where I was going. My head pointing down at the cup of coffee. Suddenly time stopped abruptly my coffee flew out of my cup as if it had life of its own. It was as if it were flying out spilling all over Mary's white blouse in slow motion. She wore a white blouse and black pants.

I remember it well. I apologized over and over more than I have ever done in that short span of time. I could feel the eyes of people on me that had just walked in on the episode. I walked up to the cashier. I looked back up at Mary and apologized again.

"I get it. I get it you're a klutz and you are sorry."

Next without thinking I took out my handkerchief. I began to wipe off the spilled coffee off her blouse. I have to chuckle a little as I write this down. As I said before without thinking I began to wipe the coffee off her blouse. My hand ran down the contours of her bosom, breast, tits, one in the same. Mary smiled I guess she must of seen me blushing when I realized were my hand was and what it was doing. She looked at me with her beautiful brown calve eyes then spoke.

"Look klutz I have a class I have to attend. I have about forty-five minutes to get back home then back with a clean blouse."

I had to do something it had been my fault. I asked here where she lived. I ask how far she had to go. She told me. I asked her the name of the professor. She gave me the name by pure luck it was the same professor I had. We were in the same class. I quickly told her that is where I was heading. She looked stunned for a moment. She smiled then there was a short pause.

"You're a little young aren't you to be attending the class?"

"Yes, but just the same I am in that class," I replied back.

"Genius?"

Call it coincidence or fate I took fate I quickly responded.

"Yes, but I am a genius with a car. So let me drive you home to change."

"We don't have much time."

"Look if you are late why not have, company." "Okay, but first tell me your name. So, I don't feel like a stranger is taking me home."

"Jeffery Mongroll, at your service." "Okay just don't get weird on me."

She smiled I was hooked, hook, line, and sinker. Our love flourished. It was as if we had known one another before in a previous life. I know it sounds corny. But that is the way I felt. Love has no restricting bounds. After college I updated some genetic principals. I was on my way. I was offered a grant by the government. I accepted. Mary followed me she worked by my side though we never married. I once hear her talking to some of our friends.

"Jeff is my better half I love him dearly," she told them.

I guess our friend must have been trying to see if he could hook up with her. I was on cloud nine. I loved Mary and she loved me is all that mattered. As I mentioned before I was born into money.

Funny thing is that she had said that even though I had money she preferred that we do things on our own. If we made millions, then we would be whole. I never quite understood that. I guess she wanted to be independent. She wanted to make her own fortune then we could be equal. I loved her so. So, on occasions I took money out of the bank. I bought her whatever her heart desired or needed.

Jacob Lee my colleague and dear friend. Jacob was a thin man of

Chinese descent. He loved to play chest. He had brown eyes he spoke with a heavy oriental accent. I found it humorous but I never smiled when he spoke. What I would do was to turn around. Of course he knew what I was doing.

He would bellow out.

"I speak the way I speak Jeff and as long as you understand what I say it is all that matters."

"I know Jacob," I would reply back as I turned around.

"Up yours Jeff I never heard people speak like you and Mary."

"You're right," I would say and everything would be as before.

After being close friends and working together for quite a while I knew he did not really care. We were family. To him I spoke funny with a southern accent he called it cowboyish. After college I divulged my thoughts with him. I told him what I had seen what I was going to attempt. He of course at the time had other plans. He explained that the time was off for he was to continue his studies under one of the prominent doctors in New York. He was to study the nervous system, blood vessels, everything to do with the heart. I understood I respect Jacob's decision. I told him that I would have a spot open for him whenever he came back. It had been four years since I had laid eyes on my friend. One day out of the blue as I drank a cup of coffee. I suddenly heard a knock on the door. There was a big button for the doorbell why hadn't they used it? I was curious so I got up went to the door. When I opened up the door I was not only happy but I was surprised as well. Jacob had returned. Of course I wasted no further time. I hugged my friend told him to come inside.

"Want a cup of coffee Jacob." "Yeah, sure I love a cup."

We sat and I offered him the job and this time he accepted. Jacob was everything one should strive for. As I got to know him I found out that while I went home to a mansion he went to a job. He put himself through school working two jobs. How on earth did he even get sleep? Only Jacob knew the answer to that. I envied Jacob especially when I found out more of his life. I found out that he would go home after work hours to tend to his mother. His mother had been hit by a drunk driver several years back. She was coming home with groceries and was blind sighted. It was the price she paid for some drunk who's only reward the next day would be to puke his brains out. I respected him. I knew he was hungry for knowledge.

I knew as well that he wanted to make a name for himself as I and Mary. I knew this for we were a lot alike. All his worries would be over for we were on our way. Our experiments and our success exceeded those from other doctors in the study of genetics. Our discoveries where on the best science magazines. But we were not done. We wanted to do something no one could ever accomplish but us. I miss my beloved Mary and my dearest friend Jacob. I am alone now in this world of sickness. My friends cradled six feet under in the securing arms of mother earth. Oh how I miss them. How lonely I feel at this moment. It is not an important factor on how I feel. What is important is for me to recall as much of the story that I can. You will soon know what happen and who and what Adam is. My thoughts weigh heavily on my soul. I now scan the interior of this drab green room. I alone am responsible for all the death that has occurred. I alone am responsible for what is still to come.

"God forgive me for what I have done."

CHAPTER 4

I don't have much time. I will begin at the very beginning of this horrible ordeal. I will relate my feelings as well as my thoughts as I go along. Disease, disease, was a curse word to my mind. Diseases appalled me so. I hated it's many existence for it had taken my beloved father away from me. The disease that took him was cancer.

Cancer ate away at his flesh. It ate away slowly until it left nothing of the man. He was nothing but a mere skeleton with dried up skin looking back at one. His eyes once full of life and joy now sunken back into their sockets. Dark shadows surround his eyes. His face stricken with what was to come. That was death. Its ugly face imprinted deeply into my brain. In my mind I could almost see the reaper standing next to my dear father. My beloved father looked more like a ghoul than human. In a way it was like seeing the walking dead in a hospital bed. I will never be able to erase the image from my brain. No, no matter how hard I try. I recall it as if it where today. The thoughts eat away at my soul. I loved my father and to see him die in that manner was devastating. All I could think of was that diseases sprout now days like wild weeds. It flourishes blooming on contact with society. Spreading without discretion. Killing no matter what religion, race, or creed. I guess it was what you would call an equal opportunity killer. Some infections were curable while others like aids, cancer, seem to get stronger with time.

In my thoughts it was as if the devil himself had sent its plague of death upon humans out of its spite for love. It sent these impurities and sickness into the people. Even one's mind was polluted with hate instead of love. And without love there was no respect. And without respect who cared what one gave or caught from another human.

Mankind was now living in his or her own hell living in fear. Was revelations being fulfilled who really knew? I just felt that it was time to help mankind. I was determined to help us survive without fear. I wanted to give that edge over illness over the unknown diseases that people were dying of. I had to help I had to do something anything. I had to stop the devil and its corruption. I became possessed. It was driving me with a blind passion. Hence, I began my research at night for knowledge. I hunted for the right specimens to begin my experiments. Humans. I quickly came across several of the so call people of the night. The poor disillusioned. They needed answers perhaps the word closer to describe their need was that they needed hope. They were the repressed the lonely beings struggling to stay alive. Fighting with in themselves struggling with their minds. They were contemplating whether or not to commit suicide. The chemicals, chemicals, man had made to keep himself at a stalemate with the world.

The drugs purpose was only to keep man at check never allowing man or woman to checkmate. There were only two ways to win. One was to go get medical attention and go through the horrible ordeal of withdraws. The other of course was death. Why would man take drugs that ate away at their very souls? Drugs a parasite that just eats away leaving nothing. Leaving only the poisoned shell behind. People of all races use drugs. But it only deceive them in believing that their problems will go away. That is what they believe but the hard truth is that their problems will come back tenfold. It will haunt them in their nightmares. Nightmares of the devil clawing away at their flesh. Clawing and clawing never letting them go. The devil is never satisfied.

Never. It wants all human minds until it destroys any decency left. The question I ask is there such a thing as a devil? Perhaps! I can only relate the feeling. I had when I went to a recovery hospital. I entered through the double doors to the building. No sooner had the doors close behind me when I felt an entity. An entity like an invisible blanket that made me feel as if my skin were dirty. I could hear awful screams of pain from several room down the corridor where the patients detoxing.

Men, women, that where just in a couple of days into the withdraw stage. It was their trip through hell from the drug addiction. The hurt, the pain, my heart died for them. The stench of puke as well as the medication that they were administering to them lingered in the air. The pungent smell hitting my nose like one of the strong nasal sprays. I took it one step further I had to know. I was allowed to talk to one man that had just made it through withdraws a couple of days ago. I asked him questions? He began to explain in detail his experiences. He recounted the nightmares of the demon he saw. He did not want to say the devil.

But he later in the conversation said Lucifer. He said it reached out to him as it called out to him as it slashed at his flesh. Who really knows what the individual really goes through? Maybe nightmares caused by the guilt? Guilt for destroying the temple that holds the blessed spirit that God has given us. Or did the devil really reach out to them. Did the devil enter their mind somehow grasping hold of their thoughts and dreams? Confusing them making sure that the person would be lost from all feelings. The only way that I could see to save mankind was to make him pure again. As in the beginning. And the only way to accomplish this endeavor was to experiment on human life. Experiment at any cost. I had experimented on animals of all sorts. They could not give me the answers I seeked. I could not wait any longer God knows that I had tried. I tried to get answers from them. I tried relentlessly but there were no signs, no hope, nothing. I tried to structure certain animals together hoping for a breakthrough. It all had to do with genetic acceptance. I could not reconstruct or manipulate their D.N.A. If their genetics where not compatible they were just not. All I had to show for my work was failure after failure. I had no choice but to use the one specimen that I was trying to save. And as I mention before that one specimen was to be man himself. There was just no more time or recourse. Therefore I began my hunt for human specimens.

Like a plague I began to stalk the streets of Portland Or. The beautiful city of roses. At night I became the grim reaper of death. I did not even fear the law. I was above it in away. If it came down to the law intervening all I had to do was show them papers. What it came down to was a matter of a signatures on a dotted line. A binding contract between doctor and patient. It would be an agreement that they chose to be my guinea pigs. Yes. By their own free will and consent. It was all legal. It was just a legality to stay out of jail. The constitution did say one had the right to choose. It is what this country is based on.

Freedom. The only two things for certain are? We are given life the other is we die. It is forth coming. It is waiting out there for everyone. I had brought forth something more horrifying than any element that this world has ever encountered. I had created Adam. I wonder now who was the real monster? Adam that killed by pure innocent instinct? Or myself that killed knowing that it was wrong? I used many excuses to convince myself that my purpose was honorable. I kept telling myself that it was to eliminate all illnesses. To make man as in the beginning. To make a new and improved man, and undying man.   Once again man could live to be in his hundreds. I was going to make it possible. It was as if something had grabbed my brain and was maneuvering it. Pulling on it like strings on a puppet. The difference between the puppet and myself was that the puppet has no choice. It moves on command of the strings. I on the other hand did. I knew what was right and what was wrong. I became the disease that I was trying to cure. I became the disease that had fallen on humanity. Every night like Jack the Ripper I preyed on life. I walked amongst the night people along the Waterfront walkway in downtown Portland. I found my first two specimens lying down on one of the benches along the waterfront next to the Willamette River. The night lamp above gave life to my shadow. As I walked along the walkway my shadow could be seen behind me.

Moving after me as the river glistened so peacefully. I walked up to a man first then to a woman. It was easier than I had thought. I offered them money they accepted without question. Yes. It had been that easy. Who would have anticipated that? The fact was how easy it was to lure them into the spider's den. The man was in his late thirty's. He wore tattered worn-out clothes that hinted he cared not for his life. And the smell generating for this man told me he probably hadn't taken a bath for quite some time.

His face was older than what it should be. The woman was in her early thirty's as well. She wore a red mini skirt, white stockings, over well shaped legs. She wore enough make up for two women. By this I determined that she had to be a hooker. The amount of perfume just added to the fact. She was a red head and very attractive. As I walked my specimens to the van hardly any words had passed between us. We reached the van where Mary and Jacob waited. Jacob brought me the briefcase then opened it. I took the papers out handed each their copy to sign. They put down their signatures on the dotted line. I said hop in. Before they entered the woman put her hand out.

"Money first."

"Payment up front wise," I said.

The man put his hand out as well. I paid them the five hundred dollars that I had promised.

Receiving the money, they climbed in. She put her money between her boobs. The man just shoved the money into his pocket. I waited for them to climb in. They buckled up before we drove away. It did not take us long to arrive at our destination. I drove slowly up on the half-moon driveway up to the front doors. I stopped I cut the engine took the keys out of the ignition open the door and climbed out. I waited for everyone. We escorted them into the mansion. I move in a rapid mode. I went in and walked straight to the lamp on the far wall. I moved it to the right. There was some sounds of creaking as the trap door lifted to one side. I climbed down the stairs leading into the laboratory. They followed me down. The woman looked around before taking a step.

"Fucking Monsters," she says.

"Good television series the monsters. Aren't you a little young to know about the monsters?" I ask.

"Yeah, but my parents watch it on one of the cable channels."

"Yeah that was a good program," said the transient in a drunken slur.

"Please," I said and motioned them to the metal tables in the center of the room as I pointed to them.

CHAPTER 5

It was now to begin there was no turning back. Mary assisted them to the tables.

"Please disrobe and put these hospital garments on then climb onto the tables."

Mary went to the computer sat down. She then began to punch in data. Like a child with a new toy, I scrubbed my hands. I prepared for the experiment I was excited. I look towards Mary and waited for the okay sign to continue.

"It's all yours," she said as she tilted her head to look at me.

"You sure have an elegant home doctor," said the transient slurring every word still in a drunken stuper.

He began to take off his clothes. His pants fell to the floor. He took off his shirt and dropped it. I turned looked at the naked man. His body was cover with sores, chest, arm, legs, I believe his entire body. This was what I have been looking for. It was the kind of illness I was searching for. It was what I was trying to prevent. He placed the hospital gown on then paused before he climbed onto the table.

"Hey, hey, doc., you wouldn't have something to drink would you?"

"After the experiment can't have you drinking alcohol it will interfere with the medicine."

"I can wait doc."

"This mansion must have cost you a lot," says the redhead.

I noticed that the woman was quite attractive in fact I caught myself staring at her. I have to say that she was well endowed in the upper region. And how well-endowed was exposed when she opened her white blouse then dropped it to the floor. She removed her bra letting it fall to the floor. I do not have a clue on why she chose to be a hooker.

But I do know by looking at her that she had everything going for her. And she could have made more by being a porn star. Funny world. She climbed onto the table.

"Not, really the mansion was a gift from my parents," I answered.

I walked in between the operating tables. I saw the look of fear growing on their faces as reality began to sink in. I spoke to them to make them feel more at ease. I ask questions of them so that they could enter the conversation.

"The metal is cold doc.," said the redhead.

"You got that right," agreed the transient. "It will warm up to your body temperature. I assure you."

Everything was going as planned. I nodded my head and Jacob placed the electrodes in position on their bodies. Two electros went to the temples, two went to the heart. Mary punched in more data into the computer. She watched the monitor's screen. Jacob reached for a syringe on the crash cart. He tilted the bottle holding formula A. He pushed in the needle through the rubber stopper.

He pulled back on the plunger filling up the syringe. He handed it to me. I brought the needle up eye level then pressed the plunger. A jet stream of formula shot out of the needle. I looked at the young woman then said.

"Girls, first now close your eyes and hold out your arm."

I inserted the needle into the crook of her arm into her vein. She flinched. I placed my thumb on the plunger and pushed. The liquid shot out freely like a tiny water fountain into her vein. If this compound worked? It would be the formula that would create the new human species. It would change everything as we know it. I gave the last push and administered all the compound into her. I repeated the procedure on the man. I watched as they became unconscious oblivious to this world.

"Jacob get them into the straps for protection."

I watched them scrutinizing every twitch every hair. I watched as they laid still as if dead. All I could do from this point was to observe and hope, hope for success. Three hours later it came there was a slight movement of the fingers. In the time it took me to jot down what was happening into the journal it happened. The patient's bodies began to thrash around wildly. If it wasn't for the restricting straps I had told Jacob to put on them after they fell into a deep sleep. They would have fallen off the tables. I looked at my watch three hours later my disappointment was my reward.

"Increase the plasma flow," I yelled out urgently.

I stood up from the stool. I began to make my way up to the patients. I could see it had been futile for all ready foam was slowly oozing out of their mouths like rabid dogs. Something was causing a chemical imbalance with in them. Something I had to eliminate.

"It's not working Jeff." Jacob shouted.

He rushed to the other side of the table. He began to work on the man. Mary looked at the vital signs as they went berserk. I watched in silent I knew it was another failure. I watched their body's spasm jerking upward with their last breath of life. A final moan escaped from their lips then the bodies relaxed with death.

"Monitor went blank Jeff."

If I could only express the disappointment. Yes, I felt disappointed instead of sadness. Or remorse for these two specimens. I had one purpose in life, and it did not matter any longer I had to succeed. My two guinea pigs had been a disaster. But like all experiments the first few will always be failures I convinced myself. I could not stop now. I had to make it right for the two that had just died. I had to release man from his weakness.

I was on the verge of rage. I would not fail again. Night after night I went out, I found new specimens. But all that happen was failure and disaster. I could not turn back. As for my colleagues? I regret to say that it was as well too late for them. They had agreed to help me. But they had not thought of what the penalty would be. They were now caught in a web without a way out. I sold them a bill of goods they bought in. Now there was no returning to the life they once knew. For that pot of gold sacrifices have to be made. Several days later the morning newspapers front page headlines read in bold black letters. "Nancy Smith missing." Her picture dead center on the front page. It had been the woman we had in the lab. I dropped the paper on the table took a sip of my coffee. I took a bite of my scramble eggs. I stood went to the far wall. I moved the lamp to the right. The trap door open I walked back down into the laboratory. Mary and Jacob where all ready in the lab taking care of the patient's disposal.

"Jacob, Mary did you see the paper." "Yes." Jacob replied then Mary.

"We have to be more careful in the future not to be seen. The less one sees the better for us."

We continued with our endeavor and still there was no success.

CHAPTER 6

A week later we brought in another young girl. She had to be in her late teens. I assumed she must have been a runaway trying to survive the streets on her own. She was one of the lost night people. Alice would be the first specimen to come the closest to being perfection. Perfection. I had approached her as she walked towards me in downtown China district. It was a few blocks of oriental stores and restaurants. It was just a few minutes before midnight. Only a hand full of bars remained open. Several men staggered out of one of the bars. But Alice walked alone without fear. It was as if she did not care of the dangers. Or the danger of being a woman along. She had blonde hair and the brightest green eyes I had ever seen. She was wearing a white poke a dot print dress. I rushed my steps leaving my colleagues behind. I quicken my steps ever more so until I was walking a long side of her. She gave me a glance then continued on speeding up her stride.

"Excuse me," I said.

She stopped abruptly gave me one of the coldest looks. There was a pause of silent. Ther was the awkwardness then she spoke.

"What? She asked.

She stopped crossed her hands in front of her chest. I could tell she was a little mift by her demeanor.

"Are you alone?" I ask.

She looked around then back at me.

"What the fuck mister? Are you fucking blind? Do you see anyone else besides you and those creepy people following you and me?"

I looked at my colleagues then back at her and smiled. "Okay. I have to say that was a dumb question. Listen to what I have to say. Just give me two minutes of your time. And if you do not think it is your cup of tea you can continue on you marry way. And I will not inconvenience you any longer."

"My cup of tea huh."

She gave a bored look as she moved her foot tapping the ball of the foot on the pavement. She spit gum out of her mouth. She looked at me for a moment.

"First mister what is your name?"

"My name is doctor Jeffrey Mongroll. And what is your name?"

"My name Jeff is Alice. So tell me mister what is it you really want?"

"I would like to hire you for a study that I am doing."

"You some kid of freak mister? Just ask me flat out if I am a hooker Jeffrey."

"Hold up Alice," I said then reached out and grabbed her hand before she walked away.

She looked down at my hand gave me an angry look. I released my grasp.

"Let's walk Alice."

"What the hell! What the fuck you think we have been doing."

Mary and Jacob chuckled softly amused. "Girl has a vocabulary," Mary tells Jacob. "Yeah, she sure does," Jacob agreed.

"What are you doing out here so late at night?" "What now you are my mother mister?"

"Just trying to have a conversation."

"I'll make it quick. I ran away from home couldn't you tell Jeffrey being a doctor and all. Now are you going to call the cops?"

Mary stepped up to walk along with us.

"Look, I am not a hooker. So if you are cops buzz off."

"No, where not cops. But how would you like to make good money."

"Money now that I can use. How much money we talking about."

"Five hundred dollars."

"I wouldn't have to do anything kinky like a three or foursome," she said as she looked back at Jacob then ads, "wait a minute you are cops."

"No, Alice."

"So, what do I have to do?"

I spewed my sale pitch. I had her all I needed was to reel her in.

"Alice what I need is people to try out a new medicine that I have created. Hopefully it can cure them from any and all sickness."

It didn't register at first when I told her it could be a cure. But I did notice a look of hope in her eyes. I did not ask then I was only concern for her to say yes.

"I am a genetic doctor. A Geneticist. I have been working on this formula. I believe it can cure."

"And you will pay me to be a lab rat?"

"We need someone to try it out first before we can tell the world that we have discovered a miracle drug. Cannot prove it works without testing it."

Alice faced Mary then Jacob then returned her gaze to me.

"Numbers it is all about numbers. You positive that the medicine will not harm me?"

"Look Alice the worst it will do is to give you a bad headache. You'll lose your hair never care again," I said truthfully and smiled as if I were joking.

I cupped my hands over hers. I guess she had been more concern with the cure than the outcome. Alice stared deep into my eyes as she contemplated what had said for a moment then agreed. I had told her the truth, but the danger lay behind the smile. I did not tell her that death lingered in the corridor. And that it would be waiting for her soul if the experiment failed. We walked to my white van. Mary opened the door Jacob scurried to the other side climbed in. He reached for the black briefcase on the floor. The brief case was filled with the papers for her to sign. He handed the briefcase to Mary. She opened it took out a pin and the contract. Alice signed on the dotted line doing what most people do. She gave trust to someone she had never met. She gave her trust to a stranger. She did not read the fine print that was detrimental to her health. After she signed the papers, Mary grabbed the five hundred dollars handed it to Alice. Alice's eyes opened wide seeing the money. It was the same money I had used time and time again. Blood money stained with deceit. And there was a lot of blood on it. Mary handed the money to her. She took the five hundred dollars. Mary motioned her into the van. She climbed in then buckled up. Mary put the pin and the signed documents back into the briefcase. She put it on the seat next to Alice then climbed in and buckled up. Jacob turned on the vehicle. We pulled out into the first lane.

"I thought you would at least have a limo being a doctor?"

"The van draws less attention to us." "Yes, I guess," Alice replied back.

CHAPTER 7

We arrived at the mansion we went inside. Inside Alice twirled around taking in the inside of my estate. She stopped smiled.

"Come Alice," I motion.

We began our descent down into the laboratory. I should say into the spiders den. I walked her up to the metal operating tables.

"Pick one then take off your clothes climb on to the table. We will prep you for the experiment. "Were do I put my clothe?"

"Put then on the ledge of the table Alice."

Mary prepared while Alice undressed. She placed the equipment we would be using onto the crash cart. I recall seeing Alice's face it was full of intrigue. She looked around as she unbutton the back of her dress. Undressed she moved up to one of the shelves. To the failures that where in huge jar floating in formaldehyde. She heard noises coming from a room on the west side. Animal mutations that lived if one could call it living. These creatures that had lived where to deformed, deformed, so bad that some could not even move or crawl. I should have disposed of them. But I still needed to study them for a possible answer. I ask myself where did I make a mistake. Alice studied the equipment the vials of chemicals at the far end of the room. She returned back to the table took off her black bra then looked at me. I could see her taking everything in. I saw in her eyes as one sees in an infant's the astonishment. Like the amazement of seeing a bug for the very first time. Yet the fear and amazement that shot through their brain of the possible danger they still would attempt to pick it up. Alice pointed to one of the animals in a jar collecting dust. The figure inside the brownish green liquid bobbed up and down softly.

"What is that?"

"Alice that is what I am trying to keep from happening ever again. Deformity is due to a weakness in the immune system. Or ones has bad genes."

I told her that if my experiments went well human's would never need to fear birth defects. She was about to say something when Mary's voice pulled me away. I walked up to Mary as she stared into the microscope.

"Look at this Jeff," she said as she pulled her head away from the eye piece.

She moved over so that I could take a look. I looked into the microscope. I stared at was in the petri dish. I stared for several moments then faced Mary.

"She is infected," I whispered.

Mary crossed her arms leaned back in the rollaway chair. Looking at me with a smile she furrowed one eyebrow up indicating that she was infected with aids. That is when it hit me. It had been hope that I had seen in Alice's eye's at the time I had related to her about the formula. I recall telling her that what I was working on could possibly be a cure for illness. She was the perfect specimen. And what better specimen than that of one that had an incurable disease.

Perfect. I said in a whisper to myself then returned to Alice's side.

"What is it? Is everything okay?" "Everything is just fine Alice."

She put on the hospital gown climbed onto the metal gurney. She lay down. I mention now that I would have to inject her with the formula. Jacob placed the electrodes in place. I picked up her clothes put them away in one of the cabinets against the wall. I returned gave the thumbs up. I recall the look on her face as she looked at me. Her eyes widen when she saw the syringe. I pushed the needle into her vein injecting the formula.

Alice squinted as she felt a little discomfort as the needle went in through the flesh. It took several minutes before she was out. I ran my hand over her forehead smoothing back her hair. I never told her that we knew her secret of the aids. I covered her with a green hospital sheet that covered her from the neck down. The other had a hole in the center for the cranial to be exposed for the operation. We were now ready for the final stage. I wondered if I would have mentioned that I would have to remove the top part of her skull off to enter her brain. If she would have agreed so willingly. May God forgive me for my, deception.

Mary put on a smock sauntered up to the crash cart. She picked up a straight razor opened it. She caught Jacob looking at her as she opened up the blade. Mary gave him a smile and a wink.

"I hope you know how to use that thing," Jacob says.

"Jacob, I can cut the hairs off your balls and you wouldn't even know it."

"Mary I don't think I want to know."

Mary turned back around and with slow even strokes she shaved Alice bald. Alice's gold blond locks fell softly to the ground like leaves falling from a tree in the fall. She then took a bottle of antiseptic. She poured the brown solution coating the top of Alice's head. It spread over her head like syrup on a pancake. The smell of the disinfectant permeated the air. Mary made sure the skull protruded through the sheet. There was no room for error.

"Jeff she is ready."

It had been my cue. I walked up to her looked down drew an outline where I would be cutting. I would have to remove the top part of the skull. I would then separate the two halve of her brain. I will separate, separating the left lobe from the right to find the pituitary gland. Here I will inject the formula. I took the saw in my hand from the crash cart. I flipped on the switch. I began. The saw came to life in my hand. Its wicked hum filled the laboratory as I began to cut bone.

Blood ran down from the wound. I moved the saw with perfection with precision along the dotted line. I had sawed through in a matter of minutes. I removed the cranial bone placed it in a pan on to the cart. I scrutinized her brain. A most glorious organ. It reminded me of sheep intestines all wrinkled up in a bowl. Carefully I took the surgical knife cut the thin membrane connecting to two halves of brain. I placed the knife down. I picked up the syringe filled it with the formula.

With my other hand I used my fingers to separate the two lobes exposing the pituitary gland. I tilted the syringe up pushed the plunger. A jet stream of liquid shot out. I was ready. I put the needle into the pituitary gland pushed in the needle. I injected half of the compound in. I withdrew the needle then injected a third into the left then a third into the right lobe and a third to the cerebellum. It was the most excelerating of moments. I felt a rush as never before. I was certain that Alice would be the one. She would be the first of its kind. She would be the mother of the new human race. Mary returned to the computer to read the vital signs. Jacob wiped the sweat from my forehead. I nodded my head Jacob then handed me the top part of her skull. It was now time to put everything back. I proceeded. I placed the cranial bone in place stitched the skin back up. I was done. I took my latex glove off placed them on to the cart.

"Jacob it is all yours," I said and walked to the computer at Mary's side.

Jacob took the gauze bandages. He bandaged her head up carefully. Now the hard part. Now we would just have to wait patiently. She should mend quickly if the formula takes. Two maybe three days tops.

CHAPTER 8

The days continued to pass quickly. I had lost all knowledge of time. Each day that elapsed was worst than the one before. Anticipation could literally kill. The wait was agonizing gut wrenching. Then it happened on the third day a sign of hope. Alice had spoke her first words. Her voice had become strong with power of the beast. The first word was that she said was that she was thirsty. Hope of our creation of our endeavor was reaching its pinnacle. I wanted to see my creation but did not dare to remove the bandages of yet.

"I want to get up," she said in her new deep raspy voice.

I told her to hold on a couple more days and that I would remove the gauze that where wrapped around her head them. It looked as if we had broken through the barriers of genetics. I had reached its fullest of potential. We were static. But then like a thunderstorm reality rushed through my brain. The high feeling of success vanished crushing my feeling like a two-ton wrecking ball slamming into a brick wall. My thoughts chattered into a billion pieces. Her skin had mutated. It looked as if we had succeeded at first. We succeeded on the outside but forgot what could occur on the inside of her anatomy. She grabbed her head and screamed. She began to pulled away at the gauze bandages. Ripping them apart as if spiders where on her face. I could see where the part of her skull had fused. It was incredible.

Like sprouting weeds on a time lap video before our very eyes her hair began to grow. It was like seeing grass growing. The circumference of the follicles before had been minute compare to what was now. It had quadrupled in size. Her skin had become like leather. It was working. It was working. The thoughts in my head ran wild. I kept myself from shouting success out loud.

Unfortunately, our excitement was premature. We had not realized one thing. Inside of Alice's body something else was occurring. Something was extremely wrong. Underneath the flesh her bones were growing at an accelerated rate. This was not anticipated. The growth continued her bones enlarging so rapidly. If we could not contain the growth she would soon parish. We did everything possible. Nothing, nothing, we did reversed what was taking place. It was just too late. I could see the flesh tearing apart. The growth of her bones were too much. I can still see it as if it had just occurred. It was horrible. I can still see her eyes looking at me crying for help. She raised her head in an attempt to sit up. Oh I can still hear the agonizing screams of pain from within her. Blood oozed out of every possible orifice in her body. Alice's rib cage expanded until her stomach tore open spilling her intestines out like molted lava. Alice moaned then fell back hard onto the metal table. Her eyes focused on me as she stared out into space. I ran my hands through my hair wanting to scream out the word fuck from the frustration caught up in me. It began to make me sick. I did not feel any remorse all I felt was disappointment. I faced my colleagues for a moment in silence then spoke.

"Jacob, put her body in the fridge for now. We will study her more closely. After you do that come to the study, we will go over our notes. We have to find out what we are missing."

I turned then walked out of the laboratory. Later that night like clockwork we brought in two more specimens. I repeated the experiments. Again, it looked as if we had succeeded in our endeavor. But it was another failure and disappointment. They had lived but they were barely alive. I could see that they would soon die. I do not know what Jacob had to do but he had forgotten about the bodies. They had been set to one side and forgotten about. They had mutated in a way they were what I had stride for. This I did not find out until later. What was I missing? I was so close I ask again what was I missing? That night my answers was given to me. It was like a wish come true. It came from the heavens. It was as if my prayers had been answered. Out of nowhere this light appeared shooting through the sky. It shot through the heavens speeding down to earth. A blessing in disguised I thought to myself at that moment. Now I wish I had not the knowledge of science. I wish I had just been a spoiled rich kid playing with fast cars and fast women. But instead, I chose to play God. I played with life, with cells, cells, the ingredient of all creation. I played with the foundation that makes all living things possible. Genetics is what I played with.

Genetics having an enticing world all of its own. It called out to me like the pipe piper calling out to the mice in the children story book. Perhaps it is true that our destiny is written in the book of heaven.

CHAPTER 9

My mind races taking me back to when I was a small child. I always loved the mystery of the dead. As a child I ask questions on why did people die? I asked if they could be brought back from the dead. Even then I played the mad scientist. I would open up the bodies of dead animals I found. I would perform autopsies on them. I found it excelerating. I studied the organs. I once found a dying bird in the yard. I wanted to make it well again. I knew what I had to do. I knew where the answers would be. I entered my father's study. I read medical book after medical book. My fathered entered his study. I was caught red handed. He had warned me that if I were caught in this room I would be punished. I   was sure he was going to scolded me up, down, sideways. I stepped away from the bookshelves and placed the book in my hand on his desk. But all he did was to say was.

"What is that on my desk Jeffrey?"

I quickly replied truthfully that I was searching for a cure for the bird I found.

"I see Jeff," he says then went around the desk sat down on his black leather chair.

I can still hear the air leaving the cushion as his body sank down comfortably into the chair.

"You want to heal the dying bird." "Yes, father that is what I want." "Knowledge is a good thing."

I just stood there like a deer caught in a car's high beams.

"You are not going to find the answer looking at me."

My father watched my every move. I searched many books for anything that could save the bird.

"Middle shelf tenth book in Jeff," he says.

I reached for the book I read what it had to say. On the cover it read medicine volume 10. I began to read its contents. I turned looked at my father as he lit his pipe then leaned back in his chair. It seemed as if his small frame had sunk deeper into the chair. I did not know at the time that cancer had begun to take him. I turned the pages until the word penicillin jumped out at me.

I knew I had heard my father speak of the powers of this medicine and what it was based on. It was a simple process it even told on how it could be made if one was in dire need. I read and understood most of what I needed. It was not the fact that my father could have gotten the medicine at anytime he was a doctor. I guess he wanted me to learn every aspect of medicine. There was more than just reading. My father helped me with the making of the penicillin from scratch. It was under his guidance that it had been possible. He had said bread alone does not make medicine, he then ads man does son. The words of a father can change many things. I knew from that day on what I would become.

Seven days later the bird was well enough to be set free. The bird had blue and gray feathers. My father said that it was a Blue Jay. I had accomplished what I had set out to do. I entered college three years ahead of schedule. My father thought it would be better if I waited a couple of years. He said that I should take my time to be a kid and have fun. Of course I was impatient like all children. I had a gold to accomplish. It was my destiny. I convinced him that it would be better that I start now. He studied me for several minutes then nodded and gave his consented. To be honest I knew he would allow me to go early for I was his only child. And what I wanted I got. I was happy. I was intrigued by the knowledge of science of chemistry. It was like candy to me. It was all I needed to be at my best. My father died in my first year of college. I met one of the most prominent doctors in the field of genetics. I remember that he stood in the center of the lecture room like a God. The bleachers circled around him like the arenas of the gladiators of Rome. All the rolls of seats were packed with students. They squeezed together in hope of seeing what the doctor held in a square object underneath a white tablecloth behind him. He talked about the new doctors and of the advancements of knowledge in medicine. He lectured for hours of all those genetics had accomplished and what it would accomplish in the following years.

He walked around stepped in back of the table. He grabbed the white cloth in between his fingers. The excitement ate away at us like butterflies trying to get out of their cocoon. But in our cases the butterflies were trying to explode out our stomach it seemed. He pinched the cloth in his fingers. He lifted his hand. He unveiled what was hidden from our eyes. The excitement grew within me like a hunger. I was in awe, dumfounded, mesmerized, at what I was seeing. It was a rat, a rodent, but this rodent had something different. What was it? My brain couldn't see it at first. Confused is the best way to explain it. It was just too unbelievable. It could not be real. My eyes focused on what materialized on its back. It was a miracle in its own rite. I thought my eyes deceived me at first. My eyes focused in on what appeared to be an ear. Yes, an ear growing out of the rodent's back.

"This ear you see before you growing on the rodent's back was constructed through genetics. This ear created for the soul purpose of using it possibly one day on a human. Ears have been grown before but not like this. Now we can do it faster and more efficient. Can you imagine a burn victim that needs an ear? Now for the first time in history a doctor can tell his patient that his ear can be replaced. One day will be able to say we can replace burnt skin. It would be minor surgery. And all the thanks goes to a rat."

The words he spoke stayed engraved in my brain. I followed in his footsteps. I followed every accomplishment every bit of his work. I took his knowledge then added mine. I went that one step further. My studies my findings brought me to the heights that where astonishing. Astonishing even to my mentor. I used this knowledge and created something that even science could not stop. In this journal I will explain in complete detail my story of woe. Not for praise or recognition but for what I had let lose in the city of roses. I want the world to know of my atrocity. Of the horror I afflicted upon Portlander's. I had acted as a God. This was and would be my downfall.

CHAPTER 10

Doctor Jeffery Mongrol II.

Journal entry: June 26th 2017

Specimen 25: Alice, experiment failure.

After writing this entry down I walked to my room. I looked out the window. I stared out at the stars for what seem to be an hour. The bright stars gleaming as if alive twinkling in the distance. Even with the beauty of the night sky I was disappointed. My stomach soured from the thought of failure. I stared out into the universe I had even lost track of time. I looked down at my wristwatch. Then out of nowhere it happened. It was a gift from heaven. The day of reckoning is what it would wind up being. I looked back out the window. Stars where a rarity in the state of Portland. In Portland Or., clouds is what one was used to seeing. I was in awe of the simplicity as well as the mysterious nature of the star's complex existence. I felt drawn in by them on this night. I pull myself away from the window for a moment.

I walked out on to the balcony. I looked at my watch again. It was five thirty in the morning. The hours had passed unnoticed. I took in the cool night breeze. The wind caressing my body as it blew softly. The curtains swayed as the wind blew moving them like a puppeteer would move the strings on a puppet. They swayed like an ocean wave as the wind pick up. I walked up to the telescope that I had bought for the soul purpose of looking at the stars when I was feeling down. It was stupendous I moved the eye piece. I focused it on one particular star. It was as if I could reach out and touch it. What happen next happen so fast. I could not believe it? At first, I thought I must have been seeing things but I was not. It was a shooting star streaking through the sky with a blazing fire trailing behind it. The chariots of fire sent to earth by the God's. The fiery tail followed it like a powerful propulsion propelling it. It was like that from a rocket being sent out of our atmosphere up into space. I followed it as far as I could. I looked through the telescope.

Seeing it through the scope made it seem closer than what it was. I could almost feel the warmth of the heat from the trailing fire. What happened next did not register into my mind at first. This projectile, meter, shooting star stopped in midflight. Yes, in midflight. It hovered above then it just dropped at a tremendous speed. I was certain I was going to see a plume of dirt in the distance, but it never came. It vanished. It was as if it had never been swallowed up. My mind raced with the thought of how magnificent it would be to fine this meteor. If that is what it was?

Oh, the hope and possibilities that it would give us. And not to mention the answers that I could get from it. I could advance my genetic knowledge tenfold. It could advance my genetic knowledge as well as the structuring of the human body. It could give me the answers I needed to prefect my formula. Helping me succeed in my endeavor. Cloning was at its highest, but I would be able to go that one leap further. I would give life. It was my redemption another chance. Money was not a deterrent I had plenty of it. I ran out of my room into the corridor up to the far wall down the stairs to the lamp on the wall. I turned it to the right. The laboratory door squeaked open I climbed down the stairs. I was startled by the light at first. I thought I had cut it off on my way-out last night. Then I remembered that I was the only one that had left. As my foot touched the ground Jacob came around the back of the computer. I jumped back looked at Jacob then spoke.

"What the hell," I exclaimed out lost for words as my heart raced.

"Sorry Jeff I wasn't expecting you for several hours. What do you think I am making out with your lady?"

"You know what I meant Jacob. Besides your dick isn't big enough."

"Up your's," Jacob replied back. "So where is she?"

"Went to the store to get us some doughnuts."

Jacob turned around walked up to one of the microscopes placed a Petri dish in place to study the girl's blood.

"Doughnuts huh. The woman does love her doughnuts."

I walked up to the far wall plugged in the radio. Jacob's eyes followed me with interest. I move the knob on the radio until I got a clear channel. Jacob knew I did not like the squeal of the radio early in the morning hours. Curiosity kills the cat.

"What's up with the radio?" he ask knowing that I did not like to hear the radio.

Jacob stood walked up to the far table next to the wall. I followed him with my eyes. On the table I saw a man that lay motionless. A man that was not there before. I guess he noticed the look of bewilderment on my face.

"I could not sleep Jeff. So I went hunting," Jacob stated.

He smiled then stuck an intravenous feeding tube into the man's right arm. Blood jetted out of the man's arm as the needle penetrated the vein. Blood hit Jacob on the chest then ran down the clear plastic apron he wore. He wipe several drops of blood off his face.

"He is prepped and ready to go," Jacob exclaimed and stood looking at me.

I remained silent for about a minute. "What the hell? Okay, let us try again."

I then realized that my Mary had been in on this. She had gone to the store yes for doughnuts and to be gone just in case I lost my temper. I divulged why I had turned on the radio to Jacob as I put on an apron. I explained that we needed to be the first to find it. We could not let the government beat us to the meteor. If they got their hands on it I would never see it. We had to retrieve it before the goons got hold of it. I continued to divulge my thoughts. I told him of what I had seen. I did not tell him the fact that I thought the meteor, shooting star, was probably a spaceship. For the time being it would be my secret. The D. J.'s voice bellowed out excitedly.

"Did you see the fiery object shooting through the night sky this morning?"

I heard a squeak turned around as the trap door open. Mary walked down the stairs slowly. She was taking a bite of one of the doughnuts. She almost lost her footing not paying attention as she enjoyed the lemon jelly filled doughnut.

"Yum," she managed to say then step off the stairs, "these lemon fill are the shit."

"Bring us any Mary?" I ask.

"Of course," she replied back with a mouth full.

She stopped stared at Jacob. Jacob nodded his head indicating that it was safe. She looked back at me. It was like seeing a kid with a guilty look on their face. She smiles at me then pushed out the bag towards me. Jacob turned back around took a tissue sample from the man. He walked to the microscope placed it into a Petri dish. He placed it under the scope looked through the eye piece for better observation. He wrote something down on the pad of paper. After a moment of studying the sample of tissue he retrieved the dish then walked it up to the fridge. He put the plate in then closed the door. He turned the knob on the side turning up the temperature. The sample would now be in deep freeze. Jacob walked up over to me then whispered making sure Mary did not hear him.

"When are you going to tell Mary?"

"It will be soon but for now Jacob just grab a doughnut. I will tell her when the time is right. For now, we have to worry about the Feds. You know they will have their own team searching the area for it."

"True but you know they couldn't find there assholes if it wasn't placed back there for them," Jacob humors him.

I agreed we then began our experiment on our new specimen. We worked on the man for three days again it was a failure. What was I missing? What element had I left out? What? My thoughts tormented me. Night was coming and sleep was what I needed. My colleagues needed this as well.

"Let's get some shut eye. Jacob your room is to the right as usual. I had Silva change the bed sheets. You know where the rest of the stuff is."

CHAPTER II

I went upstairs with Mary and fell asleep as soon as my head hit the pillow. The next morning, I lay in bed thinking on how to ask Mary for her help. It was not that she would refuse but it was just that I wanted her to be the one to agree. It would be dangerous for Jacob and myself. Mary would be left holding the bag as they say. It had been a good while since Mary, and I had a good time. I would use the ideal of a good time to tell her.

I rolled over onto my side threw my arms around Mary's waist.

"Mum," she said cooing softly then said after a few seconds, "So what do I owe this too?"

"Just because I felt like holding the one thing I love so."

"There is never a just because with you Jeff."

Jacob, you, and I have been working none stop for nothing. So far it has been depressing. Failures Jeff. I will need you more so in the coming days. Mary rolled over on to her side and faced me. She kissed me softly on the lips. I felt her warm breast caress my body. I felt at that moment as if my heart had stopped. Not from the pleasure of her body but the fact that I in a way felt I was betraying her. I was betraying her love by covering it up with a fib. I used deception I should say half a lie. I did want to go out and have fun for once. But it was still a deception in my heart.

"Today will be a day of rest." "I'm all for that," she agreed.

She climbed out of bed put her clothes went downstairs. A moment later she returned with a glass of orange juice, scramble eggs, and toast. I scooted back in bed leaned back against the headboard. She placed the tray on my lap. She turned around to leave and was almost out the door.

"Whoa, where are you rushing off to?"

"Day off so I am going to get some gardening done today."

I knew where she was heading off to. I climbed out of bed as well. I got dress went down stair to the kitchen placed the tray down on the black marble island. I walked through the dining room walked up to the lamp. I turned the lamp to the right. I waited for it to open. I walked down the stairs up to the computer where I knew Mary would be. I kissed her softly on the nape of the neck.

"I thought you said you were going to do some gardening?"

"I really was. But then I remembered something that I had to check. I needed to check the numbers on the D.N.A. But there was no mistake it all adds up Jeff."

I went over every bit of detail with her several times. It was right. I looked out the basement window noticed it was getting dark outside. Again we had lost track of time.

"Mary put everything down. Go get ready for or date."

"What about the body?"

"Leave it. We will take a closer look at it tomorrow."

I knew it would take a while for Mary to get dressed. All women took more time than they really needed. It was the look of perfection they seek.

I took a shower got out got dressed combed my hair. Mary was still trying to choose what dress she was going to wear. I went downstairs sat in the living room until I heard Mary on her way down. I stood in awe as she sauntered down the stairs. I gazed up at the most beautiful creature God had created. And that creature was woman. Mary smiled proudly knowing she had picked the right dress. She stopped looked at me for a moment. I walked up and help her off the last step.

"Looks like a new suit Jeff?" "Bought it just for this occasion."

Mary wore a white dress that showed off her cleavage sensualized the contours of her body. I felt my senses heighten. The thought of should I just take her by the hand and run back upstairs to our bedroom and screw her brains outran through my head. Of course, it would be reversed. Women out do men by a long shot. Still, it was something I had been neglecting.

"Put your eyes back in their socket. Keep the rocket in the pocket," she said coyly.

I laughed out heartedly at her words as I grabbed her by the arm. I walked her out the double doors. The trap door open and Jacob stepped out. He froze literally. His mouth fell open.

"You kids have fun," Jacob said then turned around then moved the lamp back in to place.

That was our cue. We stepped out into the cool night breeze. Mary noticed the limo moving down the halfmoon driveway up to us. The driver stopped opened the door. He climbed out opened the door for Mary.

"Impressive."

"Very impressive," Mary said excitedly. "Nothing is too good for my wife to be."

"If that is a proposal I do and I will." We climbed in. James began to drive away.

Mary scooted up next to me then kissed me softy. She stared into my eyes mesmerizing me with her beauty.

"Am I going to get some tonight?" I ask. "Yes, and maybe more than you want," she replied back.

We both laughed this night will be a night to remember. I think back now. I had everything. I should have planned for a life with Mary.

"Cosmos James," Mary said before I opened my mouth.

"Are you sure Mary?" "Positive."

"We can go to a place downtown."

"I get tired of all the kissing up out there. Oh, here is someone with lots of money let me kiss his ass. No, Jeff I want to go to a place where I know the atmosphere and the people."

"If Cosmos is what you want then Cosmos it is."

James turned left onto eighty second. We pulled up to the Cosmos. I told James I would call him when I needed him to pick us up instead of him having to wait for us.

"When does Silva get back?"

"Don't wish that on me the bitch is fine where she is Jeff."

"What did James just say?" Mary asked.

"Oh, miss Mary I think you might have heard me wrong. I said the witch is fine."

Mary looked at him not sure that he was telling her the truth. She like James but knew he was a character. But she knew he could be a cuss as well. James and Silva had been Jeff nanny and friends. They were both in their late sixties. Sometime Jeff would call him dad by mistake. James had picked him off the ground more than his real father had. I guess that is the price one pays when their parents are filthy rich.

"Oh! The answer is she will be back tomorrow bright and early. I'll be there when her plane arrives. I don't like her. But I love the hell out of that old lady. Sir if you want me to wait here I will."

"James you know what I have said about the sir business."

"Jeff you are my employer. I take care of the up keep of the grounds. I am your shuffler. And Silva is your maid."

"No, James you are my family." "Still you pay us."

"Okay, James let's say I don't pay you. You can still live with me and do shores."

"Jeffy let's not get crazy. I know we are like family, but it is the right thing to do."

I climbed out of the limo went around to the other side. I opened the door held out my arm. Mary grabbed it. I assisted her out of the vehicle. I popped in my head before I closed the door. I repeated to James that I would call him when it was time to pick us up.

"You don't want me to wait?"

"No need James. It will be at least five hours. Go home get some rest."

I turned around Mary and I walked into the Cosmos. I found a table pretty much in the center right next to the dance floor. I pulled out a chair motioned Mary to sit down. A waitress walked up asked if we needed a drink. I ordered two beers before I sat down. The place smelled I should say it reeked of fermented beer from the previous day. I scanned the place I focused my eyes on a picture that was hanging on the walls. Picture of our sister country, Mexico. I asked Mary if she felt home sick.

"My parents are natives of Mexico. I on the other hand was born here. My first language is english the second is spanish."

She did not need to finish her thought for I already knew. People began too arrived the music began. It was a good thing for it saved me from a possible argument. The band warmed up playing la cumbia de sol. Now music that is a universal language. Mary asked me to dance. I was going to play hard to get. Mary took another sip of her beer.

"You know that reward I was going to give you.

Well, it is beginning to dissipate." "I can't dance to this music."

"Bull shit Jeff. When we first met we always went to the armory to dance. You cried how much you could not understand but soon as we started dancing it was like almost impossible to make you get off the dance floor."

Seeing the scowl on her face I kept quite. I looked at her for a moment then grabbed her hand. I asked her for a dance. She smiled then winked at me indicating that what she had promise was back up on the chart. The second song was a slow piece the kind that stirs the inter emotions. The kind that makes on fall in love. After the song we returned to our table. We sat down Mary reached for her purse. She took out a pack of cigarettes.

"I'll be right back Jeff I am going outside for a moment."

She swayed to the music. She reached up undid the power bun then let her black hair and let it fall freely. And I have to say that I loved it. Especially when she let down her hair.

"Want another drink?" I ask. "Sure."

The night moved on I was actually enjoying myself. I was bewildered at that moment on how a small thing like color or a name of a race could turn people against each other. And how hate could turn them into savages sending them back to the primitive state. I could not understand this action. In my heart I wanted to make the world united the way it was meant to be. Uniting the world the new children would live without prejudice. I was close to making this happen. It was just absurd. After my father died, I would be walking along in the park. Or downtown it did not matter where I walked. I would see a black man that resembled him. I would see an Oriental, or a Russian. It just did not matter for these people thought of different races resembled my dad. A mirror image of the man. It was not a fixation.

Or a psychological need with in me. All I can say is that if one would just take time to look closely at one another and not see the skin color. Their eyes would be open. They would realize that we are of the same creation out of the same mold. We strive to be better than another. This is a normal need but we need to cure the idiosyncrasy with intelligence. I would be as God. But I would create perfection. Later that night Mary and I met a couple as we headed to our table after a dance.

Somehow a conversation between Mary and the lady had commence. The woman's husband introduced himself. He reached out his hand.

"My name is Jake Tobaris."

"Jeff," I said and shook his hand then added, "and that is Mary."

"And Jeff that is Susan my wife," he says and smiles.

We asked them to sit at our table. The man talked with a heavy Mexican accent as did his wife. He talked I could tell he was a well-educated man. He talked about his ranch and all the acreage of land he owned. I talked of genetics. He seemed to grasp on to what I related to him. I on the other hand did not know a thing about ranching.

"You know there are some things that would surprise you Jeff. Take for instance cattle."

"Cattle?" I said curiously

"Yes, genetics is involved in raising cattle.

In order to breed strong livestock, it requires that manipulation of the genes per say be used."

"Yes, I guess it would," I agreed.

"Jeff why don't you and the misses come stay at my ranch take a gander for yourself. New Mexico is not very far from here."

"I would like that Jake," Jeff says then ads, "so let me ask you do you have a place to stay tonight? My mansion is open to you."

"I as well would gladly accept your invitation, but I have very important matters to attend to. I need to rush straight for the airport. Don't want to keep my pilot waiting too long. I really would stay but I need to sign some papers tomorrow. My grandfather just left me a couple of oil wells down Lubbock way."

"I bet that hurts?"

"Yes, Jeff I am hurting all the way to the bank."

We all began to laugh. Mary and Susan had not even bothered to sit down. Mary grabbed Jake's hand Susan mine. We were dragged to the dance floor. Another hour passed. Moments later they returned to the table. They had returned laughing. Later on, that night after they had left Mary revealed what they were laughing about. Mary said that Jake was a lot like me. Susan his wife had told her that he did not usually talk to anyone.

Like you he says he doesn't like anyone. She said that for some reason he like you. The last dance of the night was about to begin. I called James to pick us up.

"Jeff we have to be leaving you're welcome anytime Jake."

We took down each other's address. I shook Jake's hand. Mary gave him a kiss on the cheek. Susan kissed me on the cheek then handed Mary a paper that had their address. We gave them ours I cannot explain it but it made me feel good in a way. I guess I felt human. Jake, and Susan, waved and walked out of the Cosmos. We danced to the last dance embraced in each other's arms. I was going to tell Mary about the meteor but she beat me to the question. I should have known Mary would know. It was as if she could read my mind.

"When are you going to ask me about the meteor?"

"To be honest Mary I was going to ask you for your help tonight."

"You know that I would help you."

"I know Mary, but I want it to be the right time to ask. I really think we can find it."

"So, was this reason why you asked me out." "No, not entirely Mary it was a small part.

But to be honest I need your help to do this right."

Jeff knelt down on one knee. "Will you marry me?"

She agreed and we kissed. I think the kiss was longer than I had thought for Mary's word brought me back to the present. We were still in the middle of the dance floor. People were looking at us then began to clap.

"I think you and I can go back to the table now Jeff," Mary says smiling.

I was somewhat embarrassed but I was happy at the same time. By the time James had arrived we had made plans to visit our new friend in New Mexico. A date that we would never be able to keep.

CHAPTER 12

Morning came quick. I woke up with the drawbacks of the previous night. It would have been good to have stayed underneath the covers longer. But I had things to do. I looked at the clock that was on the dresser. It read five a.m.

I guess one's own internal clock was hard to change once it had formed a pattern. Mary stirred in bed she would soon wake as well. I got dress went downstairs into the kitchen. I found Jacob reading the newspaper while drinking a cup of coffee. He said hello got up put on the radio.

"Someone might have reported where the meteor might have fallen," he tells me.

I nodded my head in agreement. I went to the coffee pot I reached for a cup then poured myself a cup. I sat down at the table. I drank the dark liquid any how my taste buds enjoyed the taste.

"How did it go last night?"

"Good I even asked Mary to marry me," I replied back.

"It is about time," Jacob exclaimed. "Yes, I have to agree."

Jacob had been right it was a good way to get an approximation on where the metor had fallen. I had a good suspension that it was more than just a metor. I suspected it was a spaceship. I got up went down to the lab as did Jacob. Mary sauntered into the lab a few minutes later.

"I heard what you said but what makes you think that the caller will be reliable?" Mary asked. "People in general might not be reliable source. But when they see a thing that intrigues them, they remember what and what they saw."

"I don't know," Mary dragged the word of uncertainty out.

"I tend to have to agree Mary," Jacob interjects.

"Let me explain to you two doubting Thomas." "Yes, please do Jeff. I would like to know,"

Mary says.

"When someone is attacked his or her adrenaline spikes pumps up the heart rate. This rush of adrenaline confuses them. There are not able to identify the perpetrator of the crime. They can't even remember if they were tall or short. What they remember is smell."

"Smell," Jacob interjected.

"Yes, fear has a way of imprinting odor let's say like the people that see evil, ghost, demons, and the devil persay. The odor one smell is usually sulfur for a demon, or the devil. Perfume or cooking odors are involved with ghost. Even cigarette smell."

"So, why is it you said that they are reliable on this?"

"See, Mary when people see something amazing for some reason like a U.F.O. Or a new sparkling car with a bright color that appeals to the person instant imprint of make and color."

"I get it like a marble or a top for a kid." "Correct."

I went to the far wall put on the radio in the lab. We did what we did on the norm getting the equipment ready for the next experiment. Then like an angles voice from heaven the D.J.'s voice bellowed out through the speakers. It was a woman by her voice I estimated that she was in her early thirty's. She was not going to wait for a possible caller to come forth. She was going to make sure someone would call in.

"Okay, Portland what is it that you have to say about the object shooting across the sky early morning on Thursday. Today is Saturday don't be shy I know someone saw it. Where did it fall or perhaps it burnt up?"

The sound of phones rang in the background. "We have a caller Portland. Go ahead tell us what you saw. You are on the air."

"What I saw is where it landed. I saw Government men," the old man's voice cracked with age.

"Are you sure?" ask the D.J.

"Oh, believe me I am sure. I went to the spot that I thought it had landed. Living just a short distance away I hurried there. I drove to Salvie Island the fog was dense. It was thicker than I had ever seen. Hell! I believe that it could have really been cut with a knife literally."

"That is pretty thick," says the D.J., then says, "Continue."

"I pulled over to one side I then contemplated if I should climb out of my truck. I stared out of the windshield for a moment. I knew it was a dangerous thing to do but I was already there. I was hesitant at first. I did not really like the ideal of leave my truck behind. It's an eighty-four Ford pickup it is beat up some but it is my truck. I finally climbed out I then walked about a yard up the road. I could read the sign that told one the way to White Sturgeon Lake. As the fog broke in several places as it moved along. I was about to go further when I hear cars roaring up the road towards me. I returned to my vehicle, but I did not dare to climb back in. I went around the passenger side. I squatted down out of eyesight in the thick grass. They rushed by but I made out a license plate. It was Government, issue. They drove black cars I got scared. I got up looked down the road. I could see more cars moving in. I moved quickly I knew they would be on a search mode. I made my way through the large thickets and trees. I looked back on occasion. I could see men with flashlight swarming the ground by my truck like giant fireflies. They searched the inside of my vehicle. I have to say it was my most horrifying experience. I had not done anything remotely as dangerous since Korea. I continued knowing it was safe to stop and hide. But as they say curiosity killed the cat. I reached the edge of the woods I made my way up as close as I could. I saw several men dress in black suits. One imparticular wore a white smock. He gave the men their orders."

The old man's voice broke again. He paused for a moment getting his breath back.

"Please go on," said the D.J.

"My heart pounded I knew they were not environmentalist. I heard the man in the white smock yell out that they had wasted too much time.

For now we will say that it burnt up on entry before it landed. He look mad. I guess they did not find what they were after. When I saw that they were moving towards their cars I quickly took a hint. I began to trudge through the mud and undergrowth as fast as I could. I figured I was lucky in two ways. One I made it back safely. The other was that the men did not see me. It would have been another of those he was at the wrong place at the wrong time."

"I think you mean at the wrong place at the right time."

"No, mam I mean at the wrong place at the wrong time. I do not know what they were looking for?

But it must have been important top security kind of stuff. I then walked home. I was not going back to my truck. I know they would have had someone staking out the truck just encase one came back to it. Someone would be their waiting there always is. And then the questions."

"Well, that was one hell of a story Portland," she says then says next caller.

The rest of the caller had similar stories up to where they thought it had landed. Mary cut off the radio. She turned then face Jacob and I. I nodded my head I knew we would be playing with time. I knew that the doctor would soon go out to the lake again in an attempt to find the object. I was glad they had not discovered its whereabouts.

"Let's go hunting," I exclaimed.

We hurried to get all the equipment ready that we would be needing. I did not devoludge the fact that I knew one thing. And that was if they had found it we would have be out of the loop. I and my colleagues would have been denied access to the meteor, spaceship, they would be in control. I had known who the man was that the old man on the radio had seen as soon as he said black government cars. I was not about to let him take it away from me. My colleagues and I were on the verge of success. On the verge of me being a creator like God. Nothing was going to stop me. I wish now as I write all this down that there would have been some kind of deterrent to my need. Now that there is nothing left that was good in my life. If I had not played God my dear friend and beloved Mary would still be alive. Let me continue on for remembrance is painful. I moved and bellowed out orders to get the gear for our dive. And to put everything into the van. It was an anticipated assumption, but I had a hunch.

We went over the map of Salive Island. We needed to find it. We needed to keep it a secret. We were like kids ready to go on a Halloween trick or treat run. This meteor would give us so many answers. It did not matter if it was a meteor or spaceship. The dormant life in it, the unknown knowledge it contained. To man this would be a find of a century. I was overwhelmed with excitement. I cannot say when my blood pumped through my veins feeding me with such energy. That same night we arrived at Salvie Island. I backed up the van as close as I could to the riverbank. We climbed out of the van lay out the scuba equipment for our dive in the morning.

With all that we had to prepare time passed rapidly. By the time we realized what time it was it was four in the morning. We had a lot on our minds. The dive would be a dangerous and arduous task in itself. It would not change for us when the sun came up over the horizon. If we had dove that night, we would have signed our own death certificate. Mary was used to this kind of life getting up in the morning with her parents in the fields. She was at home. She started a fire started up a pot of coffee. All I could think as I saw her moving about was that she knew what she was doing and how pretty she looked. I was as anxious as a teenager waiting to go to his prom is the best way to explain how I felt. After a moment of thought I walked up to the fire knelt down on one knee. Mary handed me a cup. I smiled back at her. I reached down took the pot off the hook that held it over the fire. I poured myself a cup I placed it back onto the hook. I held the cup between my two hands moving the cup back and forth in the center of my palms. I blew into the cup the steam from the dark liquid rose like a miniature ghost sailing upward and away. The fire crackled as the wood burn. Tiny specks of fire flew about. I took another drink of my coffee the aroma hitting my nose. I stood and moved closer to Mary. I placed my hand on her shoulder she looked up at me. I asked her for one of her cigarettes. I need a smoke now like needing a good smoke after sex. I figured that it was the excitement that made me crave for a cigarette.

"I thought you quit Jeff?"

"I did but tonight I need one to calm down my nerves."

I caressed her cheek softly with the back of my hand. She reached into her breast pocket pulled out a cigarette pack then handed it to me. I took one out of the pack then handed the pack of smokes back to her.

Jeff took a deep drag and exhaled. The plume of dark gray smoke ascends upward desipatating with the atmosphere as I looked out at the river.

Suddenly I got a revelation. It hit me. I walked up to the edge of the riverbank. I scrutinized over the surface of the water. There was something not quite right. It was something that had to do with the river. What was it? I forced my thoughts. I could not let it rest. I knew what it was it was there deep in the back of my brain. I could not see it at first. My brain stressed as it tried to recall. Something, something was out of whack. Think Jeff think, think. It was still too dark to see but I could hear movement. I saw shadows with the assistance of the moonlight above. In the night it was like a giant light an orb of energy. Energy that gave life to the story of werewolves and the effect it had on humans. The woods did not scare me but the darkness had a way of reaching the core of superstation in on. What could and would lurk in the dark. Being in the woods was the most peaceful thing that one could experience. The crickets chirped, frogs croaked, and on occasions a hoot from an owl up above in the fur trees could be heard. Small furry animals scurried away like phantoms ghost scurrying up the mammoth trees. I was suddenly startled by a hoot of an owl. My brain shot me back to my childhood. It was as if it were yesterday. I could see my father sitting on the ground with a fishing pole at hand. He would say that to catch a big fish one needed a big pole. The fishing trips were far and in between but he tried to fine time from his demanding work. He had made advancements in heart surgery. We had our father and son time. I recalled this one special night. We fished all day. I would begin to fidget from being boarded. He would look at me and says patiently that the fish would be biting soon. Of course, being a kid I would get boarded and as you can guess. I would begin to toss rocks into the water. My father would look at me sternly but not real mad. I guess it irritated him in a way, but he could see that I was bored out of my mind.

"Jeff you are going to scare the fish away please come and sit back down next to me. Keep an eye on your pole."

I remember sitting down next to him. No sooner had I sat down when my pole bent forward at the tip. It twitched several times.

"Grab your pole slowly out of the ground Jeff." "What do I do now?" I ask as I held the pole in my hands.

"Real in the slack point the tip down. Now pull back then repeat it to set the hook in firmly, Jeff."

I just looked at him my eyes bugged out with excitement.

"Pull back on the pole and real in the fish," he shouted.

I jerked the pole as hard as I could. I jerked it back I real in some line. It had taken me at least twenty minutes to real in the sturgeon. My bicep muscles ached. I was exhausted it was my first fish. My father took a cloth measuring tape from the tackle box walked up to me. He picked it up by the gills and measured it.

"It is a keeper Jeffrey forty-seven and a half inches. Yes, I think you can keep this one."

It had been the first time my father had addressed me by my entire name. I guess in my dad's eyes I had become a man. He picked up the sturgeon by the tail look down at me and repeated the words.

"Jeffrey you have a keeper."

I suddenly knew what it was. Snap instant replay. It was as if the fog had lifted clearing.

As my eye scanned the surface of the water I knew what I was looking for. I brought my eyes back to the bank of the river. I searched for a clue that I knew would be there. It was at my feet. I focused on the dead fish moving back and forth near the riverbank. It had not been fog. It had been steamed from the object that fell from the sky. The extreme heat it generated made the water steam up. The slight breeze moved it along like fog. On certain days fog was a normal thing here at Salive Island but today it was different. Whatever had landed was there in the depth of the river. It had gone undetected by the doctor. Call it fate call it luck whatever the case maybe. What mattered now was that I had been right. It was there underneath in the depth of the river hidden form human eyes.

I studied the water for a moment longer then walked back to the campfire. I took the pot off the metal hook. I poured myself a cup. I looked at my colleagues as they sat down in the lawn chairs looking up at me.

"I know where it is."

Jacob sat up abruptly, "are you sure," Jacob questioned.

"I am sure as you are sitting there. As I had estimated. I truly believe it is in the river."

"How can you be certain we haven't made the dive as of yet?"

"I just know Mary lets us say that the fog lingering around this place is not natural."

"Go on," Mary says inquisitively.

"This thing was traveling at a tremendous speed. Let's say it was on fire it landed in the river. Steam would rise up from the extreme heat.

"You saw something Jeff," Jacob says.

"Yes, and it hit me as I recalled my pass. I noticed that there was no life thriving in the waters. There were no fish jumping. I moved my eyes to the bank where I knew what I would see. I saw fish lots of dead fish just moving in and out from the river bank.

"How did the doctor miss it Jeff?"

"They did not look hard enough. The fact that they did not know what to look for helped."

Morning was breaking through eating away at the night. The radiance of the sun glimmered on the horizon. It was going to be a nice perfect day. I put my cup down on the ground then broke the silence.

"Get ready Jacob we dive in an hour."

Jacob and I got ready. Mary made sure we had the weights belts to weigh us down in the water for safety precautions. Jacob and I brought out the air tanks. The rest of the diving gear from the back of the van. We checked the air tanks pressure the breathing apparatus making sure that they were functioning properly. We then put on our wet suits placed the weight belt on. We were ready for the dive.

"I hope this weight belt dose its job," Jacob says.

"What you afraid of a little current?"

I knew that the Willamette Rivers under toe was one of the most thresrous in the state.

"You got the scared part right. The under toe can take one adrift underneath in a wink of an eye Jeff."

"Well let's hope that doesn't happen," I replied then chuckled softly.

The waters of the Columbia where indeed treacherous. But there was no way around the dive. The object was down there and that was the fact.

CHAPTER 13

Jacob put on his air tank looked at me then gave the thumbs up. I made sure my air tank was functional. We made are way up to the riverbank. The flippers flapping on the ground making us seem like human frogmen in a way. Mary turned on the double hoist. The hoist clank free as the mechanism that held it in place lifted. The cables became slack. She took the cables then moved towards us. She dropped the cables with the hooks to the ground then ran back to the van. She cut off the switch to the hoist. I put the weight belt on. It was just an extra precaution. Jacob hooked the cable to his belt. We were ready for the dive. Mary restarted the hoist. We turned and slowly walked into the water. We began to disappear deeper and deeper into the river. The water was now to our waist. We moved further in cautiously. The heat generating from the object made the water bearable. The warmth of the water embraced us.

We were now chest level with the running water. The under toe was strong. It pulled at our legs. I looked back at Mary. She blew me a kiss I remember thinking how lovely a creature she was. I loved her free flowing auburn hair in the wind. She puckered her lips turned her back toward us. She wrapped her arms around herself as if it were me that was holding her and kissing her. I laughed then I yelled out that I loved her. I put my diving mask over my face. Mary wore a denim jacked over her long John shirt. Her wrangler jeans would keep her warm. The morning brought a cool breeze through Salvie Island.

I heard Mary shout the words good luck. I submerged under water. I wondered how we would find anything in this murky water. The rains had made a mess of the river. I guess where there is a will there is a way. We searched using the high power 200 watt flash lights. We searched for an hour. That hour seemed as if it had been three down in the depth of the river. We had searched the entire river bottom it seemed. Nothing. I was about ready to give up the search and give the sign to go back up when Jacob spotted something. Jacob had stumbled onto the object's opening. It had been the blind leading the blind. We had been lucky on sparse occasions the dirt broke. We were able to catch a glimpse of what was in the water. I could only see a few feet in front of me. I saw Jacob come around the sphere. I saw him moving his hand as if to motion me to follow him. I followed his light until I was up next to him.

The impact had been greater than we had imagined. The ship had landed with tremendous force. It had kept on moving until it stopped and had been covered completely by the rivers mud. We just happen to be at the right place at the right time. In the passing days the under toe of the river had washed a good amount mud off the sphere. It was still submerged halfway in mud but I could see what it was. As I had expected it was a spaceship. It was smooth on the exterior reminding me of a giant jaw breaker. Jacob had found an opening to this thing. He pulled at me to follow him. I moved slowly looking at the object in amazement as we went around. Jacob stopped and pointed. He shone his light into the opening. Hell, I almost had an orgasm. Though the water was murky I caught a good glimpse of something.

Something that I could not believe. As I got closer I knew now positively what it was. I stood in awe. I was dumfounded but as they say curiosity killed the cat. I motioned Jacob that I was going in. He looked at me with hesitation. I moved he grabbed my arm. I shone the flashlight to my face. I told him that I would be careful. He shone the light to his diving mask then said that we did not know what waited in there. I replied that I knew but it had to be done. He stared at me for a moment then nodded his head and released his grasp. Jacob knew as I that there was no way around it. The opening was the doorway. Somewhere in the riverbed lay the hatch to this spaceship. The water was clear enough inside to allow me to make out the instrument panel. I as well could make out what appeared to be writing on the far wall. I shone my light on it. I followed the writing I stopped. In the center of the writing right above the console was what seemed to be a picture of a creature. The words or writing where strange. I knew it was not the language that was from or earth. Jacob walked up beside me. He stared in amazement. Strange letter on the instrument panels. I dared not touch them. Who knew what they would cause the space ship to do.

Jacob shone his light to his mask. He asked what the fuck was that. I related that I did not know but it appeared to be a creature of sorts. Or light seemed like a light show in the spaceship as we search the interior. My light came upon what seemed to be a holding room. I walked inside I saw a small flying craft. This ship was inhabited with an alien. I walked around the craft. On the other side was something not of this world. It was a creature with four arms and a huge head. It was a strange alien, with human like features. He lay with his back split open. The four-arm creature had attacked the humanoid like alien. He or she I could not tell and I was not going to look. It had shot off its weapon it had killed it creature. It had bug like eyes. Yes, like that of an insect.

What went wrong in flight was its cargo. I believed it was the only explanation. Jacob and I moved into another room. I saw three compartments I think this would have been loaded on to the small flying craft to be delivered on some planet. Blue electrical charges shot out in all direction from the holding compartments. No, let me retrack it was a holding bend meant to keep something inside. I took a better look at the containment area. I saw three tubes of medium size inside the containment bends. These containment bends had been of glass with a wire mess of some kind inside the glass for extra protection. One of the small tubes inside had been broken. Whatever it held was gone. The question is, was it in the water at our feet. What made things even harder to comprehend was the fact that the small tubes inside these holding bins had been fused shut. What on earth did not need air to breath to live? I took my flashlight shone it on the small vial. It had the same writing. Inside was what appeared to be a sperm. I know it sounds crazy but that is what it looked like. I took the other vial. It had the exact writing as the other. Whatever they were? I knew it would be a find of the century. We were running out of time. I would have to try and decipher the writing at another time. Find of a century but still this made me feel uneasy. Jacob pointed up. I began to reach in and as I did blue small electrical charges shot about. These small containment bends where just that to keep something in. Whatever they were they did not want them getting out. They contained something but what?

What would these sperm like creatures evolve to. There were two containers intact. I followed through I reached in retrieved the two small containers put them into my diving pouch. I looked at my watch as did Jacob his. We had about thirty minutes left of air. About seventeen would be wasted on our climb back out of the river and on to land. We began to make our way back out of the spaceship. And as we made our way out my brain was already in the process of deciphering the writing. I came out with the conclusion that the writing was very similar to ours. Except that these alien words did not have vowels. I recall the words, "dngrs lffrm dstry." I knew what it meant but like a simple puzzle that baffles the mind. The answer lied right in front of me. The puzzle so simple that you cannot find the answer.

Later as the weeks passed I figured out the meaning of the words. The words read as, "Dangerous life form destroy." We stepped out of the ship suddenly I saw something move from the edge of the doorway. The life form from the broken tube. It was alive it shifted from one side to the other. It was as if it were agitated with our presents. Then in a split second it shot out like a tiny missle at an incredible speed. I could not believe it. I moved it shot by in a straight line in a collision course with Jacob. It shot directly at Jacob's face mask. It was as if it knew where it needed to attack. It was trying to penetrate the glass. It seemed that it wanted to get to Jacobs mouth. But why I asked as I saw this scenario. The funny thing was that this thing was like a human sperm but about a thousand times bigger. It swan back then shot forward and stop. It repeated the onslaught at Jacob's mask. Its small suction like lips opened and closed. It was as if it were trying to make its way through. I shone my light on Jacob I could see his mouth as he shouted with fear to get the thing off him. There was only one thing to do. I got closer I shone my light at his mask again. I began to reach out with my hand. It shifted as soon as the light hit it directly. I retrieved a small vial at my side on my weight belt. I handed it to Jacob. He unscrewed the lid. I counted one, two, three, and placed my hand over it so it could not move. Jacob moved the container under my hands. It shot straight into the container. Jacob quickly closed the lid. It stopped it turned and faced toward me. I guess it felt danger whatever the case had been. It shifted then darted two the bottom. It just laid still. Maybe it was the security of the vial. I do not know. I could see Jacob mouth open wide with relief. He said a few words. I was able to distinguish the words as if he had yelled them in my ear.

"What the fuck."

He repeated the words several times the air bubbles from his air tank came out sporadically. His fear had taken over his breathing at that moment. I would have freaked out as well if it had attacked me and had tried to get into my mouth. I grabbed his shoulder. I retrieved the other two vials then handed then to Jacob to put in the pouch. I told him to relax his breathing. I pointed up. He had understood nodding his head. I just hope he had not exhausted all his tanks air. I paused for a moment then seeing he had calm down I pointed to my weight belt unhooked the cable from my belt. Jacob nodded he knew what need to be done. He unfastened his cable. We wrapped them around the spaceship. We secured them in place then we began to swim upward. We made it back to land safely. For Jacob it was a good thing. He only had about two minutes of airtime left. Jacob quickly headed for the van to put the life form into one of the containers.

He picked up the container and placed the vials in a safe place for transportation. Jacob took off his wet suit then put on fresh clothing. I on the other hand had to make one more dive. I had to tie on the small straps of cable that would fasten the ship in and secure it for lifting out of the river. I climbed back into the water. When I completed my task I climbed back out of the water. I asked Mary to turn on the hoist. It was a slow tedious task to pull it up and out of the river. It hadn't been more than a few minutes when up the road two black limosense and a white mobile van like that of an ambulance drove up. It had not taken the doctor long. The question I ask myself is why? Or how did they know when to show up. I turned around quickly told Mary to shut off the winch. The hoist clanked to a halt. I could not see Jacob at the time. Jacob had vanished from site of the vehicles approaching. The cars stopped and four men climbed out. I noticed Jacob climbing back out of the back of the van. I looked out in his direction I did not have to ask the question in my throat at that moment. I knew he had gone back in to hide the life forms from the intruders. I just hope he hid them somewhere that they would not find. They had planned their arrival and timed it perfect. Who or how had the information leak out of us being here?

Mary no. Jacob no, not with all that we had done. Then who? I saw the doctor I knew him well he was my mentor and professor. Then it hit me somehow when we were away they had entered my home. They had planted bugs in my mansion. Not the bugs the creepy crawler kind but surveillance equipment. The bastard the fucking cock sucking bastard. They had infiltrated my home and my lab. They knew what I was experimenting on. Who else could it have been? Yes my dear professor. I had divulged my finding my theory on the possibility of creating a hybrid life. Not, a hybrid as a plant or animal but a hybrid human being to the doctor. I had surpassed his knowledge. He knew it as well. And he was jealous of my work of my accomplishment. What better way to get control and call it his baby.

Doctor Skyosky doctor of alientology. He had known as I what had fallen to earth. For the time being there was nothing I could do. He had government agents that where ready to enforce his order without hesitation. I watched on as the doctor gave the men orders. I could not hear him but I knew. No, sooner had the doctor turned his head back in my direction. When two of his goons swiftly surrounded the van. It was like seeing a herd of hungry hyenas waiting to attack a fallen animal. The doctor wore his white smock over a blue pin stripe suit. I would wager the man was wearing white tube socks underneath the pants. He approached us in a slow confident stride. He had us. We were not going to go anywhere. He stopped just inches away from me. I could smell his breath as he spoke. I would have told him that his breath smelled like shit but I knew that the consequences would be worse.

"Doctor Mongroll if you don't mind I would like you and you're colleagues to step away from the van."

Fucking foreigners, I thought to myself then did as he requested. I figure I would oblige him there was no use in resisting.

"Good," he said then ordered one of the men to search the van.

"What is it you are looking for?" I asked nonchalantly.

"What is it you have found Jeff?"

"What we found is still in the water Jim."

I stared into the man's cold blue eyes. He studied me for a moment then spoke.

"We will see if you are telling the truth soon enough."

The doctor stood at five eight. He had a pointed nose and was overly thin. The students had given him the nick name Greyhound. Put floppy ears a tail on this man and yes he would look like one indeed. As I said he was my mentor. I knew this man well. This doctor would steal an ideal if it meant his fame. He would get his information at any cost. He did not care for those that surpassed him. The doctor smiled as if he had read my thoughts.

"You placed bugs in my house. Why?"

"Yes, doctor Mongroll I don't want you to get a big head and keep the findings to yourself."

"You are an asshole Skyosky."

"Now doctor," he said then turned his attention to the agent making his way up to us.

"Doctor we searched every inch of the van. The equipment every corner all the inside. Nothing worth our effort doctor."

"Well if the doctor doesn't have it in the van let's see what the doctor found."

"Doctor Mongroll I need you to turn on that hoist. Pull out what you found in that river."

We did as he requested. We would bring the spaceship up out of the water.

"Ah, so it was a spaceship as I thought," he says as he opens his eyes wide.

"Yes doctor it is a space ship." "I will need my assistant."

"Yes, by all means doctor."

Mary turned on the hoist Jacob and I made sure that the cables stayed firm. We brought up the object after about fifteen minutes. Then suddenly one of the cables became slack. I looked at Skyosky he saw the cable then spoke.

"Do whatever it is you need to bring it up safely."

"Mary cut off the hoist." "Got it."

"Jacob bring, me my tank and face mask. I need to go back in."

I dove I had to make it seem as if I were following his orders. I reached the spear and went inside. I pulled out the alien life and the hedious four arm creature and laid then down on to the riverbed. I made sure they were firm in the mud. I placed my weight belt on top of the alien and creature. I scanned the ship for something I could use. I spotted a rod on the ground next to the escape pod. I picked it up went back to the body. I placed it between the alien's belt and my weight belt. I pushed the rod down as far as I could. He would get the ship, but I would make sure he did not get the life forms. I quickly tighten the support cable. I swam back up to the surface gave Mary the okay to restart the hoist. The hoist cranked on and the cable became taut. I took off my face mask, tank, and lay them on the ground. It had not taken long for us to bring the ship up and onto dry land.

"Okay doctor Mongroll you and your two colleagues can go back to the van. Don't try to leave."

CHAPTER 14

Jacob, Mary, and I made our way to up the van. I knew I would soon hear his voice for he had not inspected the ship as of yet. I knew the man he like the torment game. He moved his head then one of the agents join us. We waited patiently for the doctor to begin his inspection. He turned vanished as he went into the spaceship. He took his time.

He examined the spaceship he saw the writing inside then focused his eyes to the room with the containment compartments.

"Hum, three empty compartments one with broken glass," he said to himself.

He walked to the room were the dead alien and creature would have been. He then turned around walked out of the sphere and up to me. There was a pause of silence before he spoke.

"There are three empty compartments Dr.

Mongroll. One has shards of broken glass. My question is where are the other two? Do you have any ideal doctor Mongroll? And the ship flew itself doctor."

"Maybe it only had one passenger aboard." "Doctor I am curtain that the escape pod and the weapon on the floor had to belong to the pilot of this ship. But it is funny no pilot aboard. Maybe there in the escape pod? We will find out the answer to that question at a later time. For now doctor Mongroll I don't have the time for this bullshit. So let's cut the fucking games Mongroll."

"Look Skyosky, I know only of the broken vial nothing else. I of course lied. We had two of the life forms. It was deserted, vacant, no one around but the one broken container. Whatever was inside vacated it."

"But I do believe that the lifeform in the broken vial is free in the water."

"You saw the alien life form?"

"Yes, Jacob and I saw it. It swam freely in the river. I saw it face to face as did Jacob."

He mulled what I had said over for a second. I could see the anger growing in his face. Perhaps it was not us but the fact that whatever was in the space ship was free and out of his control.

"Oh, one more thing if you are going to look for this alien life form. I would put on protective gear. Whatever it was attacked Jacob's face. It seemed it wanted to get into Jacob's mouth. One more small bit of information for you. This thing you will be searching for looks like a giant human sperm just a thousand times bigger."

"I will take care of thing from here on out. I think it is time for you and your help to leave."

I moved slowly not to give him a hint that inside I wanted to hurry and get out of there. I did not want him to know that we had two of the alien life forms. As I picked up my face mask and tank. From my peripheral vision I saw the doctor say something to one of the men. In moments he was heading back to the van. I do not have the slightest hint on how Jacob had accomplished it.

But somehow, he had given Mary the containers with the life form. One of the agents opened the driver side then told Jacob to climb back out. He then went over to Mary's side. He stopped and glared at her. I continued to walk towards them.

"Stop right there Mongroll let us finish with the search."

I looked on that was the only thing that I could do. I saw Mary squirm. I had no inclination at the time why it appeared she was so uncomfortable. Jacob moved up to my side. He knew what I was thinking. He whispered softly to me.

"Between heaven and earth."

I frowned not understanding what he had said. I knew that he could not say it out loud. I looked at him again and he could see I was bewildered.

"It lays in the valley of pleasure."

I knew what he meant then. Mary had placed the containers. I should say one of the containers. The other had fallen out onto the ground in our rush. She had the one vial between her legs. With deep anxiety I watched as the agents rummaged through our equipment once more. I glared at the agent. I wondered if he would snap in half like a twig in his rigid frame. I noticed a funny expression shoot across Mary's face. If I have to be honest it almost looked like she was ready to unload a baby. The agent at Mary's door began to open it. He was about to tell her to get out of the vehicle. But like all men he ask the wrong question.

"You okay miss."

"I'm just hunky dory. What the hell do you think is wrong with me? Can't you see the expression on my face, asshole. I just had an awful cramp. You know like the ones women and your mama had. It is called a period. You did have a mother did you not? I have to sit here for a moment then I will get out. You would think you men would get the hint the first time you inspected the van that we are not hiding nothing."

Mary then gave the man an angry look. She shook her head then looked at him with her eyes open wide as to say well can I have time alone. The man scanned the inside then closed the door. He walked back up to the doctor. He told him that the van was clean. The doctor looked at the van then at Jacob and me.

"Doctor Mongroll you can leave."

I wanted to reach out and tear the man's head off his shoulders with my bare hands. I needed to remain silent so I bit my tongue.

"Let's get out of dodge Jeff," Jacob said.

Jacob climb into the back seat. I climbed in put the key in the ignition then started up the van. Mary made a funny face again as I began to drive off. I pulled off the dirt road. I looked out the windshield at the doctor. It pissed me off that they would allow a pompous fool like him to take over the discovery. The spaceship would have been an added plus. But the life organism in my possession would suffice. It would suffice enough that I that we could get a Pulitzer for our discovery. If they wanted an alien life form, then the doctor would have to go into the Willamette as I and Jacob had. The only thing is that they would come out empty handed. Knowing the doctor he would play it out. He would wait for us to make a mistake or say something that he could use. This thing we found only God knew what it would become. I drove slowly not to bring any more attention to us. I turned I then pulled out on to the paved road back onto the main highway.

"Its cramps I loved it Mary," Jacob exclaimed then repeated what he said and laughed out loud.

Mary raised up her skirt for me to take a look. Between her legs was the life form moving, wiggling, up her enter thigh. It was inching its way up to her private region. I did not know whether to laugh or shout for her to kill it before it got any further. It had been extremely fast in the water. But out of water it was like a slow snail. I was quite amused.

"Quit gawking. Stop the van and get this thing off me and back into its container," Mary interjected apprehensively.

I knew that if I did not stop the van she would soon scream. I pulled over to the emergency shoulder. I saw Mary biting her lower lip I needed to hurry. She squirmed uncomfortably as the thing got closer to her privates. I abruptly stopped to a halt. The tires screeching as the rubber grabbed at the pavement. I unfastened my safety belt reached over pulled Mary's dress up further all the way up to her waist. The life form was to close for comfort.

"Oh, my God, oh, my God," she whimpered.

I reached between her legs grabbed the open container then separated her legs a little more. I placed the container next to it. I scrapped it off her thigh with the lid. I placed it in and secured the lid on firmly. I looked at the small vial and at the life form for a moment. Mary thanked me softly for she was relieved. I smiled I could only imagine the eerie feeling she felt as it squirmed up her thigh. And at the time she could not make a move without letting the doctor know. How had it managed to escape its confine? How did it break the vial? It was closed and they had a wire scream securing it.

"Give me one of the small containers from the briefcase Jacob."

He handed me the container then handed me the lid. I placed it in position. I looked at it for a moment longer. I then used the lid to assist it into the container and handed it back to Jacob.

"Where is the other one Mary?" I ask.

"I did not think of it at the time Jeff. But it must have fallen to the ground."

I would not press the matter for it was what it was. I could see goose bumps popping all over Mary's leg and arms.

"We now know it can live out of water." "Yeah, and it was at my expense," she said slightly miffed.

Jacob laughed and I put the van in gear then gradually I made my way back on to traffic.

"You wouldn't have thought it was so funny if this thing was crawling up your ass trying to get some poon tang."

"You have a point," Jacob agreed.

As the word from Mary mouth registered into our brain we all began to laugh. The thought of the other life form out there on the ground worried me. I did not think that the doctor would search the same area for the life form they had already been at. Skyosky wanted to be known, remembered, as one of the best. He was a smart man but with intelligence sometimes dumb things happen. For now we need to get home and our work must begin. I have the Ace in the hole and I am going to use it.

CHAPTER 15

That was the beginning of our nightmare. These last days here on this Coast Guard Ship I had plenty of time to reflect on things. I had done so. So that I could write relate what happen up until now. I was in despair, my attempts to protect life was a failure. But in the game of poker when you are dealt with a good hand everything seems to come together. This is what I thought but should of realized. It started off being one of those weird weather days. It was strange from the word go. It was as if the moon, stars, and all living things of our world pull at my very soul. Pulling me in the direction of deciding what I should do next. Perhaps it was the Nino effect on this world. Whatever the cause it was warmer than usual in Portland Oregan where the weather is usually cool. Maybe it was El Nino or possibly the world was experiencing a change of its own. Changes like those of human's. Like us the people of this world going through what we call the change of life.

Maybe the evolution chart meant something? Something, we could not comprehend. And maybe it was time for the world to cleanse itself from what was killing it. That of course would be us the people. Who really knew with all the explosions, then digging, and not to mention the contamination of the drinking water. The cutting down of all the trees? And maybe the price for our own selfish needs will be too high of a cost. It is possible that Mother Nature could retaliate against us.

Against the so call keepers of this planet. As I said the world seemed to be in a turmoil of its own. Thing just were not the same. I guess the best way to explain it is that if evil existed then a veil of darkness surrounded our world. I say this for people were killing like animals.

Killing for no apparent reason. Perhaps it was just for gratification. Killing without purpose killing just to kill to feel power over someone. And God, God, was just a word that people heard on occasions. The meaning behind our savior was forgotten. Gone from people's beliefs, morals, and the way we live. Can you believe that belief was now becoming a crime? A crime to believe in a better place. They had become intimidated by this world and our savior. The wick finding any reason to destroy rather than to preserve. The question that we need to ask is if we the people are superior to another. Are we superior to that of another race? Then why is it we all bleed. Again the question to be ask is why? Is blood from another race not compatible to all races.

Aggression instead of kindness. Had we become more like animals? Have we made a step backward and reverted back to the primordial state? Had we become predators of the weak? We as people need to understand the simplicity of our own existence. And that is that we all became. It was my determination to make man stronger a new breed. A breed that would withstand any adverse condition. A creature that would be able to care for itself. A subhuman that could tap into its own D.N.A. like that of a lizard. A new creature able to rejuvenate a hand or a leg after dismemberment.

Many theories are out there. I could jot down the hundreds of possibilities. The thousands, the million theories. Rejuvenation still is new. All theory out there are or could be possible. Many scientist have come to the same conclusion that the brain is the answer. And that it has the ability to cure itself hidden somewhere in the inner part of the brain. Studies of the brain have been ongoing for years. Now is the time to study it in depth. Explore it like a new universe to an astrologer.

Scientist experiments with rats and human tissue where miracles of the century. My mind races back to when I sat in the lecture room listen to my professor. I recall setting quietly as I stared in awe as he displayed a rat. A rodent with an ear growing from its back. On its back constructed for human use. It was stupendous. It was wonderful. It was the first stage of being like a God. Like being a God in all its glory.

The power to create life can you believe that? This, this, was to become my own person hell. My studies began I became possessed with the my work. Hour after hour I toiled in my laboratory like a mole hidden below ground. I had equipped my father's wine cellar with the best equipment available on the market. I have to say it was better than many labs around the world. I bought it all, microscopes, incubators, test tubes, chemicals, and one of the best computers around. Money was no problem money was what I had plenty of. Let me explain I acquired millions from my father. Night after night I burrowed deeper into my lab. I searched for that one answer for that one clue. What was life? And where and how do I create it? I had to find the answer. Hearing my father's voice hearing him boosting to his friends that one day I would create a cure for cancer.

This reason drove me. Cancer killed him, it kills love ones without warning. It crept up on man, woman, child, like a blanket of invisible death. And that is exactly what it was death. Cryosurgery was becoming the leading weapon to fight liver pancreas and prostate cancer. I could have gone in this direction. But I was reaching for the stars. I was to create life that would not have any flaws. A subhuman with the D.N.A., that would kill any invader to its body. To make a tail or an arm when it had been severed off. It would grow back. I was disillusion with the world with humanity itself. I believe that God wanted me to create such a new life. The sins in the Ten Commandments would be a thing of the past. This new life would just kill for food. It would breed when it was time. It would kill just for food and to protect itself. No jealousy or language barrier. No hate of color or religion. No more terrorist or the need to fight over oil. The atrocity of this world was man. No more. I would create the new protector of this world.

So, thus I began my experiment in the construction of the new Adam and Eva. Little did I know what I was getting into or the horrible price I would wind up paying. I had committed the ultimate sin against God. And that I can never be forgiven for. I pleaded with God for forgiveness. I pleaded for forgiveness from the people of Portland Oregon. There is not an hour, minute, or second, that passes that I do not think of the blood spilled. I write with regret in this journal while on this ship as we wait like scared rodents for our demise at the claws of what I created. I think of the evil that I let loose upon the metropolitan area. On the evil that spawned from my blood. What I created was neither good nor beautiful. What I had created was hideous. Yes, and it was a killer. In my own glory I had not anticipated or even had dreamt of conceiving such a monster. I should have stopped. I should have killed it when I saw what was taking form from my blood and the alien organism. In a way I Jeffery Mongroll II was its father. I know some of my words are confusing to you right now.

But as I go on I know my words will help you understand the horrifying tale behind my ambition and of my God complex. The next words I write down will be my last for my time is running out. I lift my head up from the journal for a second. I see a Navy Seals moving about taking their positions for the assault on Adam. I had no idea, it would come down to this. I will find my own demise at its hands. Poetic justice. I find peace in a way for it will be the purest justice given. We hear the phrase that blood is thicker than water frequently. How true these words are. My heart weighs heavy with sadness. I cannot explain the way I feel only someone that has caused such grief and pain as I could know of the true feeling I am feeling inside. This feeling of true horror and of hell. I will try to remedy my wrong. I know whatever I do cannot bring back my beloved Mary, and my dearest of friends Jacob. Or the innocent people that succumbed by the creature hand. Please I ask with all my heart please forgive me for what I have done.

CHAPTER 16

When we arrived at the mansion. I pulled into the driveway I cut the engine off. I opened the door and climbed out carefully making sure I cradled the small vial in my hands like a precious jewel. Jacob and Mary followed me up to the house. Once inside I walked up to the far wall turned the fake lamp to the right. Jacob quickly moved the persan rug out of the way for the trap door to open. Once the trap door had open we proceeded down into the laboratory. I stopped I then turned around.

"Mary go back upstairs get us a bag of coffee. It is going to be a long night."

We would be needing the extra boost of adrenaline. I told Jacob that once I put the life form into deep freeze. That we would need to look for the surveillance equipment that Skyosky had placed in the mansion. It would be like finding a needle in a haystack but it was imperative that we find them.

"Miss Mary," says Silva as she notices Mary rummaging through the cabinet.

"I am just looking for some coffee." "You want me to make you a fresh batch."

"No, thanks Silva, I need a bag of coffee to take down into the lab."

"Next cabinet Miss Mary third shelf up." Mary grabbed the coffee thanked Silva. She returned back to the laboratory. I grabbed the bag of coffee then took the coffee pot filled it with water. Minutes later I took a sip of the freshly brewed coffee. I returned to my experiment. I made sure that the lid to the vial was secure. The life form had tried to impregnate Mary I am certain of this. But I dare not mention it to her. I opened the freezer made sure the lid was fastened on tight. I put the organism back in deep freeze for the time being. I took my cup of coffee and went back to the computer. I told Mary that the coffee was made. I looked at my colleagues for a moment before speaking. I was still in awe of what we had discovered. I took a little more time to focus my thoughts.

"Okay, let's do it," I exclaimed.

We prepared for the experiments that we would be conducting the following day. We did not and could not waste any more time. It was our dream. It was our time. The opportunity had fallen in our laps. Nothing was to impede the experiment or the making of a new life. Nothing must impede our plan. I calculated every bit of information. I made sure that the equation for each of our experiments were precise down to the last detail. We had no room for failure. We needed to be prefect with our calculations. There was no room for mistakes. I continued on with such zeal. Not wanting to stop not wanting to yield to fatigue. I stood up from my stool after several long hours of tedious writing and configuring of the equations.

Everything needed to be written down as we went along. I closed the journal I looked at the tired faces of my colleagues. Fatigue brought mistakes that we could not tolerate.

"Let's call it a night guys."

"Jeff that sounds good," Mary replies back. "I concurred," Jacob agreed.

"Okay, then let's call it a night."

Mary yawned stood up. She and Jacob followed me out of the laboratory.

"Get a good sleep we start bright and early," I interjected.

"Early, early, it already is," Jacob says. "Guess you are right," I said looking at my wristwatch I then looked at Jacob, "guess rooms ready and waiting. Silva put fresh linen on the bed as well as fresh towels."

"Remind me to thank her Jeff."

I nodded my head I looked at my watch again. It was five o'clock in the morning. I knew Jacob did not mind sleeping over in fact he loved it. He would tell me that the rooms in the mansion I took for granted. He said it was five time the size of his bedroom. And the king size bed in the blue opaque room to sleep on was a Sultans dream.

"It took money to buy these thing Jeff," he said then added, I will someday accomplish my dream."

We went upstairs. Mary opened the door to our bedroom. I stopped told Jacob to have a good night sleep the said morning sleep. Mary stepped into the room skipped up to our bed on one foot. The king size bed with a brass headboard looked pleasing at that moment. I looked at the white silk sheet spread over the bed. I knew that my body would be in ecstasy as soon as I lay down.

Next to the bed was my nightstand with the alarm clock and it had just gone off. I hurried to cut it off. I took off my shoes walked on the soft green Persian rug. I then walked up to my dresser reached in to one of the drawers. I pulled out one of my monogrammed robes. As soon as Mary sat on the edge of the bed, she began to rub her feet. She moaned several times as she massaged them.

"Oh, that feels good doesn't it my puppies?" She ask her feet.

She went to the closet. I stared as Mary stood and began to undress. She turned then looked at me I felt a lump in my throat. She knew and purposely began to take off her white smock slowly then her blouse. She smiled again I felt my heart skip a beat. I looked on as she removed her white panties and bra. She smiled again then tossed them my way. Her eyes met mine it sent an electrical impulse through my flesh. It had been days if not a month we had even kissed. And a longer time went by sense I held her in my arms the way I should have. We were scientist therefore she did not complain.

She knew we had test to make. Test after test, it seemed. The work seemed to drain our sexual needs. I looked at her on the bed as I walked by from the edge of the bed. She sucked on her finger. I knew exactly what that meant but today I was going to play hard to get. I walked into the bathroom to do my business. I sat down on the toilet without looking at the important things. I reached for the roll of toilet paper.

"Shit!" I said softly for there was none.

I felt foolish like a kid caught with a porno magazine in his hands. There was only one thing to do. I would have to eat crow.

"Mary, Mary," I shouted. "What?"

"I need some damn toilet paper," I shouted somewhat embarrassed.

"Use a finger save a tree," she quipped.

I did not reply knowing if I had she would have teased me the rest of the night. She made a joke and it just now sunk in. I began to laugh it was funny. She brought me what I needed of course. I was truly indebted to her. I knew she went back into the bedroom to take off her jewelry. I walked out Mary was stark naked. I swallowed hard as I took off my robe. I walked back into bathroom I turned the shower on. I entered the warm water relaxing the tension in my body.

"Are you mad at me?" "No, of course not."

I knew Mary just wanted to make small talk. I played the hard to get card and it was working. I knew she was anxious and so was I. I felt like taking her there where she sat. Patients I told myself. Moments later Mary climbed into the shower with me. She cooed as the water hit her skin. I could feel her body's warmth as she looked at me.

She looked down then looked back up at me. "I see what you have been thinking of."

Again, she cooed. She hugged me tight then shivered. She laid her head softly on my chest. The water caressing our bodies like tiny fingers. The tingling sensation awaking or flesh. She looked at me then gave me the look of invitation. She stood on her tip toes and kissed me. I quickly bent forward to meet her full lips. We did not need to speak for our bodies spoke out our need. She leaned against the east wall away from the spray of water. She raised her right leg straddling my waist. I did not need any more encouragement. She had enticed every fiber in me.

I wanted her with a never-ending passion. I leaned close to her. The water hitting my back. My hand became sensors picking up the impulses from her body. We became in tuned with one another entering a world of our own. A world that I should have visited with her more frequent. A world call heaven where time stops and it appears that one was floating in the sky with the clouds. We were like angles embracing each other. In our rapture I forgot about time about the alien life form. The water splashing down on my back making time absent.

We woke up just in time for the evening meal the next day. We were young but sleep, sleep deprivation, now that was something that no matter at what age, young, or old, it would defeat one. By the time we dressed and went downstairs Silva had breakfast ready. I entered the kitchen I walked up to Silva kissed her on the cheek. When I look at her, I remember the granny from one of the cookie pack. She had gray hair except she was a dark virgin of the woman on the cookie wrapper. James walked in handed me the newspaper. Silva brought my breakfast and Mary's. She did not have to ask what we preferred to eat. She knew she waited on us many years. She placed the plates before us and smile. She told us to eat up. She returned just a few seconds later with a plate for Jacob as well. Jacob's eyes open wide with joy as soon as he saw the huge T-Bone, two scramble eggs, and pancakes on his plate.

"Pancakes with walnuts in them. I love pancakes with walnuts."

"Silva you making breakfast is better than the restaurants."

"Ah, you are silly Jacob. Eat."

"Silva if you were not married already I would ask you to be my wife."

Silva laughed the said, "ah, you say that to all the girls that cook food for you Jacob."

"Silva," Jacob said as he turned slightly in his chair.

"Hold Jacob up I am bringing you something else."

"What?"

"I bring you the biggest bowl of grits ever." "God, I love you Silva," Jacob exclaims as

James her husband walks in from out in the garden. "Jacob do an old man a favor don't play like that. Take her and don't bring her back please." "What did you say you old fart," she said as she moved up to the sink.

"I said scratch my back."

"Why you asking Jacob I will scratch your back old man," she says to James knowing what he had said.

James smiled at Jacob as if he had won some unseen prize. James walked up to her kissed her on the cheek then drank a glass of water and returned to his gardening.

"Who, in the hell bought grits?" I ask surprised.

"I did Jeff. You can use a good meal for once.

Too much T-Bone, prime rib, is not good for you. Jacob knows what I mean huh Jacob."

"Yes, I do. I was raised on veggies. They are the best food around."

"That is you culture Jacob. My culture was raised on cattle. Hell! I almost want to start singing oh give me a steak from a buffalo or cow."

"Jeff you know that is not the way the song goes," Silva says.

We all started to laugh out loud. I thought I saw a little bit of sadness behind Silva's smile.

"Okay, Silva if you cook it, I will eat it."

I stood then went up to her and hugged her tightly.

"Yes, boy I love you too."

I smiled then walked out to the foyer and up to the lamp. Mary took a sip of her coffee placed the cup down as did Jacob. They stood up then followed me down into the laboratory. The following sequences of test would be crucial no mistakes could be made. I told myself over and over. We were like kids with a new toy we were elated.

Elated with the mystery and the thrill of new life. We would be exploring this life form from space. It had been given to us on a silver platter as they say. And we were going to take advantage of it the best we could. Jacob walked to the container.

Took it out of the deep freeze. He brought it up to the table then handed it to me. I carefully opened up the container. I took some tweezers in my hand. I picked the life form out of the vial I placed it into a Petri Dish. I placed the small electro's on the Petri dish. I gave the okay Jacob began the procedure to thaw out the organism. Next I placed a syringe with the formula I had created ready to be administered in to the life form on my right. It contained three different D.N.A.'s from three creatures that I believed had survived the worst disasters, wars, wind, fire, water, plagues. Creatures that had beaten the odds of our world.

Creatures that had proven there will to live. We were not ready to slice and dice as they say. We wanted to make a new life that would stand for something. We wanted to make life. Life like a God. That was to become are misfortune. We forgot the laws of Mother Nature. The law that we should not attempt to be as God. We needed to remember that we were just scientist with knowledge that we had accumulated. Only a true God had all the answers.

CHAPTER 17

The first of the D.N.A, that I choose was that of Rattus. Rattus is one of the largest of all mammalian genera. Rats belong to the group of vertebrates animals call mammals. This would keep my creation more on the human aspect. Mammals are different than other vertebrates by various structural and physiological feathers. Mammals have for chamber hearts. A true palate in the roof of their mouth. They have red blood cells without nuclei. Mammals have a lower jawbone that is attached to the bony mass of the skull. They also have mammary glands that produce milk for suckling their young. Rats are alert, intelligent, animals that quickly learn. They can grow to be the size of a domestic house cat. They are aggressive, omnivorous, and can adapt to its environment. It can, gnaw, climb, jump, and even burrow into most places. It can squeeze through a hole as small as the size of a quarter. Or even burrow through concrete undetected giving it the advantage. It has adapted to living with humans. I hope this one trait will help.

They can eat practically everything and anything in sight. It is believed that they carried at least twenty of the most deadly diseases ever found. Bubonic plague, rabies, typhus, tularemis, are just a few. If we could just come close to making a superior creature a new race of man. A new life that can be exposed to the deadliest of diseases. Exposed and still be able to flourish. Able to live would be the ultimate creation the ultimate dream. Most would cringe at Rattus appearance or shriek away at it sight. A rat is an incredible animal for it has already proven itself by surviving, surviving, the utmost of disaster and to boot in some countries it is even a delicacy.

The second of the D.N.A. that I chose was that of the krait sea snake. This water reptile as well an incredible animal in its own rite. An animal that had altered its state and moved back into the water. It descended into the depth of the ocean.

It adapted quickly to its new territory, environment. It removed itself away from the danger of man. How many animals could do such and incredible journey from land to water. We have heard about the opposite of reptile's leaving the water and moved to land. But to reverse the process was a stupendous foot. Incredible is the only word I can use.

The D.N.A. of the third animal that I had decided to use was small but pound for pound the deadliest I think of all. It is a magnificent creature. It is the Piranha. It is the most horrifying of the animals I picked. Looking at this exotic fish in a fish tank one would not even give it a second thought. Looking at it in the fish, tank. Yes, in the fish tank it was harmless or appeared to be. Reality sets in when its jaws opened. When it expose the triangular teeth.

Teeth that lock firmly together when it bites. In a way it is like a Pitt Bull of the Amazon. Piranha's take clean bites of flesh they bite into. They nibble about a cubic inch {16 cm 3} at a time stripping their victims down to the bone. Piranha's have short stocky bodies that are deeper from back to belly than most river fish. These fish are found in the lower basin in South America. The largest is the {Pygocentrus Piraya} the best know species of this fish is the white spotted Piranha. This fish is sold mostly in pet stores. {Serrasalmus Rahombeus} The one with the worst reputation is the {Natterer's or the Red Piranha} {Roosevettiella Nattereri} Piranha's are cable of growing about seventeen inches long.

It is small but yet most powerful. It is able to devour a water buffalo in minutes as a group. Its teeth are like sharp porcelain that can strip the flesh off the bone in minutes. It is noted for its ferocity. Its skin ranges from silvery blue, green, brown, or black. I picked this Rooosevettiella Nattereri Piranha for that one purpose and with the other two D.N.A. of Rattus, and the Sea Krait I knew it would be the ultimate creation.

Mary," I said letting her know to start the procedure.

I returned my gaze back to the microscope as she placed the organism in the Petri dish under the scope. I took the syringe held the life form with the tweezers. I slowly inserted the point of the needle into its skin. It squirmed as I injected the formula into its body. It squirmed almost thrashing about. It reminded me of a small worm coiling before placing it on a fishing hook. I placed the syringe down and waited. I remained glued to my stool. I remained in the same position for at least an hour in front of the scope. I stood I ran my hands through my hair as Mary took her shift at looking at the life form. Nothing seemed to be happening. It had just lay there without a sign of life. It seemed dead to the world. I was getting worried. What was I doing wrong? I asked myself. I could feel the frustration clouding up my ability to think straight. It was beginning to overwhelm my thoughts. I felt a rage I felt like breaking all the equipment in the laboratory. I knew it would not accomplish anything. I was not about to quit not yet. I could see signs of fatigue as well as disappointment on my colleagues faces. I knew they wanted to say something. I knew they could see the disappointment in my face.

"What do we do now Jeff," Mary ask as she put her hands in her smock pockets.

I looked around the room my brain ran wild calculating equations through my head.

"Okay, let's sit down and access the problem together."

"Why of course," Mary agreed then ads, "three heads are better than one," she interjected.

Mary and Jacob grabbed a stood sat down next to me. Jacob moved over one of the vial steaming with chemicals running through a tube and put his arm on the counter. We discussed and evaluated every bit of information until morning. We were getting nowhere I took the coffee pot placed it over one of the burners used to heat up chemicals. I heated the coffee then pour each one of us a cup of coffee. We did not sleep we continued on with our sequence of test. We waited for something from the life form. I knew inside I had calculated every equation perfectly. So why in the hell was there no response? Why? Again I ask myself what? What was it that I was missing? What on the element chart was I not seeing? I needed to find the answer. I had impregnated it with the different

D.N.A. It had to accept the D.N.A., before I could continue on with my endeavor. I could not administer it to a human not yet. I needed evidence that it would work. I was disillusioned with failure. I wanted positive feedback.

Nothing, still nothing, not even a hint not a glimpse of a flinch from the creature. Again I felt like smashing my fist down crushing even the organism for just laying there. Still I was not ready to give up.

"Prepare for a second dose," I said as I stood and went to the get another syringe with formula A.

I Came back sat down in front of the telescope. I placed the syringe down to one side. I looked into the eye piece in hope of seeing movement. Somewhat miffed I jerked my hand back. I felt a sharp pain as the needle stuck into my flesh. My finger stung a droplet of my blood ran down to the back of my finger as I looked at it.

"Shit, shit," I barked out.

The blood bubbled up to the surface as I squeezed my finger.

Mary brought me an antiseptic alcohol pad. I did not a see droplets of my blood fall into the Petri dish next to the life form. I wiped my finger with the alcohol pad. I felt the disinfectant instantly working. What happen all of a sudden was pure luck. It was glorious, stupendous. When I had pricked my finger with the syringe, I had not noticed that blood had fallen into the dish. After bandaging my finger, I had returned to the microscope. To my surprise the life form pulsated with life. It was alive. I did not see it at first. Then I realized that it was feeding on my blood. Yes, it was feeding. The missing ingredient, answer, was blood, that was the answer to life. Simple is what it was. Organism + blood = life. Yes, my blood was the God given answer. It would be in all genetic books known as the Mongroll theory of life. Perhaps I was reading ahead. Yes, my blood was the answer. I knew exactly what to do next. On occasion I wonder if this organism would have lived no matter if it had human blood or not. If we had not tried to impregnate the girl now with the blood and with the different D.N.A. Would it have survived? From what I know I can say I truly believe it would have stain life one way or another. It had lay in the Petri dish in a dormant stage like the mud fish that lives in the Amazon. And as soon as the rains come it as well comes back to life. Its mission was to survive this is when I should have ceased all experiments and killed the life form. I became mad with the ideal of creation. I was mad like Dr. Jekll and Mr. Hyde. There was no stopping now.

The girl we had inject the previous day was still alive. I had been getting closer to my creating a subhuman. I had become mad as I mention. Mad with the ideal of creation. I placed the equipment on the crash cart. I moved it into place next to the steel table for the soul purpose of operating. The girl was in her late teens another runaway. A runaway and as the say money talks and bull shit walks. She lay disrobe she moaned on occasions. I injected the needle into the life form it squirmed violently I withdrew the fluid within it. I then injected the girl with the formula and alien D.N.A. It did not take. Fuck, fuck, fuck, the word ran through my head bombarding every corner of my brain. My mind raced back to the van and Mary. I saw the life form as it inched its way up to Mary's privates. As I said before I was certain it had tried to impregnate Mary. That was the answer. I was frustrated there was only one recourse. I ask Jacob to bring me the vial with life form. I poked the needle through the rubber stopper I pulled back on the syringe plug. I then picked up the alien life with the tweezers. I injected it with the formula B I had created form the three different specimens. Jacob pull the girls legs apart and put them in to the stirrups. I bent forward placed the sperm into position. I inseminated her as one would do with a human sperm injecting it to an egg. The only difference was these doners where not of the humankind. I placed the life form into position, and it did the rest. It was as if nature had take its course. Now we would wait. If I was right about the alien life form it would start to grow rapidly in the girls womb. It did not take the normal nine month for this life form to grow into a fetus. It had happen in a matter of weeks give or take a day. We did not move her for the following two weeks. We continued to feed her through the I. V. feeding tube.

CHAPTER 18

We watched her day in day out. The fourth month on the last day as I wrote down the progress she screamed at the top of her lungs. It was as if she was being ripped apart. I gave her something to take away the pain. I could see the infant moving in her. I could see it shifting. Seconds later Mary cried out that the infant inside her was now crowning. Jacob stood at the ready. I thought it would be a normal birth. It began to ripped her apart. It had birth like all babies into this world. I grabbed its head securely. With my other hand I assisted it out. It was a natural birth.

Natural birth except for the fact that it tore her apart. I looked at the girl. I knew she was dead. I was glad it was over for her. I was glad her pain had ceased. Jacob took the newborn from my hands and Mary wiped it off with a towel. We would take a few weeks to examine it through. We would study its demeanor, its intelligence, and its muscle structure. It looked like a human baby but some parts seemed altered. We examined it closer we were amazed at what we saw. It had gills on the side of its neck just below where the ear should be. For now it looked like a human but we needed to put it in a fish tank for the fact it had gills.

"We will be needing a fish tank." I said out loud.

"Yes, Jeff I have to agree Jacob says. "Why a fish tank it looks human?"

"Look closer at the side of its head Mary."

She bent down looked at the neck. She saw the gills pulsating moving in and out. It appeared it was still able to inhale the air comfortably. I rolled the baby over onto its side. I pulled back on its gills to study them. The black gills moved in and out taking in oxygen.

"I'll be right back Jeff," Jacob says as he begins to leave.

"Where you going?"

"I believe it is more aquatic there for to be on the safe side I am going to go get that fish tank."

As we waited for Jacob to return Mary and I studied the infant's skin thoroughly. Its eyes, and ears as well. An hour later Jacob returned with a huge fish tank the kind that needed to be install for the customer. Hide the infant for a while until the men leave he tells Mary. Mary places the baby in the other room away from human eyes.

"How," I asked. "Yes, how Mary ask.

"Money, your money Jeff."

The two men that had delivered it had it up in no time. I ask them to put it close to the double doors of the wine cellar leading out to the back road. We brought them a hose. They filled the tank with water. The air pump to kept oxygen flowing into the tank. After the two men left Mary brought back the infant. She placed it into the water slowly. It floated down it lay at the bottom motionless. A day past still there was no movement. The only thing we saw was its gills moving in and out. It was alive. I did not understand. I did not know what to do. It began to seem as if we had failed again. I was just about to tell my colleagues that it was time to throw in the towel. Mary said it is still alive.

Jacob said to give it more time. We gave it another week it just lay there. Abruptly as we looked at it we noticed that it twitched. Jacobs, Mary, and my own eyes opened wide with excitement. We stared at the infant. We saw what appeared to be a tail that had grown. How had we missed this happening? Mary smiled and nodded in approval. I do not know what made it decide to swim but it just started to move its hands and feet. The only explanation is that this life form. This new wave infant had been in a hibernation state of some kind. It had slept and had grown a foot taller.

It was a growth spurt. I noticed it had developed several other characteristics we had not seen of as yet. It swan, but I did not notice it had grown arms or legs. Yes, it was alive and it was growing fast. Though it looked like a deformed child at first it now resembled a human being created in a woman's womb. In this odd case the womb was that of the fish tank. Its movement where sharp and the small tadpole like mouth open and closed as if it was trying to feed. Now, the question was what do we feed it?

"What do we feed it?" Mary asked.

"What we feed it is fish food," Jeff states.

"Fish food I would say is correct. It is aquatic," Jacob agreed.

"Then fish food is what we will give it first. It has gills therefore it has taken the traits and characteristics of the Piranha. Therefore fish food." I said.

It was a good assumption we looked at the infant that was forming before us with each passing day.

"Who is going to go get the fish food?" Mary asked.

"I thought about it on the way there," Jacob say and to be sure I bought a box of fish food."

Mary took the fish food from Jacob's hand and began to open up the box. She sprinkled the fish food on top of the water as one would do for a regular fish in an aquarium. In the next couple of weeks, it had grown as much as a three-month-old.

It was growing at an accelerated rate. It opened its mouth. I saw what where teeth growing. Sharp teeth I felt something that was strange as if I knew that it was a monster coming to be. It was growing at an excelerated pace fast taking on more human traits. I felt that it needed to be confined to the tank. I went to the hardware store. I returned with some wire mesh. The next day I worked on the tank. Jacob drilled holes on the metal part of the fish tank as I placed the wire mesh screen on top of the fish tank. I held one corner down in place. I began to insert the screw. It was astounding amazing this creature had intelligence. It seemed as if it had known what I was up to. It darted from the bottom of the tank like a speeding bullet heading straight for my thumb. My thumb barely submerged underneath the water. It hit I felt a searing pain shoot through my thumb. I looked down at the infant as it sucked away at my blood. It sucked at the blood like a kitten suckling its mother milk from her tit. I jerked my hand out as quick as I could. Instantly blood trickled out and fell into the water. The droplets floating down slowly then separate. I cut off the supply by squeezing my thumb tightly. It shifted and darted back down to the bottom of the tank. I had to see again. I squeezed my finger bring up the blood again. A few more drops fell into the water. It was as if the droplets of blood had been slowly animated in time. It shot up lightning fast. It hit the droplets like a hungry fish hitting a worm. It seemed as if it had devoured the blood in a second. I quickly slapped the wire mesh down on top of the fish tank. Jacob moved swiftly and finished putting in the screw that would hold the wire down. The infant dove to the bottom then swam around the tank and propelled upward towards Jacob. I had to tell Jacob to move his hand.

"Jesus all mighty," he exclaimed as it hit the wire with a thud, "I don't think this fucker likes me much," he said, to Mary.

"Oh, I think your are wrong Jacob I think it likes you a lot. I think it would like to eat you," Mary tells him.

"Why did it not attack you," Jacob questioned. "I think it kind of did. I think it thinks I am its mother in away. I gave it the first taste of life, of blood. Just that one droplet of blood changed its whole being."

By the next morning it had grown it was the equivalent of a five month old. It now resembled that of a human infant with some animal characteristics. I now know that it was not I or my colleagues that had created this life form completely. Yes, my blood played a good factor. This creature, alien, it had been alive waiting for its benefactor. I it's father the giver of life blood and the D.N.A. that would make it more dangerous, menacing, than any animal alive. I put the final ingredient needed like a cook cooking a pot of stew. I needed tissue samples from our creation. We needed to take a closer look at it. I told Mary to sedate the creature. There was no way to put our hands in the water without being attacked.

"And how am I to accomplish that?" she says.

I contemplated what Mary said then after several minutes of thought I came up with a solution.

"The wire mess gloves from the knight in the dinning, room," I said firmly.

I went upstairs and returned with the gloves. I asked Mary if she preferred me to do the task. Mary reached out I handed her the gloves. She placed them on. I opened the cabinet took out a tranquilizer gun. I loaded it. I went up to the tank and shot the tranquilizer into the infants back. It moved so fast and violent that it caused the water to churn. After a moment Mary grabbed the creature in her hands. Still not quite out it squirmed and made a high pitching sound. The sound was different none we have ever heard before. It was the hideous the kind that makes one's blood curdle with fear. Mary took the tissue samples. It squirmed then it was out. Mary looked at the infant for a moment.

"I think I have enough samples for now."

She put the infant back into the water placed it at the bottom of the tank. If I was right I would be able to use its genetic makeup to complete the formula to use on humans. Time was the essence. I have to say it looks like a six-year-old child. Its muscle growth stupendous. Its muscles slightly different than ours. Its muscle's structure were chiseled in like stone. The strands of muscle fibers like tiny wires running along its arms and body. As I look at it at the bottom of the tank chills run down my spine. I will give you a visual description of its appearance. I will describe this abomination that spawn in my lab.

CHAPTER 19

Its eye's have a metallic silver around the rim of the deedless black eyes. A fine membrane closes and opens like a blind. The pitch black of the eyes reach deep into your soul. The cold stare of no emotion penetrates every thought of evil.

Lifeless eyes that stare back with malice. There is no hint of love whatsoever. Just that cold hate emanating from this creature as it looks through you. Now that the taste for human blood grows the fish food is becoming absent to its mind. It lingers at the bottom of the tank and it seemed as if it was deteriorating. New symptoms = No hunger = it would die. The question now what do we feed it. On the side of its head where slits, just holes that are its ears. At the base where the neck connects to the head are black gills that move back and forth sucking in the oxygen from the water. Looking at this it reminds you of someone opening and closing small doors. Its head was almost human round in back, but slightly thinner from the ears to the nose. It stands erect like man. Its torso elongated slightly. Its feet and hands like that of a rodent. Except these had webbing between each of its digits. Its skin is thick almost leather like a mild green in places.

On its stomach it is white with a hint of shade at the beginning of each scale. Its tail is that of a white Sea Krait snake with black and white markings. Its tail reaches the ground but that was not the concern. The problem was its most horrible trait, terrifying, and unholy characteristic. It was that it had white jagged porcelain like teeth that of a piranha but ten times bigger. Not to mention the mucus like silva that it had in its mouth. Its silva was poisioness. Once bitten there would be no cure. Death would be the only way out. Yet though hideous it was still beautiful in a way. Again at this time I pondered the ideal of killing it. I could see it looking back at me from the corner of the fish tank. Small bubbles escape upward to the top of the fish tank. The membrane opens and closes over its eyes. I was compelled by some unknown force to continue on with the evaluation of our new creation. Days past by the end of the week it had grown another foot. The following day I entered the laboratory and caught it clawing at the wire mess. It had cut through the wire mess in several places. And it was out growing the fish tank. It was time to get a much bigger tank. So, the following days Jacob and I constructed a new tank for Adam. A special tank that went three quarters of the way up to the ceiling and was circular like a tube at least seven feet in diameter. It had been confined in a small vial that had been completely close. I constructed this one hoping that maybe it would not want to get out of the tank. Maybe it would feel at home as they say. After completion and several test for water pressure making sure it was strong enough. I told my colleagues it was time to move Adam into the new one. I went to the cabinet took out the tranquillizer gun loaded it. I shot it twice. It jumped the screeching sound permeated the cellar. It went to the bottom of the tank. Bubbles floated up in a speratic urgency. We waited for the creature to go into the coma state before we handled it to moved it to the new tank. I put on the wire mess gloves I had removed from the armored knight. It looked up then as if had known something was up. It sat down placed its head between is knees into a fetus position. It was like seeing a child sulking when there feeling where hurt. After it fell to its side, I reached in cradled it in my hands like a father picking up his child.

"Mary get another syringe draw blood enough to make three different formulas. I do not think we will have another chance."

I lay the creature on its back on the metal table. Mary placed the syringe down then grabbed a cotton swab dipped it into alcohol. She rubbed the crook of its arm then placed the tip of the needle into place. There was no way to determine exactly where to place the needle into the vein. Or if it had veins running down the center of its arms like humans. She positioned the needle then gave herself the sign of the cross. She held the syringe firmly between her index finger and thumb. She pushed the plunger down there was a hesitation for a second then the needle broke through. She estimated the depth and hoped for the best. She pulled back on the plunger. Perfect she whispered to herself then repeated the word perfect. Mary knew it had been luck, luck, that it had some human qualities. She filled the syringe with fifty c.c., of the creature blood. She pulled out the needle then quickly moved out of the way. I took the creature climbed the ladder climbing up to the platform that I had made at the top of the aquarium for us to observe it. I was just about to say something when I noticed it moved. I had underestimated the dosage. In a human infant it would have been more than enough to put it under for several hours. It opened its eye stared inquisitively at me. I could tell it was still in a daze but wanting to know what I would do next. I looked at it as it opened its mouth. In that instant of seeing the jagged teeth I dropped it in to the water quickly. There was a slight splash.

It floated to the bottom of the tank. It remained still for a few seconds then began to move its arms. It stood then began to swim around the tank. We had placed a small wreck pirate ship, a Davy Jones looker, seashells, and pebbles. I hoped this would make it feel more at ease in its confinement. Though it hand never seen or been in an ocean or river. Mary took the vial filled with the alien's blood. She walked up to the scope placed the vial down for a moment. She picked up the syringe next to the scope injected the needle through the rubber stopper. She placed the vial, and the syringe down. She walked a few feet then wrote down Adam's D.N.A., on the small sticker.

She walked back placed the small label on the vial. She repeated the task three times. She walked up to the center fuse placed them in secure. She pressed a button and watched as the centrifuge began to spin. Jacob meanwhile worked with me securing the new wire mess in place. Now all we had to do was to get the right specimens. I divulged my thoughts to Jacob. Jacob nodded his head in agreement as we observed the creature from the platform. For the next few weeks we would spend hours studying it. Studying it in the water in its new habitat. One after another we studied the creature. What I write down next was amazing and scary as well. Mary had left for a short span of time then returned. She held a sandwich in her hand. I guess she must have been hungry. She took a bite of the ham sandwich as she climbed up the ladder up to the platform. She just happen to take another bite as she leaned to take a look at Adam. A small piece of the ham fell out of the bread onto the wire mesh. It happen so fast. First there was a stream of bubbles floating sporadically upward.

Then like a lightning bolt it shot up off the bottom. Adam hit the wire mesh. It clung to it while his other hand franticly searched for the dangling piece of ham. It cried out in a high pitch. The pitch startled Mary. I had to reach back and grabbed her before she fell over the edge. It grabbed the ham then rapidly ate it. It looked at Mary and what was in her hand. I told Mary to go back to the edge of the platform and to drop another piece of the bread. She took a piece dropped it on to the wire mesh. Nothing it just looked at her. I reached over pushed the bread through. It floated to the bottom slowly undetected. No response. I then told Mary to drop a piece of the ham. The fear in me grew I knew what it would do next. As it saw Mary getting the ham out of the bread it shot up grabbed on to the wire mess with one hand. It screeched out more erratic than before. It was more demanding. I saw Mary's eyebrow furrow up as a hint of anger entered her. Or maybe I saw fear. No sooner had the ham hit the wire mesh it started grabbing what it could. I pushed it through it let go of the wire mess darted off towards morsel of ham. In a matter of seconds it devour the meat. Incredible. It screeched out then sank to the bottom of the tank. It sat on its hunches looking up at us. I needed more I needed to understand its reasoning. Later I would understand the riddle of life. Or the riddle of its existence. I would understand Adam did not have life it just existed. Its one instinct was to feed. And it would feed on flesh. Adam was a true killer. Killer or not I was closer to my dream than ever. I just hope that we could make it understand. Like a dog to listen its masters command. I needed answers as I mention before. I went back upstairs to the kitchen. I returned with a T-bone out of the fridge. I went back down into the lab. I went to the microwave at one of the tables next to the wall. I thawed it out. It had cooled down by the time I had climbed back up on to the platform. I told Jacob to unscrew the wire from one of the corners and to keep an eye open for Adam. He did as I asked. My colleagues watched me in anticipation like kids waiting for candy. I saw its eyelids close and open. I could tell at least that it blink, as it scrutinized my every move. The cold menacing stare was all I got. I told Jacob that as soon as I tossed in the meat to fasten the wire mesh back in place. And to do it quick. I told Mary to grab her camera to record what the creature would do next. I waited for Mary to set up everything on the tripod. She was ready in a matter of minutes. "Here we go."

"Wait one minute," Mary says then a small pause, "what are we going to name it?"

"Adam, as I have been calling it for it is one of a kind, the beginning.

"I agree," Jacob interjected.

"I just wanted to make sure to write down the right name. So all we need is Eve," Mary says.

I opened the wire and began to toss in the T- bone Jacob began to fasten the wire mess back in place. It hit the wire mess. Jacob jumped back startled. I felt a good jarring sensation from the force of its ferocity. It attacked the meat and as it devoured it, it caused the water to churn

as if boiling. It had been as if a thousand Piranha's were feasting on the red flesh. It gave the sensation as if the water in the tank had come to a boil. After it ate it let the bone fall to the bottom of the tank. It swam to the top of the water popped out its head. It looked at me then made a soft gurgling sound them returned to the bottom. It sat in the corner watching, studying us. The nightmare was to begin. The reckoning of what we did with life was to commence. We saw it become what it is now and that was the unmentionable. It now stood at four feet five inches weighed at least a hundred and twenty pounds of solid muscle. Night was falling there was nothing more we could do this night. As I have written down that its structure was more human.

Its bone structure surpassed than that of man. I guess it was only one third human, one third fish, with the quality of a rat. It had jagged sharp teeth under its fish man lips. My brain was in turmoil tormented by Adam day and night now. It did not matter all I could do was to think of our creation. My mind was raveled up with fear of the unknown. Of what it might really become in the coming days. Fear for the people of Portland for my colleagues and myself. I was intrigued by this creature. I knew what was coming still I did nothing. My own guilt for what we had done was what tormented me. Adam plagued my thoughts my sleep every breath of life I took. It was the guilt for the crime that God would not forgive. I had done the unmentionable. The unconceivable sin. I played God but I was not the creator, nor could I reverse what was born. I knew what I had done. I need to sleep. I need to count sheep to imagine them jumping anything to take my mind off Adam.

I was going crazy I fought with my thoughts. I was near the threshold of insanity. I went to the bedroom window I felt something calling out to me. I reached between the curtains unfastened the sliding door leading out to the patio. I stood on the patio I looked out over the city. I watched as the sun began its descent. It seemed as if the sun were at the edge of the world. It was as if one was peering at a picture. The beautiful setting sun setting to rest bringing in the night sky. It was spectacular with an array of colors accenting the background of the sun rays as it dropped out of sight. I turned to look at Mary as she stirred in bed. A lovely creature she was indeed. How beautiful she looked this night I thought to myself. If I knew of the price, I would have to pay for playing God, maybe things would have been different. Funny isn't it? Funny how it is always after the after fact that one says.

If I had only known the outcome. I brought my gaze back to the setting sun. I returned to my bed climbed in put the blanket over me. I then snuggled up next to Mary. I felt as if something was not right. Maybe it was just in my head I convinced myself. I lay looking up at the ceiling hoping to fall asleep. Again I tried to count sheep I was desperate. I felt trepidation a premonition as if I could sense a presences coming. I erased the thoughts from my head somehow without knowing the fatigue took over. I fell asleep. All I remember was that the ceiling began to spin. I slept but with my eyelids slightly cracked leaving a small slit to see. In my subconscious mind I was guarding myself from danger I suppose.

CHAPTER 20

At first I thought I was dreaming. I could see the interior of my bedroom as the moon light shone through the window. Suddenly I saw a face. I could not make it out I could not move. It was as if I had been paralyzed from the neck down. I could see the doorway. I could see something peering in. It slowly began to open the door to let itself in to the room. I needed to wake. I fought with my brain. I needed to wake Mary up.

The feeling of danger swept over me with a horrifying reality. It was as if I were in a coffin and dirt being thrown on top of it. I was still alive calling out for help. Calling out but no one there to hear me. No one really knows how the subconscious mind works. There are ideals, theories, that surround the study of the mind.

They know that the brain can smell, feel, and see as if one were awake. I had to be awake for I see it I told myself. I see Adam making its way in to my bedroom. It is inching its way towards us. I moaned still fighting to grasp reality on what was true and what was just a part of my dream. I know that in dreams all things seem so real. So real that the hairs on my back began to tingle as if a small electrical static had swept over my spine. I asked myself if it was my imagination. Why? I asked myself several times why was I getting scared. Why? Why would I be scared of what I made? Why? I wanted to jump up but I could not.

It was at my bed side. Adam gurgled softly it grabbed the silk blanket piercing the silk with its clawed hands. It bit down with its teeth as it inched its way up onto the bed. It crept up slowly to me. I tried to focus my eyes on it. The image was a blur. It was a blur but I know what it was. In my dream state I refused to believe it was real. I refused to believe it was Adam. It was impossible there was no way it could have escaped from its confinement. I told myself this over and over in my head. I rolled overthrew my arms around Mary. I felt its claws on my face as it tried to roll my head to one side to look at it.

Oh, oh, let me wake up. I fought with my brain. I finally rolled over onto to my back. I heard a faint sound and through the narrow slits left by my eyelids I saw the creature. It tugged at the blanket again I felt this coldness as its claws scraped along my chest. They felt like steel knifes moving across. Its face was now next to mine as it looked into my eyes. I felt the fear of death at that moment. The kind of fear in a dream state where it could give one the feeling of falling off a cliff to one's death. I heard it gurgle softly again as its clawed hand ran along my face. Open your eye I told myself. I felt Mary stir as she shifted into a fetus position. Adam shifted at her movement and snarled. It abruptly jumped off the bed to the floor. It hit the floor with a solid thud. Cumbersomely it made its way towards the door then made its way down the corridor and down the stairs. I could hear its claws scraping along the wooden oak floor. I shot up I opened my eyes. I felt my heart pounding away. I thought it would explode. At first glance in the dark as I scanned the room the shadows came to life. Monsters jumping out at me. I moved my eyes from shadow to shadow as my mind pictured the absurd. Focusing my thoughts and eyes I noticed that these monsters had only been my furniture. I seconded guessed the ideal that if Adam had been in our room. It was impossible for it to break out of the fish tank. I felt a sticky substance on the edge of the silk blanket. Must have been my drool. Then I heard glass breaking. It was thin glass not from the tank. I got up and out of bed. I turned on the light. As I looked at Mary I noticed several wet spots on the blanket. I reached down ran my finger along the center of the globs. weird I thought.

"Adam, Adam," I said loudly.

Adam had been inside my room. I moved to go to the door. I slipped on the sticky mucus like substance. I scrambled back onto my feet. I lifted my leg ran my hand along the edge of my foot. I knew for certain now that Adam had been in our bedroom. The question was why? It had just stared into my eyes. Why? It could have ripped my throat out. For now the answers would have to wait. I got dressed then placed a pair of red slipper on.

"What is wrong Jeff?"

"Think our pet broke out Mary."

"Adam."

Mary did not wait for an answer she quickly climbed out of bed and got dressed.

"Watch your step Mary it left something behind."

She made her way to the door but before she got there, she lost her footing slipped and fell flat on her buttocks. Mary got up carefully reached for the door behind me again slightly losing her step.

I reached out and I grabbed her hand. "You okay?"

"Yes, I am fine," she said as she supported herself on the door frame.

She wiped the bottom of her foot with her hand. "Yuk! She said discussed then said, "Shit!"

I walked a few steps up grabbed a towel from the hallway bathroom. I returned handed it to Mary. She wiped her shoes off then tossed the towel by the door. She said it was for us to use when we came back. Jacob ran up to us.

"Did you hear the glass shattering?" "Yes, I think Adam has escaped." "Impossible."

"Adam was in my room Jacob." "How?"

"That is what we are going to find out."

We made our way down to the corridor and down to the main floor. I opened the trap door we made our way to the laboratory. As soon as we enter Mary shouted.

"The window Jeff."

It was a small basement window but at Adam's size it would be able to squeeze through without any problem.

"How did it make its way out of the fish tank?" "Looks like he clawed his way out," I told him as I stared at the torn wire mesh.

We were dumbfounded it had escaped captivity. It had cut through the wire mesh like wire snips to chicken wire. It had not been chicken wire though. It had cut through the thick wire mesh used on barbeque pits. The reality of what had gotten away permeated every inch of my being. Now what else was it capable of doing? What would it do next now that it was free? It was now imperative that we capture it before it hurt someone or worse and the worst was to come.

"Fuck! I exclaimed out my frustration.

I scanned the place I focused on the water puddles on the countertop of the table. I followed the water up to the lamp then to the window.

"It is a lot smarter than what we give it credit for."

"Why is that?" ask Jacob.

"Adam jumped from the top of the tank to the platform to the table then to the lamp. It went into our room came back jumped up on to the table then to the window and escaped to its freedom.

"Impossible," Mary interjected.

Jacob went to the wall ran his hand on the lamp. He looked at his finger for a moment.

"Hum, what is impossible seems probable." "And that makes it intelligent and dangerous," I said.

We all knew it was true. It was viscous it would kill to stay alive. In the distance dogs yelp there last breath as death found them others just barked franticly. Adam gills worked hard to extract the oxygen out of the air. Its lungs began to hurt. Its instincts took over it would have to find water for the pain to subside.

"Time is against us," I said.

"It is part fish Jeff. It has to make its way to the river," Jacob said quickly.

I told Mary to find something on the computer to slow it down so we could capture it. I felt as if I had let hell lose on the world.

CHAPTER 21

Adam's first victim was Betty a young woman.

She had black hair and was on the plump side. She was in her mid-thirties. Betty would give Adam its second taste of human blood and the love of the hunt would begin. It would hunt for the sweet human flesh the red liquid that it held. A taste that Adam would never forget. It would not forget that sweet pungent taste of the red liquid. The savory taste of flesh that it would crave like an addiction. Betty walked her trash to the edge of her driveway. She talked to herself even made herself laugh. She had awaken that morning feeling especially energetic full of life. She looked around then took in a deep breath of air enjoying it. Abruptly she heard a trash can tumble over into the street just a few house up from hers. She put her trash into the trash ben turned her head squinted her eyes to see if she could focus on the moving shadow.

"Hum," she said to herself then added, "it is bigger than a cat. I would say about the size of a grown Labrador."

There was something strange though about it. She could not see it clearly. Still her brain shot a spark of fear into her. Suddenly panic overwhelmed her. Betty tried to convinced herself that it was just a big dog.

"Calm down, calm down," she whispered to herself. She looked around nervously her eyes open wide. It seemed she was scared for no apparent reason. The object had vanished from sight. She looked around again she saw nothing. She put the lid back on the trash can. But before she completely closed the lid her hand moved back at the sight of what was charging her way. The lid dropped out of her hand hitting the can with a twang then falling to the ground. Betty stepped back as a fear entered her body like a wave of cold water. It was not real it was not possible. It was not real it couldn't be. The creature suddenly stopped no more than three feet away from her. It remained still like a statue on all fours just looking straight at her. It starred with its cold piercing eyes. It scrutinize the area and assessed the kill. It opened its mouth wide showing the deadly gagged teeth behind the fish like lips.

Betty wanted to run but couldn't her feet became paralyzed. It was as if her mind and body had become frozen. She felt tingling along her forehead. The thing before her was not real she told herself again. She had to run she told herself repeatedly in her mind. Somehow the creature had known what she would do next. Its next move was from pure instincts. Its claws dug into the ground like small backhoes. It pushed off its hind legs as the front grabbed the ground sending small puffs of dirt sailing out from beneath its claws. With each maneuver it gain speed. It was coming into range for the attack.

It lunged forward. It leaped into the air. It reached out with its rat like claws. To Betty it looked like a small deformed infant. An infant with glistening skin and razor sharp claws, and teeth.

"What in God's name," Betty cried out.

The creature's onslaught had been too fast for her to move. Its jagged teeth lashed around her neck. She wanted to scream but the teeth closed around her throat keeping her scream in her larynx. The searing pain shot from her ankle to her heart. It continued to take bite after bite of her flesh. It had brought Betty down like a tiger taking down a doe. Adam struck at her face cutting deep gouges across her cheek and lips. The pain in her was gone. It continued to gouge, cut, spilling her blood onto the ground. It then bit down ripped her throat out completely. She made a soft muffled moan as the life left her body. Adam thrashed, ripped, rapidly devoured the sweet tasting morsels of flesh. In a matter of minutes, it had eaten from Betty's neck up to her head. It left only the ivory white bone of her skull exposed. Her black hair remained untouched. Betty was static number one.

Jeffrey nightmare had begun. "Fred, Fred, Fred, wake up."

"What the hell." Fred exclaimed out loud to his wife as he rolled over on his side.

"I heard a scream coming from outside Fred. It sounded like Betty."

Fred climbed out of bed only wearing his boxer shorts. He walked up to the window separated the blinds with his fingers and looked outside. Martha looked at her husband thinking how much he looked like the comedian W.C.Fields. He notice what appeared to be a dog leaving from Betty's thrash can then shoot down the street. He noticed that it ran but its movements were strange. Maybe Betty had yell at it. What Fred did not know was that Betty lay on the ground hidden by the rose bush and the trash cans hiding her body. "Did you see anything?"

"No, Martha I can only see her trash can from hear on the ground."

"Talking about trash cans will you take ours out Fred?"

"Fuck! Martha is there anything else you want me to do? Can't even rest on my days off."

Martha pulled her blankets over her head rolled over onto her side. Fred put on his robe tie it close then walked into the kitchen. He took a plastic bag with the trash out of the trash can in the kitchen.

"Hell, what we been eating? Shit. The trash smell like vomit," he says out loud so Martha can hear.

He open the door then walked outside to curb. He dry heaved a couple of times from the smell. He opened the trash can placed the trash in. When he turned at first glance he noticed pink slippers. Thought of the Wizard of Oz ran through his head. He scratches his head.

"Those slippers look like the ones we gave Betty for Christmas last year," he says to himself.

He looked closer then noticed something strange it was how the slippers where positioned. The only way that the slippers could be at that position was if someone were wearing them. At first he could not see Betty. He walked up to the rose bush moved her trash can.

"What the hell?"

He saw Betty's ankles exposed connected to the furry pink slippers. He carefully walked close to her then froze in place. He stared down at the once attractive face of his neighbor. There was no face now except the white bone of her skull. Tiny splotches of pink left behind hinted that there had been flesh on the skull once.

"Jesus oh mighty," he says to himself then looks up to the second floor window of their bedroom, "Martha call the cops. Call them and quick."

She climbed out of bed rushed to the window looked outside. She could see Fred shouting. She pulled the rope on the side of the blinds they traveled up. She opened one of the windows halfway stuck out her head.

"What is it Fred?"

"Call the cops and do it quick, Betty's dead."

Martha did not have to ask the question again if she was dead. She knew by the urgency in her husband's voice. She rushed outside to where he stood. Fred stopped her before she could see Betty. Martha was a thin woman in her late fifties with graying hair. Fred thought it would be better if she stayed away. She did not need another heart attack. From where Fred stood, he could see his wife's hands shaking with freight.

"Martha go and put on a pot of coffee. I will stay out here until the cops arrive."

The neighboring lights began to come on. Some walked out on to their porch to look on. Twenty minutes later the cops arrived. They took down the information from Fred. Fred then walked back inside his house went to the kitchen sat down at the table. Martha placed a cup of coffee for him then hugged her husband tight. In the distance dogs howled at the strange intruder not to protect their parameter or territory but from the unknown. Adam's claws dug into the pavement making a dull rasping sound. It sounded like that when one is sanding something with a low grate sandpaper.

Sirens filled the morning air. The news crew arrived on the scene. Forensic and the M.E.T., moved about taking the smallest information and the slight clue into consideration. The M.E., Jennifer five seven, blonde hair of German parents arrived on the scene. She climbed out of the Medical Examiner van and made her way up to the body. She walked up to an officer stopped at the yellow and black tape that barricaded the area off from pedestrians.

"Sam where is the M.E.T? She asked. He pointed in her direction. "Good or bad Sam?"

He moved the tape for the M.E., then said, "I think you better take a look."

That told Jennifer all she needed to know for the time being. It was another bad crime scene.

"Sam, has anybody touched anything."

"No, when I saw the body I knew it was not an ordinary murder. The Emergency Medical Tech was with the body. I.D. did their thing as well. There is Susan and it looks like she is in a rush mode."

"Body is over there Jen I have to get things ready for transport. You have about twenty minutes. Let me know when you are done with the corpse," she says before Jenny could ask about the body.

"Will do."

Jenny walked right up to the body that lay about two yards away from where she stood. She began to look for clues. She would take a better examination at the county morgue. From the corner of her eye, she noticed a black unmark car approaching then stop. She recognized the driver instantly it was Johnny. He was young stood six four, good physic, Latin and good looking and had a hell of a tan. He made his way up to the corpse.

He stopped towering over her as she knelt down over the body. She looked up at him and smile. The thought of if he was just a few years older she'd do him ran through her head.

"What do we have?" Johnny ask.

She stood up walked around the corpse then faced him.

"I do not know Johnny. But the scenario of the crime is not of the ordinary."

"Fuck, from here it looks like flesh termites."

"I see you got jokes Johnny. So tell me are you working on this one alone?"

"I heard the call over the two way. I was close by so I thought I take a look. But the answer to your question is no. I am to work with some burn out from the Great State of Texas."

Johnny took out a note pad then began to make a rough sketch of the area where the body lay and the surrounding to use for later. He was not a good artist, but his stick figures would work fine. He put down anything and every think. Marks on the body and he wrote flesh gone from face. Jenny put on the latex gloves that she had in her black medical bag at her side. She knelt down next to the corpse. She ran her index finger down the side of the woman's face. She reached into the black bag pulled out what appeared to be a blunt looking knife. She scrapped the bone where there was once a cheek. She then scrapped off the knife onto a small flat container. Meanwhile I.D., was investigating every inch of ground. Lights flashed on and off as the bulb from the photographers camera flashed as the woman took over lapping pictures of the crime scene. She took several pictures of the dead woman. Jenny looked at Betty's neck for a few minutes. She faced the woman taking the pictures.

"One more for the road and I'm done," she tells the M.E.

One of the I.D. team made a plaster cast of the animal print. He poured a white glob mixture into the crevice of the print. He would have to wait several minutes for the plaster to thicken before taking the printout of the ground.

"Looks like everyone is getting done," she says and stands.

She puts her equipment back into the black bag. She walks away for a moment then returns with a gurney.

"Johnny give me a hand with the body. Help me take it to the ambulance."

"All most done just let me put this line on my stick figure," he said the closed the note pad and put it into his breast pocket.

He studied Jenny for he knew that if the body needed to be transported to the ambulance several officers were still on standby. This indicated that there was something she did not want anyone to hear.

"Sure," Johnny say then followed her to the ambulance then mentions as they get close, "morgue on wheels."

"That is what it is Johnny."

"Susan, open the double doors to the back of the vehicle."

The back doors open Susan stared at them.

Jenny told Johnny to pick the edge of the gurney up. Susan grabbed the front of the gurney helped them push it into the ambulance. Susan grabbed Betty's legs secured them strapping them down secure with the leather straps. Jenny jump into the truck while Johnny stood outside watching the two women work. Jenny lean forward as if she were going to touch Betty's lips with hers. Johnny felt a little uneasy. It was freaking him out.

Meanwhile Jenny scrutinized Betty's chest to see if it moved up or down.

"Do not be freaked out Johnny I'm just checking to see if the corpse was still breathing, it's is just protocol. With her face gone as far as we know she could still be alive."

Jenny jumped back out of the truck as Johnny held on to her arm. She thanked Susan then closed the double doors for her.

"That was dead weight. No pun intended Jen." "So, Johnny you thought I was getting kind of kinky with her?" "Well!"

"I always get those looks but it is what makes it easier to visualize the movement if the chest is moving."

"So, what is it you did not want anyone to hear?"

"Damn, you are a detective. You read me like a book."

"Okay so what?"

Look Johnny I did not want to mention anything yet not until I am positive of what it or who just killed this lady."

"Dog attack." "No.

"What's different?"

"Johnny the area around her neck was ripped out. You see the skin has tell, tell, signs like any other part of the body. I thought I might be seeing things at first. But when I look closely it was jagged teeth marks penetrating deep ripping apart her flesh."

"And you got all that from just looking at her?"

"Yes, and the truth being said dogs bites are different."

"I say dog open and shut case. Dog attack." "As I said before Johnny dogs devour their prey differently and as far as I know we have no wild dogs on the lose."

"Still you believe it might be some kind of animal."

"Yes, people see what they want to see. When you wake up. If you're the type with an expanded imagination you could see a numerous of things that go bump in the night. Human equation not eliminated as of yet. But.

"I knew there would be a but thrown in there." "Johnny dogs have canines that poke and gouge shit out. Whatever kill her was a machine. I have never seen flesh torn away so clean."

"So I guess for now it will be the unknown." "Maybe the Chief will let you work alone on this one.

"No, such luck. Like I said Jen I am to work with a detective that I just mention. He is from Texas a burn out. Should be here in a couple of days. I ask the chief if I could take the case. What he said was that he wanted me to get more knowledge and experience. I said working with this burn out I will learn more. You know what he said then."

"What?"

"He said that is exactly right. I ask the chief to tell me the detective story."

"They had one hell of a murder massacre down in Austin Texas a year ago. Turns out the killer was not human but a creature. A predator teeth and all. A creature. He said that he had received a call from the chief down there in Texas. He asked the Chief if he could help him out."

"So they don't want a crazy fuck running lose down there so they send him here. That's not heard of I guess the chief of Austin is a close friend."

"That sound about right Jenny."

What the chief did not tell Johnny was that the call was from his twin brother. He had asked him to help get Pete back up to par.

"That's all I need is to work for a wacko Jenny. He then says, "Johnny just listen to what he has to offer." "To a Wacko?"

"Johnny you are not too far behind," the Chief tells me. He told me I am not far behind. I smiled turn and made my way out to the corridor. I walked to the elevators and out of the building. I am a detective and if the Chief says I have to work with this man then I will."

"True dedication Johnny."

"I will bring him around to introduce him to you."

CHAPTER 22

Detective Pete Rodrequiz boarded on to Continental air flight to Portland Oregon from Austin. He was greeted by the flight attendant. He entered on to the plane. Pete felt his phobia coming on. He did not like to be confined in his words. Confinement gave him the willies. It had been a good while from the last time he flew. If he remembered correctly it was his flight home on a c-130 cargo plane from the Nam. He walked down the isle looked at his flight ticket seat 15-B.

"Fuck it was a middle seat," he said to himself softly.

He put the ticket back in his coat pocket. He made his way into his seat. He sent his luggage through so all he had to worry about was who would set next to him. He relaxed for the time being.

His mind jump to the past. Eagle Warrior, Monster Killer, he thought to himself. What would be the odds of what happen to occur again? Impossible his mind ran on. He scanned the people as they boarded the plane. The turbines hummed softly the hatch door closed. He noticed an oriental lady walking in front of two large women. The old oriental lady was on the thin side and walked with a slight limp. She took the open seat across the isle. Pete's eyes open wide as he saw the next two women in line. The first was a white woman she had on a small black hat. She had red hair pultruding from underneath the hat. He estimated she weigh at least two hundred and eighty pounds of flesh easily.

"Oh! God be good to me," he mumbled.

Suddenly the phobia set in a little more when the woman stopped in front of the role of seats he was in. She glanced at her ticket then smiled.

"Right here Dora," she turned and said to her sister.

She turned back around put her carry on bag in the bend over head.

"Give me your bag Dora."

Her sister handed her the bag. She put it in the bend above looked down then smiled at Pete once more. Lord do you hate me his mind raced on. The woman forced her rear end into the seat. Her buttock flesh rubbing Pete's arm as she squeezed in. Pete felt uncomfortable in the seat especially when her sister Dora stood at the isle. Fuck, no there is no way in hell this woman can sit on the other side of me without both of them suffocating me to death his thought running wild. Maybe he was being a little over dramatic. The flight attendant stopped in front of Dora in the isle. She smiled at the two women then me.

"There are three empty seats in the back," she said as if to tell the two women.

It had been a full flight except for the three seats at the back. Pete was about to stand up and say he would take a seat.

"We will take the seats," said Dora as she looked at her sister.

"Yes, that would be fine," agreed Jone.

Jone stood rubbing her thigh on to Pete's arm. Dora made her way out her butt cheeks rubbed against Pete's cheek. Pete laughed out loud at the weirdness of the feeling. The flight attendant chuckled and tried to refrain from laughing out loud. Pete felt a sudden relief.

"Enjoy your flight," she say then the attendant walked away.

She walked to the microphone at the vert front of the plane. She grabbed it into her hand and spoke.

"The emergency doors are marked for if there is an emergency evacuation. If you feel that you might not be able to fulfill the task. I can assign you another seat. In case of a crash floating devices are attached to the bottom of each seat," she continued with the procedures.

Pete looked out the window most of the flight. He never been to the state of Oregon. But he had heard stories of the rain from Bill Gomez. I was born in Portland Oregon he had mentioned it to him. I lived there for twenty seven years before I decided to transfer here to Texas.

"Why? I hear Portland is beautiful."

"Let me tell you that Portland is beautiful.

But it rains Pete. I have three boys and a promise is a promise to a boy or girl. But especially to your sons. I would tell them that I would barbecue on a Saturday or Sunday. Sunday would come around and it would drizzle like clockwork. I'd promise them next week and again rain would come down. I finally got fed up with it and barbecued in the freaking rain. Hell! I even barbecued in the snow once. Should have seen the snow as it hit the barbecue pit. It sizzled as soon as it hit the lid. The boys would began to laugh they thought it was halarious. But was I their hero? Why, yes the fuck I was."

After a moment of laughter Pete ask. "So, how do they like Texas?"

"In the ten years Pete I would have to say they were born here. They love going to the river the sunshine and the hunting. They love it here. It beats the rain and cold anytime."

It had been a quick description but somehow he believed Bill. After four hours the planed landed and they begin to unboard the plane. The same attendant stood at the doorway.

"Have a good visit sir," she said and smiled.

Pete made his way out and down the corridor into the terminal. He went straight to the car rental before grabbing his bags. He stood at the counter for about fifteen minutes before an attendant walked up and said.

"Can I help you?"

Pete felt like saying no, "I have been waiting here for at least fifteen minutes while you play with some fucking paperwork," but kept it inside.

"Yes, Pete said then handed him the fax he received with the conformation of his rental.

The woman looked at the papers for a moment then stood up straighter than before as if in attention. Pete wondered if a broom stick had been inserted up the woman's ass at the time.

"Just go out there to the small shed. The attendant will help you to your car."

She handed Pete back the papers. He walked up to the baggage area grabbed his bags went out the double doors to get the rental.

"Before you leave I need a map of Portland," Pete said to the young man escorting him to the vehicle.

"Your lucky day sir one of the costumers just left this one behind," he says as he reaches back to his back pocket then hands the map to Pete.

"You are a life saver. How much?"

"Like I said it is your lucky day there is no charge."

"One more question where is a good place to stay?"

"There is a Ramona Inn kind of expensive."

The young man pointed and told Pete to drive straight out and to take a left onto the high way then to go about five miles. It would be expensive for the department Pete thought to himself. Pete took the keys climbed into a white Malibu. Fifteen minutes later he found the place. He turned in and parked in front of the building. He went inside and reserved his room. He went upstairs went straight to bed. The next morning he found himself walking into a new precinct. He walked straight up to the information desk. The women behind was a young women in her twenties. She had blue eyes and a good figure.

"Excuse me." "Yes."

"I am here to see the Chief of this precinct." "Does he know you are coming?"

"Yes."

She reached for the phone.

"Tell him detective Rodrequiz from Texas is here." Moments later she put the receiver back on its base.

"The chief said go ahead. Just get on the elevator to the second floor go straight down the corridor until you see his name. It is printed on his door."

"What is his name?" "James T Golds."

Pete made it to the end of the corridor. He looked in through the window. He could see a young Latin maybe late twenties. Johnny noticed Pete.

"I think the new man is here. Come on chief get someone else. I don't want to play driving Miss Daisy."

"Johnny he is going to be the senior detective on the case. You will treat him as so," he interjects firmly, Johnny step outside.

"Come on in detective." Johnny say theb closed the door behind him and stood outside.

Pete walked in and up to the desk he stood at attention. Right before him was a man that he knew well. But it was impossible the man he knew was back in Texas.

"Relax detective it looks like you just saw a ghost."

"I know you can't be Golds from Austin." "No, you are right. Mike is my baby brother.

We are twins. Can you tell," he says then chuckles softly then ads, "yes, twins like identical. I am the oldest by a few minutes."

"Damn I thought I had gotten away from that sour puss."

"What was that detective?" "It just came out Chief."

"Yes, Mike can be a pain in the ass." "I agree."

"Detective I am glad you are here. The man outside will be you're partner. He is young I hope you can teach him some new things. He is good but a little impatient."

"Chief I don't even know my way around here. And you know about what occurred back in Texas." "The streets here go east, north, south, and west. You will be fine Pete," the man say ignoring what Pete had just said.

This one is a bit funnier than his brother he thought to himself.

"Mike related what happen Pete. And if you can live through such an ordeal this will be a piece of cake for you. You will feel right at home. Hell, you will think that you are back in Austin."

Chief Golds walks to the window he taps on it for Johnny to come back in.

"Johnny get Pete acquainted with the place.

Get going there is no time to waste. Have to get you back to work a.s.a.p. detective Rodrequiz."

"We have the same last name," Johnny says.

Pete could tell the young man was not happy to be under a newcomer. Johnny took him around the precinct to the different units. He introduced him to the S.W.A.T., team. Johnny told the leader of the S.W.A.T. team he would be the lead on the investigation.

"Detective if you have any question just ask."

On their way-out Johnny explained the details of the crime scene. Of Betty's mutations. He divulge his thoughts, "the perp was probably carrying a tool of sorts pretending to be and animal. And that he was trying to send them in a different direction of the investigation. One day he left a half smoked cigarette he tossed it on to the ground. I believe to this day that if it had not been for that we would not have caught the perp. The killer is human."

Pete just listened quietly for he had just seen a young man possessed with a demon. The creepy the odd and the unmentionable were out there. Whomever or whatever it was would have to be stopped. If it is animal or a psychopath murder with a garden claw still they needed to stop it or him.

"Look! Johnny it could be a human but we have to make sure. We investigated a crime one years ago. We investigated every clue and each time it seemed it was an animal it was not. Until he left a clear clue. And a year ago when it pointed to a human. It was not. As I said we have to collect all evidence first."

They made their way out of the basement then up to the vehicles outside. Pete noticed the sign with an arrow pointing to the Medical Examiner's office and her name. Jennifer William.

133

CHAPTER 23

Night gave Adam the invisibility it needed from human eyes. It made its way down through Washington Park cumbersomely. Adam was still getting acquainted with his arms and legs filling awkward on land. In the water it felt at home. It would have to learn how to maneuver to survive. It crawled through several shrub making its way in to the clear. It then made its way down the stairs releasing several loud gurgling growls of frustration. It reached for the next step. It lost its grasp slipped falling back to the bottom. It made a second attempt to climb onto the top step. It looked around moved eastward through the tall fir trees and the green foliage that was up ahead. Adam disappeared through the foliage then continued its way downtown. It avoided the highway traffic. It then made its way towards the river. Adam was still in its infant stage. It was tiring as all infants when exhausted from play. It was no longer confined to the fish tank. Freedom was knew, exploration, was new. Adam was alive and tuning his instincts as he went on. It made its way undetected. It looked around at the tall building standing like a giant monster above leering down at it. It walked through an alley.

Now it stood at the edge of stairs leading upward to the double doors in the center of the city. The Catholic Cathedral lay several yards up ahead. Adam moved east it needed rest. It did not fear humans. But it was weak it was getting harder to breath. Its gill moved and strained. It felt pain. It cumbersomely made its way down the pavement around the cars parked against the shoulder next to meters. Its claws making a scrapping sound like that on wood. As it dragged across the asphalt.

Adam's keen hearing picked up on human footsteps coming it way. Adam moved underneath a Ford pickup in the shadow of its rear tire. It waited patiently until the person was out of sight. It popped its head out from under the truck then its torso. It stood on the sidewalk looking in all directions to see if anyone was coming. It was getting hungrier with each minute that past. It had nothing to eat for a day now. Its journey had been a tedious one. Night was coming. It could see the clouds eating away at the horizon like a billion locust filling the sky. Rain began to fall. Adam moved up to the Cathedral as if it were a beacon. It stopped in front of the double doors looked at the enormous building that loomed over it. Adam tilted its head to one side then let out a soft gurgling sound. It looked up at the church as if it called out to it. It was as if it understood the meaning behind the structure and of what it represented. And the power it held.

A power that was invisible to the cultivated mind of intelligence. A power that only the innocent can see or feel. It remained staring up from its throat eminated a soft gurgling sounds. Was it possible that it could sense the power of God? Or was it just instinct that linked it to the higher power. It turned its head searching for a place to hide for the night. It walked a few steps. It saw stairs that lead down to the basement portion of the Cathedral. It clawed at the side walk making its way slowly to the edge of the first step leading down. It again looked over its shoulder scanning the area around it to see if someone might be watching it. Adam made its way down the steps to the bottom of the stairs. At the bottom it moved to the far corner hiding away from view. It curled up next to the door in a fetus position. It longed for water and food. It hurt when it inhaled. The rain began to fall down faster and faster allowing a few drops at a time to hit its gills. Adam took in the water and was able to breath more relaxed. Hunger gnawed at his insides but he would have to wait. Like all infants it was tired, and sleep took over. About three hours into its deep sleep it was abruptly startled. Awaken as a car door slammed shut. It listened for a moment then fell back into a deep sleep. Morning had come Adam was well rejuvenated. In the early morning hours it would be free it would be undetected.

Its stomach growled in the anticipation of finding prey. It climbed up to the second two steps watched as several people walked by to their jobs. It felt the first pang of pain. It forced its gill stretching them as far as they could go. It needed a full body of water to fill its lungs completely with life. It was the size of a four year old child now. But this one had the strength of five grown men and it would get stronger with time. It would kill now to satisfy its need to live. Its ears caught a faint sound. It honed in on the noise. It was getting closer Adams eyes focused on some kind of animal. It was new to Adam but it was prey. It focused its attack on the large orange and white calico as it crossed the street. Meawo, meawo, the sound emanated from the cat. Adam stiffened up his hind legs. Its hands grasped the concrete as it waited to pounce on the cat. It pushed off its hind legs. It pushed with its arms sending it in to the air. In one swift moment its claws sunk deep into the cat's hind quarters.

It's back arched upward. Its hackles stood straight up on the cat. The cat meawoed frantically shifting from one direction to the other. It try to free its self from the claws in its flank. The cat hiss and clawed then suddenly out of pure luck it shifted. It managed to escape death claws at that instant. It darted down the street but to no avail for it heard Adam's claws coming and getting closer. Adam lunged forward with its claws extended to their fullest. They sank into the cats flesh like hooks grasping on like a vice. The cat's hind legs buckled under its weight. As they rolled on the ground again it managed to free itself. It knew there would be no escaping this creature. Its hackles and tail shot up. The tip of its tail curled. But for the Calico cat there was no magic to follow. Adam opened its mouth wide exposing the white porcelain teeth in a vicious snarl. Before the cat could think of an escape Adam grasp the cat set its claws in deeper. The sound of flesh ripping off resounded out as if hearing paper being torn apart. The cat's fur refused to be pulled apart from the red raw meat. Adam bit into cat's skull the sound of bone being crushed echoed out.

A hole appeared on the top part of the head. Adam thrashed from side to side in swift rapid movements. Brain mater shot in every direction on the ground. It was like a thick heavy soup from Adam's mouth. In seconds it had devoured half the cat then tossed the remains on to the sidewalk. It screeched out a cry of victory then made its way to Waterfront Park three block from where it was. It moved on as if on a mission. It could smell the water. It made its way up to the edge of the river. It leapt off the edge. A splash brought the river below to life. The river calmed and moved on its way as before. Moving as if nothing had just entered into its arms.

CHAPTER 24

"Friday night time to let down our hair and have some fun," Gwen says happily then looks at her sister sitting next to the vanity, "Beverly do you think this green dress looks better on me than the black one?"

"Oh, no! Not the green. Definitely the black dress Gwen," her sister says then turns back around.

She puckered up her lips as she looks into the mirror then puts on some plum lipstick. She smacked her lips together making a soft sucking sound. She stood then motioned her sister to sit down. She smiles at her through the mirror then grabbed her sister arm and sat her down. She then grabbed her sister's hair pulled it up in a bun.

"That is the look for tonight sissy," Beverly tells her.

Gwen approved Friday was what they called club night. Beverly the oldest of the two. Gwen two years younger loved the ideal. She loved getting all made up and turning heads. There was a small difference in their body structure. They were both outstanding knock outs. Beverly was tall blonde and well formed. Gwen was as well a blonde and a few inches shorter and full figured. And they both where at least a D cup.

"Ready."

"Let's do it Gwen."

One hour later they found themselves at the night club downtown Portland. They were bombarded with music from a pair of large speakers on the stage. The music seemed to bounce off the walls literally. Every fifteen minutes Beverly scanned the place for Johnny.

"Waiting for that brown night in shinny armor?" ask Gwen.

"Hoping Gwen just hoping he is on time for once."

She knew Johnny had crazy hours he was a detective. And it went with the job. It would not have been the first time he would have canceled their date because of a crime. She was madly in love with him and if late so be it. Just show up Johnny she thinks to herself.

"Bev," a voice called out to her.

She turned around to see Kwok approaching her.

"Hey, where is lover boy?"

"He will be here soon enough I hope."

Beverly sees Kwok eyeing Gwen. Well, what the hell she thought to herself.

"Kwok let me introduce you to my baby sister."

"Gwen this is Kwok. Kwok this is Gwen," she says then turns to the entrance in hope of seeing Johnny walk in.

Kwok reached out his hand and ask Gwen if she would like to dance before he had to go to work. His shift would soon start. It had not been a romantic pickup line but it was an honest one. They went to the dance floor danced to the music playing from the juke box. After the dance Kwok walked her back to the bar then excused himself.

"Do not forget to call me," Gwen exclaimed as he began to walk away.

Kwok looks over his shoulder smiles then continues on and vanishes into the back out of sight.

"Beverly did you know he was Chinese?"

"He is half Gwen his mother is Chinese his father is Mexican."

"Not a bad combination huh."

"You know Gwen the man is quite handsome."

Gwen notices Johnny walking in as she is talking to her sister.

"Look who the devil brought in," Gwen exclaims.

Entering the establishment Johnny recognized Beverly and Gwen instantly. He noticed her long legs, sensuous body, moving in poetry. The black dress she wore clung to her body like another layer of skin. Her legs exposed several inches above the knee. The v-cut dress delightfully holding in her voluptuous bossom. And her light blue eyes enticing him. Inviting him with love. He gazed at her full lips as she open them to say high. Next to her he noticed Gwen. She looked quite attractive wearing a black dress with the same low v-cut as well exposing her knockers. It must run in the family same genes he thought to himself then smiled. He walks up to the bar kissed Beverly on the lips softly.

"What will it be Johnny?" ask the bartender.

"Jimmy give me a Mui Thi and a wine cooler for Bev. and her sister."

"Yes sir, coming right up."

It was perfect timing no sooner had Johnny moved to the bar when Jimmy placed their drinks on the bar.

"I'm glad you were able to make it Johnny," Beverly tells him then hugs him tightly.

"I was sure you would be late as usual," Gwen interjects.

Johnny pulled away from the bar looked at Gwen then said, "Who put your panties in a bunch? Lighten up doll. I feel hell freezing over. I am going to have to tell this establishment to put on the heater. Fuck its cold."

Beverly chuckled amused at Johnny's remarks.

"Johnny you and Gwen try to get along for once."

"You wish is my command hon."

"Let's go sit down at one of the tables Johnny."

They found a table at the edge of the dance floor. Seeing Johnny one of his friends walks up to him and greets them. He then ask Johnny if he was going to play poker later that night.

"No, not tonight Gibby. I am spending time with Bev."

"I understand dog." "Who was that?" "That was Gibby."

"Why didn't you introduce him properly to us?" "You mean to Gwen don't you?"

"Well hells bells I am fucking sorry your friends are too good for us simpletons."

Johnny knew that the conversation was going south immediately.

"Okay I will call him back from the stage." "No thanks Johnny," Gwen says then adds, "I already met someone today and I think I can like him a lot."

"Who was the poor soul?" Johnny says holding in the word bastard.

"Who?"

"I see now you want to know who?" "I'll tell you who it was Kwok."

"Trying to ruin my friendship with the guys."

Johnny could see the dismal look growing on Gwen's face from his remark. He rapidly thought of something to say. He like giving Gwen a hard time but not to hurt her.

"You know Gwen I have to say I think you made a good choice."

"Really?"

"Honest Gwen," he says then adds, "let's make like the birds and flock out of here."

"I will be just a few minutes I have to say by to my new guy."

Outside of the building Johnny shoved Beverly softly. In turn she shoved him then they crossed the street where she had parked her Lexus. She could see Johnny had parked his sixty-six corvette convertible behind hers. Gwen rushed across the street. Beverly gave Gwen her keys. Then told her she was going to stay with Johnny tonight. Gwen looks at Johnny. He asked what she was looking at. He tells her it was freaking him out.

"Tell me Johnny why do you always wear a trench coat?" Gwen asked.

"Would you believe I like it?"

"I think you wear it because it gives you the gangster, spy look."

"I know huh, shotguns, machine guns, guns, I never really thought of it that way."

"See you tomorrow sis."

Beverly climbed into the passenger side as Johnny held the door open for her. He then waited for Gwen to start the car and pull out. He ran to the drive side of the vehicle jumped into the car. He started the car then pulled out and began to drive off.

"Shit, I love this car. You know it is like the one Mill-Mascarras drives in his movies."

"Who the hell is Mill-Mascarras?"

"Him and El Santo are the first Mexican heroes. He was awesome. My grandmother gave us the tapes she bought too, look at. He was awesome. Hell him ane El Santo are awesome now."

Beverly laughed she enjoyed the cool night breeze caressing her body. Her hair blew in the wind like gold ocean waves. Johnny put on some romantic music as they drove to his apartment. They held hands in silence the rest of the way. She wanted to be with Johnny forever. She would wait for him until he was ready to pop the question.

CHAPTER 25

Mary, Jacob, and I continued with our search for Adam the following morning. We searched through the alley ways, parks, and the walkway, down by the Waterfront Park. We walked up and down the streets of the city. I walked from first to ninth up and down Everett to Emerson. I found myself in front of the cathedral. I stopped I turned to faced it. I stared at the entrance to the structure. The double doors began to slowly open. A priest walked out the doors. He walked to the edge of the steps. He looked at me smiled then spoke.

"Can I help you with something you seemed to be a little lost?" He asked in with a heavy Irish accent.

"No, father I was just looking for something that escaped from home."

"Yes, we all look for something. Today I look for the sun. I like to see the sun come out more often."

I sighed then replied, "yes, father it would be nice."

"You sure you don't need anything? Something seems to be weighing heavy on your shoulders my son?"

"I must find what has found freedom father."

"Ask God for a little guidance he will help you," he says looks up at the sky he takes in a deep breath then looks at me and says, "Well I hope you find it," he says and walks back into the cathedral.

The doors slowly closed behind him it was mythical in a way. The power of good. It had been the same power he felt standing there in front of the building. It was as if I were feeling something looking back at me. The eyes of God perhaps. I had not imagined that it could have been Adam. I had felt something looking at me. It was an eerie feeling. I know that the eyes on me where that of Adam now. Adam had been there at my very feet. How stupid I had been. Why had I not known. I shrugged the feeling off then continued to search the city for any clue. I past the same stairs leading down to the bottom part of the Cathedral were Adam lay. I had heard a scraping sound I turned looked down and stared into the darkness. I could not see it for the dark cloak hiding it from me. I scanned the steps nothing. I saw nothing but it saw me. I felt its presents I knew it had to be close by. Where? Where the word ran through my head over and over. The thin hair on my back let me know I was on the right track.

It had passed through this area. Again the thought of where could it be ran through my mind. Was I too late had it already made its way into the depth of the Willamette River? If so are hunt would be harder than expected. I met my colleagues at Lauderman Park later that day.

"Nothing," I said as I approached them. "Nothing here as well," Mary said. "Diddly squat here," Jacob exclaims. "What do we do now Jeff?" Mary asked.

"For now we go back to the laboratory before it gets dark. We put are heads together and devise a plan to capture it."

Three weeks passed and still we had not found it. The thing that horrified me the most at the moment was that I knew it would had grown bigger and stronger in strength by now. I knew it would climb back out of the water and kill. It would feast on human flesh to live.

And as I said in the early morning as the sun began to break at the crest of the east. Adam climbed back out of the Willamette River. Adam swam to the surface. Its head bobbed up and down in the water as it made its way up to the park. It was hungry it needed to fill its belly to subside the pain. Adam made its way back to where it had left the mutilated cat.

The blood the sweet taste of blood of human the thought ran through its head. It remembered that sweet pungent taste of the woman it killed. It would wait for now the decaying cat would do. Adam's mouth opened as soon as it had lifted the rear half of the cats remains. Its head began to thrash violently jerking devouring the rotted flesh. It ripped away at the cat. It ate but was not satisfied. Its hunger for flesh like that of the woman caused hunger to gnaw at its insides as if there was a void. Suddenly a horn blew and several cars passed by. It had never seen the metal object move. Adam moved into the alley. It heard voices coming from the street. It spotted a dumpster halfway into the alley. It saw more and more humans moving about. It was all new to Adam. It made its way along the edge of the building making its way up to the dumpster. The lid on one side was open. It jumped up barely catching the ledge of the dumpster with its claws. It scrambled urgently with its hind legs to climb in. It pushed and fell over the edge into the trash below. It looked over the rim it remained looking out over the edge down the alley. Morning had broken and everything became more visible. It could not take a chance to be seen. It turned around like a dog circling to make its bed studying the trash. It began to pat down the trash. In the middle of the bend in the trash it made a small dip to where it would lay down. It grabbed a plastic bag placed it over the indentation it had made. It moved some more trash, paper, cardboard, and a few cans making a border around it.

Again it patted down the trash in the center firmly. It walked around in a circle several times. Rain began to fall. Had it known and how was it able to detect that it would rain. Water began to fill the indentation swiftly it filled with water. It had made the paper, cardboard, food, more durable. It began to pat the material into place. It circle around the center then curled into a fetus position allowing its gills to extract the oxygen from the water filling it with new life. The water in the pocket it had crated reached its ear line. It would hide for now. Night came and Adam stirred awake as it heard a lid close from one of the smaller cans next to the dumpster. It could sense and smell someone walking toward it. Adam swiftly stood on its hind legs moving against the dumpsters wall. It hunched down on its hind quarters here it would not be seen. Here it would attack its prey. It could here two men now. Kowk and Cho stood by the entrance of the restaurant joking around with each other. Cho grabbed the small trash can in his hand then stopped.

"I am telling you Cho she was a looker," Kwok says.

"Now Kwok come on who in the hell would want to go out with your ugly dog face. Fuck, it scares me from here."

"I see you got jokes tonight. Cho do you have a girl yet. Or is it you like boys?"

"Fuck you Kwok!" Cho says and then they both begin to laugh.

Cho turned around and continues to make his way up to the dumpster.

"I am telling you Cho I danced with her and her body felt like soft silk. I thought I was going to cum right there on the spot. You know she is Beverly's sister."

"Our buddy Johnny's girlfriend sister." "That is right Cho."

"Hum," Cho says under his breath.

"I have to go Kwok they just called an order out. Talk to you more about it later."

Cho walks back into the kitchen. Kwok laughed then opened the dumpster door to throw in the trash. He turned over the small trash can into the bend then tapped the back of the can. He placed the can on the ground then reached for a pack of cigarettes. He took one out of the pack put in his mouth then put the pack back into his breast pocket. He took his lighter lit it then took several long drags before he put his lighter back in his trouser pocket.

"Fucking Cho," he says out loud.

He began to close the lid but from the corner of his eyes he thought he saw something move. He reopened the lid all the way. Adam moved closer still cloaked by the shadow of darkness where the sun had not reached yet. A rat scurried over the trash and up Kwok's hand.

"What the hell?" he yelled out then seeing the rat run away he says, "fucking diseased infested rat you better run."

He laughed for a second for the rodent had scared the hell out of him. Adam moved out of the shadow stared straight into his eyes. The piercing black abyss looking straight at him. He could not believe his eyes it was inconceivable. Adam mouth open wide displaying the deadly jagged teeth within. It gnashed its teeth together before fear could enter Kwok's brain. Adam sprung off its hind legs sailing out at him. Kwok began to open his mouth in a scream but Adam was too quick. In that split second it would take Kwok to open his mouth. It lunged forward with its claws from both hands stretched out. It fingers immediately grasped on to his face. The claws sunk deep into the flesh.

It pulled back ripping the flesh off Kwok's cheeks. The gouges open up like several extra mouth on the sides of the face. The gouges stopped just at the edge of his lips. Blood gushed out covering his jaw. Adam moved to the left side of the man reached out grabbed the man's eyeballs that dangled freely from just a strand that of flesh remained that connected it to the eye socket. Adam plucked the eyes out like one plucking a plum or a cherry off a tree. It then popped it into its mouth.

It moved back as if to study the man. It moved its head to one side just starring at the torso hanging on to the edge of the dumpster. Kwok's body suspended by his arms that were all the way into the dumpster. Adam moved forward again rapidly thrashing eating half of Kwok's face off until only the white of the bone was exposed. It scrapped the flesh clean. With each bite the teeth grating sound emanated into the night. Adam then jumped out of the dumpster falling to the ground with a thud. It made is way rapidly along the wall of the building. Its claws scraping along the pavement as it moved down and out of the alley. Several beer cans echoed out the tin sound of an empty can. It cumbersomely made its way out of the alley and up to the river walk. It jumped into the Willamette River. The ringlets of water waves and bubbles where the only hint that it had entered back into the river. Adam spread its fingers and toes. The membrane between its digits caught the water allowing it to push itself through the waters current. It swam down to the depth of the river floor into the dark abyss. It began to claw at the mud. Air bubbles ascended upward like bubbles from a champagne bottle. It worked its claws laboring at the wet earth tunneling boring through like a rat preparing a place to live. A place to hide. A place where it would bring and eat its victims. The taste of the human's was all it could think of. The man it had just killed the red flesh. It continued to labor at the earth. It had made a den for it but like an infant it was exhausted. As soon as it lay down it fell asleep.

Small air bubbles ascended upward to the surface. The following day the front page of the newspaper headline read, "Woman dead killer unknown." In the article it said that a full investigation was in the process to find Betty's killer. In other words they were stumped for they did not have a clue. In the following days pictures and small articles as these were printed. Pet vanishes, Dog slaughtered in broad daylight. It was only the beginning of the true horror that would come. Adam was still growing as its appetite. It did not fear man, man's flesh is what gave it a burst of energy.

Adam moved to the opening of its dwelling. It watched curiously at a fish passing the opening. After a moment of scrutinizing the fish it switched its tail forcefully darted out into the river. Bubbles streamed upward again it switched its tail following the steal head that just past in front of it. Adam shot after it. The steal head darted to the left trying to avoid it and to get to safety.

It shifted down then up but it was to no avail. Adam was toying playing with the fish just staying a few inches behind it. Suddenly from the corner of its eyes it spotted a five foot sturgeon swimming by. As soon as it saw Adam it shifted and darted to the surface. With a swift thrust of its tail Adam changed direction moving after it. In seconds it was upon it piercing its flesh with its claws. It flung the fish up into the air just to see it hit back into the water in a daze. Adam repeated the scenario watching the sturgeon plop back into the water with a hard splash. It tired of the game. It grabbed the sturgeon in its hands placed the head into its mouth and bit down. The sound of crushing bone pleased Adam. But the fish flesh was not that of man. The flesh did not give it the vigor of red meat and blood. More reports of missing dogs and a few cats were reported.

Several of the people interviewed claimed that they last saw their pets at the edge of the river walk. They claimed they heard a loud splash then their dog or cat were gone. One man said he remembered seeing bubbles and that a huge fish stared back at him from within the water as he looked in. It was Adam. Adam waited patiently like all predators. It waited until they had come to the edge curious to find out what the soft gurgling sound it made was. Then at the right moment it attacked taking them from the edge of the walkway down into the depth of the water to their death.

CHAPTER 26

The next morning Pete and Johnny headed out of the precinct. They walk to the elevator went down to the basement floor. They past several doors Pete read the writing on the doors as they walked. He stared at the sign that said Medical Examiner's office and focused on the arrow indicating the direction in which to go. He knew he would need to spend time with the examiner as the case went on.

They turned left they walked up to the door that read Medical Examiner's office. They walked in Pete eyes opened in an expression of whoa. Jenny was as pretty as they come this he was not expecting. Being the medical examiner Pete figured she was probably old and eccentric like Sally.

Pete smiled but kept his thoughts to himself. And the fact was he was attracted to her he liked his women different.

"Johnny," she says.

"Jenny this is Pete Rodrequiz the transplant detective," he tells her.

She stood up from the stool and as she did Pete saw she wore a blue dress underneath the smock. She had shapely legs his thoughts ran on. Jenny was blonde with thin lips she had and oval face. Her tan accented her hazel eyes and her natural beauty. He looked at her chest as it heaved up.

She was well endowed he could see. She smiled at Pete. He felt a connection between them instantly.

"What is new on the case Jenny," asked Johnny.

"What I found is that this is one of the strangest things I have come across."

"Same," Johnny said.

"I heard you are from Texas way?" she asked Pete pulling away from Johnny's remark.

"Yes! Word gets around quick Jen. It is okay if I call you Jen?"

"Quite all right Pete."

"I heard what you told Johnny. Can you bring me up to para on the investigation?"

She walks up to her telescope. At first Pete thought she was going to ignore him. She grabbed a small note pad then looked at Pete.

"I will tell you that it is not normal. What I found detective is that it is the strangest thing I have seen. I found slime shit, on the body. I have not tested its contents as of yet. I do not think it is what we think it could be. Human."

"What else could it be?" Pete ask feeling as a rock was weighing down his intestines.

Hell of a way to meet women Pete's mind raced.

"Let us take a ride to Water Front Park and see what is happening out there," she says

They arrived at the Water Front Park later that afternoon.

"Now investigate these mysterious pet vanishings," she says as she looks at Pete.

Johnny looked out over the river wondering what Pete was staring at in the water. They searched the area as if searching for a needle in a haystack. Pete turned faced the Medical Examiner.

"Anything."

"To tell you the truth cowboy. No."

An officer approached her with his cell phone.

She had a bad feeling as she grabbed it from him. "Hello."

"Jenny."

"Chief."

"Jenny finish up as quick as you can. Head over to Damascus A.S.A.P."

"What will I be looking for Chief?"

"A cougar. Get the zoo people out there."

"An elderly couple walking along the path next to the river had an encounter with a cougar."

"Park ranger would do better don't you think chief?"

"Yes, but they are the ones who called. Look two attacks and strange footprints. It stinks Jenny. Find out what where up against."

Johnny reached for his phone answered it then listen to the voice on the other end. He turned towards Pete.

"We need to head out to Damascus Pete another attack. Possible perp big cats that kill."

"Chief wasted no time in calling you," Jenny comments as she handed the officer back his phone.

She grabbed her black medicine bag she began to walk to the M.E's van. When Pete and Johnny arrived at the scene Jenny was already at work. The old man that had been attacked was being placed on to a gurney to be hauled up to the ambulance.

The old woman trembled with fear from what had just happened. She kept mumbling on how the cougar waited patiently for them on one of the tree limbs. It waited watched their every move. They had made it up under the huge fir tree. It could smell them every muscle twitched with the anticipation of its next meal. Like a bullet out of nowhere. it sprung off its hind legs at the couple. As they reached the striking zone its teeth shone as it lips moved back into a vicious snarl. Its sharp claws protruded from its paws as it lunged forward. It sailed suspended in air for several seconds.

"Oh God!" The old woman cried out several times as she recalled the onslaught she continues with her story, "the claws from the cougar hit him squared on the shoulder hurling my husband back.

Its claws ripped the heavy cloth from his jacket cutting through it like a pair of scissors. Its claws dug in about a half inch into his flesh. It bit down. I heard my husband scream out in agonizing pain. He screamed for help I could see him losing the battle. My husband kicked wildly trying to dislodge the predator's teeth that ripped at his flesh. I don't know how but he turned and yelled for me to run. I thought at that moment it would be his last words. Without thinking I did the only thing that I could do to try and protect him. I spotted this large branch I grabbed it into my hands. I started swinging it wildly with all that I had. I do not know where I got the strength but I am glad. I hit it I hit it hard twice in the head. It staggered then just ran away. It just ran away just like that."

"Nothing like a woman's scorn huh," Pete interjected.

Jenny looked at Pete then replied. "I guess not."

"Johnny I am going to hitch a ride with the M.E."

Pete faced the M.E. she nodded her head. "Okay, see you back at the precinct." "All right be right behind."

An hour later they arrived. Johnny arrived five minutes later. Pete and Jenny waited for him to enter the room before they started. Jenny handed the chief the pathologist report. She looked down then reached for a doughnut on the chief's desk. The old German Sheppard just lied there looking up at her. It was curled up next to the Chief's chair. The Chief looks at Jenny then quips.

"By all means help yourselves."

Johnny knew he was being sarcastic, but it was that one opportunity he could not let go. He walked up to the desk reached in and helped himself to a doughnut.

"Thanks Chief," Johnny says with his mouth half full of doughnut.

Chief Golds sat down behind the desk opened up the file and read its contents.

"Hum puzzling," Golds says out loud. "What's up Chief?"

"Well for beginners Jenny there is a cat, cougar running loose stalking people down. The other is whatever attacked the first victim could not have been a cougar. The plaster prints where from two different animals. The first prints where small. The second larger. It stinks the whole thing reeks."

"I don't know if this pertains to the case Chief."

Golds studies Johnny for a moment, "Let's hear what you have to say Johnny."

"When I woke up this morning, I remember the smell of tuna. It smelled musky like a fish smell. There are now a total of four dead victims."

"I'll keep it in consideration Johnny for now I have to find answers to give to media."

Golds reached for the phone and began to dial. It was his cue for us to leave. Johnny looked down at the dog then said.

"Hang in there boy,"

They walked out of the office. The thought of dog stars ran through his head. In the movies the dogs played the side kick to the hero. They were young, healthy, dogs. Golds really must love his dog he thought. Golds dog could barely stand on its old wobbly legs. The next day they received another call another dead body at Damascus. The M.E. walked the edge of the river up to where Pete stood.

"What are we thinking of detective?" "Water."

"Okay, water and?"

"Jenny seems everything is near the water." "Yes, I thought of that as well. The killings are becoming more frequent as well."

The following day another dead body in Rohdadendrome. A small city east of Portland. Pete stared at the river. Pete's mind ran wild this was the third body. But this time it had been a small calf. Jenny released the edge of the gloves snapping snugly to her wrist.

"Jesus, this does not look good at all," she says to herself.

She knelt down next to the corpse. She reaches down into her bag and retrieves a small recorder. She begin to speak into it.

"Young calf. Half of right thigh missing.

Gouges and deep cut. Cause of death loss of blood and eaten. Death approximately one p.m., four hours ago. Time six p.m."

She placed the recorder back into her bag. She moaned she turned her head for a second as she looked down the river. She looked at Pete. She like the Texan all ready. It did not help she found him dark tall and handsome. She smiled at the thought. Johnny walked up to Pete. Now there is trouble she thinks to herself. She then brought her attention back to the corpse. Identity. She wrote down calf on a tag and fastened it to the right rear leg.

"Blondie," Johnny calls out to her. "Johnny don't call me Blondie."

Johnny chuckled then said, "I promise I will not call you Blondie cross my heart and hope to die," he says knowing that she did not like to be called Blondie.

Pete smiled then thought it did not make sense. Cross my heart and hope to die. Just did not make sense to him.

"We will see Johnny."

Pete walked up to her and asked bluntly.

"So Jenny what do you have?"

"Right to the point waste no time."

"Yes, my dear that is the detective creed for time is of the essence."

Johnny knelt down next to the dead calf trying to figure out what had slaughtered the animal so savagely. But still the question was what killed it. Man or beast.

"Jesus all mighty look at this calf's rump," he says out loud.

"Looks like something ate it," Pete replied saying the obvious.

Pete scrutinized the hind quarter's bleached bones remains. The calf's intestines sprawled out like large slimy rope. Its liver and heart exposed. He could see gouges and claw marks at the top next to the right ribcage. Why had it only eaten half the calf? Did it not find the rest of the body taste worthy. He did notice that from the waist down was the area it had chose to feast on.

More meat perhaps he thought. Meanwhile identification section has been taking pictures of the area, fingerprinting, in this case paw printing, and collecting evidence that could be helpful. For now what they had was a possible group of felines down right mean and hungry. That's is the theory until something comes up from the test.

"Any eye witness Jen?"

"Yes, a ten year old boy," she said as she pointed in his direction, "said it started coming towards him he got scared and ran inside. That is when it turned back around and attacked the calf.

"Damn it to hell that is all we need is to have state officials worried and their fears growing."

Pete scanned the grounds then back to where the boy stood.

"Now, where was it that the boy saw it approach from Jen?"

"See the fir trees over their? He said it came from the north. There was something the boy said that did not make sense though Pete. He said it was white and it stood upright like man. I asked him if it could have been leaning against the tree scratching its claws on the bark. He was sure he said it was just standing there staring at him. He said it started towards him.

"Maybe it was studying the boy's movement hoping he would wonder off in its direction for the kill," Pete says.

Pete's mind raced on trying to filter out what the M.E. had said.

"White," Johnny says out loud.

"White, that is what we have to figure out Johnny."

"Pete I can tell you this if it is white then it must be an albino. In turn it will make it valuable."

"What," Johnny says.

"Johnny if it is an albino you cannot kill it.

It has to be captured something to do with them going instinct. As I said cannot kill it. And as far as I know one of these tigers remain."

"You mean cougar," Pete interjects.

"I say tiger because of the description that

the boy gave. Still there is a flaw to his description. It is white with black patches. It has stripes on its tail and body. It could be a rare type of cougar I do not really know. I have been trying to figure out what black patches means. I am speculating it means shadows."

"Jen I do not care what color it is. I do not care if it is an albino. I do not even care if it is the last fucking cat on this planet," Pete says firmly.

"Shit look at this fucking stuff," Johnny says as he stands up with mucus running down his hand and fingers then adds, "freaking wicked."

"Saliva," the M.E. answers back.

Pete hoped she was not right it would mean it would make the investigation that much more difficult. Unidentifiable substance ran through his mind. He began to recall Two Souls and the clear mucus it left behind. One of the officers approached him.

"Detective there was nothing anywhere that we could see but we did find a footprint. And I believe we saw a beaver jump into the water."

"Officer Williams what color was it?" "White detective."

"Any dark patches," said the M.E.

"It might have but it was too fast. It vanished almost as fast as it hit the water. I do know it had a big tail. Yes its tail was thick and it glistened."

"You want me to go pump the boy for more details Pete."

"No, I think the boy said all he is going to say Johnny."

"Poor dumb calf," Johnny exclaims. "What you want to give it a name now." "Well Pete we do have to give it an identification," Jenny replies.

"Johnny just get one of the officers and I.D.S., and let us take a walk up to the river."

"What's up Pete?"

"Johnny I think there is a lot of housing going up around here. Therefore, there is less land for the cats to live on. This thing is getting less and less fearful of man. It will kill again to protect itself and like the M.E., said if it is an albino then it is protected by law. We have to find it before they have measure eighteen pass and special kill program is initiated. We do not need the media or gun nuts out here. We have too kill it and kill it quick before they step in," Pete tells him.

At the edge of the creek bed Johnny squats down run his finger along a footprint of whatever it was that jumped into the water. Johnny noticed that the footprint was bigger this time. Pete walked up to where Johnny was as he stared out at the water as if looking for something. Johnny looks up at Pete.

"Pete the size of its footprint is getting larger."

Just as Johnny and Pete where about let I.D.S. handle the print they here a splash in the water. Adam surfaced. Its tail, back, and head slightly above the water level. Abruptly with a forceful thrust of its tail it went under and vanished. It had been watching them.

"Look like a beaver to me," Johnny quipped. "A big one at that," Pete agreed.

He looked at the water with uncertainty. It did not even come close to being a beaver. It had been too big to be a beaver. It was the right , but it was too big for a beaver. It was the size of a large crocodile or man. It was the same color the boy described. Pete wondered if the others realized the abnormal size of the animal. And again death near the water.

"Pete."

"What's up Johnny?"

"Pete it was too big to be a beaver."

"Yes, partner I believe you are right. And I believe we are going to get a big surprise."

Pete did not known what they were up against but he knew it was not normal circumstance. He knew it would soon show its face but when. Two Souls ran through his mind again and again. What he believed to be man had been a monster. What you see is not what you get his mind raced on.

CHAPTER 27

The following day there was another murder up in Rhododendron Or.

"Here Pete. Turn left up that hill.

Rhododendron was about fifteen miles away from Sandy Or., and about thirty from Portland. It was small secluded and peaceful with an abundant of fir trees. Pete took in the scenery as he drove slowly. The enormous fir trees towered over mother earth like Giants waiting to be awaken for battle. There limbs seemed to move as if to want to reach out and grab one as they passed by. Johnny knew this was a different landscape for Pete. If he was right the only tree that grew thirty feet was a cotton wood tree up in Texas. And they were far and in between. Johnny began to whistle the theme to the Wizard of Oz. He looked at Pete. Pete smiled then nodded his head as if to read Johnny's mind. Pete's mind race with the words, "there are no ghost, there are no ghost."

"This is a loggers dream," Johnny says.

"Yes, I guess it would be," Pete replies back. The town was on the right before they turned on to the dirt road a few miles up. They turned left onto a dirt road drove about two miles before spotting the sheriff's vehicle and the others on the scene. It was like one going to a monster truck show.

"Look at those fucking trucks," Johnny quips.

Each of the trucks were fixed up with mud flaps, tire racks, fog lights, raised suspension, making them sit higher off the ground. Even the Clackamas Sheriff Department had a four by four. Next to the sheriffs vehicle was a news van with its logo in big bold letters.

"Hey Pete. How much do you think they paid to have the trucks built like that?"

"Well I would have to say more than we make in a year Johnny."

"That is what I was think as well."

They parked beside the sheriffs vehicle climbed out of the vehicle. They began to make their way up the hill. A few yards up it began to level out some then it began to incline again on and off for about another mile. Pete could see the man holding the camera. He could as well hear the news reporter talking. They continued up the incline up on top they rested for a moment. They made their way between the men around the news lady.

"Do you have any ideal where the predator is hiding or where it could be?" she asked the group of men.

"It is up there just a few hundred yards between those fir three up there," he says in a heavy Mexican accent and points.

"What brought you up here sir?"

"The Mow-neey of course," George tells her.

She yelled out, "cut," then told the camera man that they needed to interview one of the other men.

"Sir, sir, what brought you up here," she ask as she stuck out the microphone at the man.

It was a tall thin white man that held his gun over his shoulder like back in the day. Back in the day when one went out squirrel hunting. He chew some tobacco then spit. He looked at her for a moment then spoke.

"I am just tired of these things eating all my livestock."

"Do you think you will capture this cougar mister?"

"Lady I am not here to capture anything. I am here to kill it. If you want to follow me? I have to say you will see old Betsy here in action," he says and pats his rifle softly as if it were a pet, "lady you will see it die right before your very eyes."

"Who's in charge of this cluster fuck," Pete interrupted.

"The sheriff is," said a short fat man as he pointed towards the sheriff.

Pete and Johnny made their way in further. Getting a few yard away shouting distance Pete yelled out.

"Sheriff."

The man turned around then took off his smoky and wiped his forehead. The man was tall medium stature reminded Pete of the main character that played in gun smoke.

"Tom," Johnny greeted the man.

"Johnny," says the sheriff stretched out his hand.

He shook Johnny's hand then Pete's.

"Tom this is detective Rodrequiz from Texas." "From the big state of Texas huh," he says then was silent for a moment before he spoke, "yes I saw you in the paper. You are that detective that had some unworldly creature slaughtering folk. Right? Yes, I remember the name you made headlines. I think I read they called you, "Eagle Warrior."

And the other name they gave was let's see. Oh yeah the, "Monster Killer."

"Yes, sheriff and I hope the names will disappear from every ones memory."

"Yes, I guess you would want the names not to be remembered. So detective you are here to see if this is the cougar doing the killings," the sheriff say changing the subject.

"Where do you have this thing pined at Tom." "Just a few feet up Johnny."

"Circle the tree," Tom said and waved his hand for the men to move in he then looks at Pete and Johnny, "Let's go hunting boy."

Pete pulled out his Springfield. Johnny pulled out his forty-four magnum pointed it out in front as he held it with two hands.

"Jesus all mighty it isn't an elephant young man," Tom exclaims.

"It will stop it in a heart, beat."

"That it will," Tom agreed he got a glimpse of the men and told them to fan out.

They inched forward a twig snapped in half as one of the men stepped on it. The snapping twig warned the cougar of the danger approaching its safe perimeter. The cougar pushed up on all fours. In a swift rapid jerk it pushed off its rear legs. It sailed through the air. Its front feet hit the ground and in a blink of an eye it shifted in a different direction and vanished. The men began to talk out loud some began to worry if it would attack them.

"Stay calm men. Quite down so we can hear if it is nearby. Let's pick up its trail you news people can stay behind," the sheriff ordered.

Pete held his Springfield in his hands securely.

"After all this I hope it is the cat you and your partner are after detective."

"I hope it is as well. Another man was killed two nights ago close to downtown. If it is the one it will have tale, tale, signs," Pete says.

"These cats are getting braver by the day," Tom says.

Somehow it had made its way up another of the trees. It was perched on one of the tree limbs. And as we got in target range it sprung off its legs like a cannonball. One of the man just happen to see it as it squatted down.

"Get the hell out of the way," the man shouted as he saw the cougar leap in Johnny's direction.

"Get a shot of the cougar," shouted the reporter excitedly.

Johnny's eyes barely focused on the descending cougar heading at him. Out of instinct he grabbed the lapel of his trench coat quickly pulling it over his face. The cougar hit him hard sending him down to the ground.

"Roll, Johnny," Pete shouted out as he aimed.

It was as if the cougar had known for as soon as he saw Pete lift his gun it shifted and darted away. Leaving a small dust cloud behind. It wanted man dead as much as man wanted it dead.

"Oka0y, let's move out carefully. This time do not wait to see the white of its eyes," shouted the sheriff.

Pete walked up to Johnny then reached out his hand.

"Not, the face, not the face," Pete joked.

Johnny stood and brushed the debris from his close he smiled.

"You are right Pete. Can't touch this face.

Pete I would die if something happen to this face." "And you called me vain."

Pete knew that Johnny was only half kidding about the face. The other half he was serious. "You all right Johnny?" ask Tom.

"Yeah, I think my ego is hurt the worst. Were in the hell did that cat come from," the adrenaline through his veins shooting through made his limbs tremble. He could feel himself shaking from the rush.

It would be dark soon. If they did not get the cougar soon it would be for nothing. Again it climbed up another tree. It just stood froze like a ceramic statue and just watched us. It waited not for prey but for man. Undetected it waited for anyone to be in its target range. It sprung off its perch sailing down on George below. Its claws spread out the force of gravity as well assist its two hundred pounds of mass. It hit George the man screamed out as the claws sunk into his face.

"Chinga to madre, chinga to madre," he cried out.

The attack had been that of a desperate attempt to escape. It pounced off the Mexican man then shifted in a different direction. It desperately tried to find a way out between the men. Its feet sending out puffs of dust and debris as its claws dug deep into the ground for better traction. It saw an opening its front paws grabbed at the ground. It was about to shift when a blast form one of the guns resonated out. The bullet echoing out the sound of a victory. Echoing out and death written on the projectile. The bullet hit about an inch behind the cougar's left shoulder. It entered in an angle up to the heart. A plume of fur shot out as it entered its body. The cougar fell face first in a dive then stopped two feet from where it hit the ground. The news crew moved in for a closer shot. The reporter stepped forward with her microphone in her hand.

"The cougar gave its last breath."

She saw the tall thin man with the rifle and pointed the microphone in his direction.

"Like I said lady follow me and you will see it dead."

"Well it looks like we can all sleep a lot better tonight," she says as she looks into the camera.

The camera man focused the camera on the dead cougar then on the men standing around it. The camera man followed the reporter up to the man that had been attacked.

"You all right there George?" ask Tom.

"I will stay alive," he said in the heavy accent.

"Tom the cougar needs to get to the M.E.," Johnny says.

"I will make sure she gets the cougar a.s.a.p.

Let's hope it was just a rogue and not a trend setter Johnny. It took four men to carry the cougar to one of the four by fours. Two of the men flung the body into the back of the sheriff's truck. Its body hit the bed with a thud. Its head rolled to one side. Its eyes lifeless staring into space sending a cold chill down ones spine. Blood seeped out of the edge of the cat's mouth slowly forming a small puddle of blood next to its mouth on the truck bed.

CHAPTER 28

Three hours later back at the precinct at the morgue the medical examiner studied the cougar sprawled out on the metal table. She took pulled a small recorder from her smock pocket turned it on. She looks at the cougar for a second then speaks into the recorder.

"Female cougar, the date, time and the weight."

She cuts it off and then placed it on one side of the table out of her way. She took a black marker then made a line down the center of the cougar's stomach up to its neck. From the shoulders she made a small Y mark connecting the lines to the center line of its chest. She then continued down to its pelvic.

"Hum," she sighed then moved towards the metal tray at the edge of the table.

Now the good part she thinks to herself. The crash cart held her tools to her profession. She picked up the surgical knife.

"Okay kitty let's take a look at what you snacked on."

She then placed her index finger on top of the blade. She looks up at the clock at the far wall 11 p.m. She leaned forward placed her left hand on the cougar's belly. She poked the stomach several times with her fingers as if to find the right place to cut. She pushed down firmly on the scalpel in her hand.

"Let's see what you can tell us kitty."

She put pressure on the blade the skin opened up with ease. She followed the black marks making deep incision cutting from the neck to the back legs. A small pocket of gas escaped as the cougar belly opened pushing freely to the sides. Its intestines floated up quickly begging to protrude out of the cavity. It was as if one were seeing noodles expanding in a boiling pan swelling. Jenny turned placed the knife back into the crash cart.

The faint sound of metal hitting the metal as the knife hit resonated. She moved back to the cougar her fingertips stained with blood as well as her smock.

"Ah, now for the good stuff."

She turned on the recorder walk back to the cougar. She puts her hands into its belly. She shifted the intestines to one side then pulled out the stomach. The rancid smell hit her nose immediately. If it had not been that she was accustomed to it she would have puked. She reached for the surgical knife then cuts the end connecting it to the upper intestine. She placed it on a weighing plate.

"Four pounds two ounces."

Seems to be empty her mind races. She placed the intestines onto the crash cart. Again she moved in precision cutting the stomach open. She placed her right hand in to its stomach.

"Into the belly of the beast," she says to herself. She smiled remembering a child's song they use to sing on recess. Put your right hand in take right out. The song rang through her head. She spread the stomach open then placed her hand in again. Her hands searched like a hungry parasite for anything that linked it to the murder victims.

Nothing, not a damn thing she thought.

"Nothing," she says to herself again furrowing one eyebrow up.

It appeared that this was not the killer. This cougar has not eaten for a couple of days. She repeated the procedure with the upper, lower intestine, the liver, heart, saying the item then the weight. She cut off the recorder walked up to the sink at the far wall. She turned on the facet then took off her gloves. She then tossed them into a small waste can. She took off her plastic apron put it on a hook on a coat rack. She returned to the sink washed her hands then went back to her desk.

"Pete is going to love this," she says out loud.

It was weird she thought. He was new yet he was the one she found important. Her mind continues to race.

"Well if it wasn't you there has to be another one out there," she whispers as she looks at the carcass sprawled out on the table.

I feel sorry for you cat. We take and clear out your homeland for us to build for us to live. Yet in return we forget to give back. We are the protectors of this world. How easy it is to say the words yet so hard to follow through. No, wonder why you cougars are on the rampage. You come down from the hills for food. We as well hunt most of the game you feed on. I wonder if there was to be another evolution period what would be in stored for us. Her mind continued to run on. The whole thing ate away at her and time had pasted unnoticed. She looked up at the clock on the wall time seven 2 a.m. She got up and at that time her assistant walked in.

"What's up Jen? What are you still doing here?"

"Time crept up on me Gary."

"Go home and rest Jen I will close up," Gary says knowing the morgue never closes. "Hey, I like your hair Gary." "Yeah, green does something for me."

His normal hair was red on a thing face covered with freckles. She happens to like it more than the shade of green. Or the colors he came in on occasions.

"Where can I go and get my hair done like that."

"You have to have balls of gold to color your hair like this. You know damn well you would not get your hair dyed green."

"So, you are saying I got silver balls?" "Yeah! That is right. Jen go home and rest."

She looked at him then nodded her head in agreement. He was right she would never have the guts to get her hair dyed. He was a little eccentric in a way but he was good at his job. She recalled the first time she had talked to him. She was making her way down the corridor to the morgue. Several of the officers as well as the custodian made their way down the hallway as well. She remembered asking him what had moved him in the direction of pathology. He said as they walked bluntly that he did not want to be a cop and maybe have to kill someone. He said he decide to work on the dead to help catch the predators doing the horrendous crimes. She recall having to go fight in his behalf. She had been summon to the chiefs office. The chief had gone ballistic seeing the kid with purple hair at the time. It was the ninety's I had to argue with the chief. I as well had the opportunity to see Gary at work. And I have to say he was a natural. The next time the chief saw him he had changed his hair color to a yellow. I recall the chief looking at me. He did not say a word he just gave us a run down on the victims and what we where to look for. And I have to say he found the clue I missed. That was it Jenny says to herself and stops abruptly. She turns back around and rushes back into the morgue.

"Gary, Gary," she shouts out. "What? You gone crazy."

"I want you to leave your beeper on." "Calling for a date," he says joking.

"No, but you are going to go out into the field with me the next time."

"Why and how did I know you were going to say that?"

"Maybe you are pshyic?"

"No jenny. Pshyco for doing this job perhaps."

Jenny knew Gary loved his work as much as she did. He did hate the outdoors elements especially the sun. It toasted him red as a lobster. Most of the time it blistered his lips. It went with the fair skin.

"Two heads are better than one Gary."

"You are right Jen. You know I will do it no matter if I suffer."

"Gary I need you. You are almost as good as I am."

"No, Jen I am better," he says and waits for her come back.

He waited for several moments then spoke, "you must need my help that bad. You had no come back."

"I do need your help Gary. I need you to help me find out what the hell is masacareing all the innocent people. Perhaps I could have tried to butter you up a little but the fact is I need your help."

"I will get gear ready Jen."

She turned back around walked out into the corridor. Meanwhile Gary took a notepad out of his breast pocket then a pin. He began to write down what he thought he would need for the field. He pushed up his glasses with his finger using the bridge to move them up. He wrote down sun block, bug spray, and lots of it. He put the pin and note pad back into his pocket.

"Ticks, spiders, and snakes, shit," he says out loud.

He went to the cougar and began to put things away. He would push the gurney to the incinerator to dispose of it. The thought of animals that he would have to deal with sent a chill up his spine. He grabbed the gurney and began to whistle as he pushed it through the double doors.

CHAPTER 29

Days continued to pass like the flipping of a page to a book. One month then another now the New Year was coming in. In a matter of hours another year gone. And who knew that the New Year would bring a sighting that Adam was back? Its sighting would mean more death would come like the horseman on a black horse. It would be horror at its best. It had survived the cold this was something we did expect. We wanted it dead gone from our world but instead death was coming at us with a vengeance. It had survived the cold, the snow, on the balance of fish, dogs, cats, rodents, and a small calf.

What I dread at this moment is to mention that it had taken two humans as well on New Year. The taste for human blood awaken its mind. It rolled its eyes back as soon as it tasted the sweet pungent taste of blood. In its dreams in the depth of the Willamette it dreamt of its teeth scraping against a skull eating to the white of the bone stripping off the flesh. For unknown reasons it did not stay in Portland. It made its way up to the Dalles up to the Columbia River. It made its way up to Bonneville Dam. Through thicket and trees. It made its way around the dam and back into the Columbia River. It swam back to the Willamette River. There had been no killings and to this day it is not know why it went to the

Dalles. The only thing we could think of was that perhaps it was warmer in that region. At the edge of the Columbia River it turned right back into the Willamette River. It slowed down its pace. Its body half submerged the other half above water.

Two month and now it was the fifth of March. Its tail moved in slow even strokes as it made it back to its abode. It looked at the opening of its dwelling. It had seemed it had gotten smaller for it had grown. Adam was now at least seven feet and three hundred and seven five pounds of solid muscle. It scrutinized the opening for a moment then went to work. It thrashed violently burrowing like a backhoe tearing away at the mud. In a few minutes it had vanished into the depth of its dwelling of its new home.

CHAPTER 30

Ken and old man in his late seventies walked along the embankment of the Willamette River on the other side of the river. The sun rose in the east bring life to the city below.

"Georgie, Georgie, you get back up here now," the old man's voice cracked with age as he shouted out to the black and brown dachshund.

The dog waddled when it started to run up ahead ignoring the old man. The dog had one speed and it was not very fast. The dog stopped sniffed the air as if it had pick up a scent. It tilted its head to one side then to the other. But there was no one in sight. It stopped suddenly as the water in front of it began to bubble. It watched the form of the creature emerge from the water. It began to stand. Water fell from its body. The sun made its skin glisten reflecting off the sun. The dog moved back its hind legs kicking up small debris of sand. The debris from its feet scatter out. It began to yelp then yelped more franticly. The old man being further away could not see the figure clearly. The dog rubbed against his owner's leg letting him know it was at his side.

"See I tell you stay next to me. I do not know what you saw boy. But maybe you will listen to me the next time. Now let's go home," the man tell his dog as if speaking to a child.

Adam watched the man. He watched as the old man struggled just to walk away. Adam's tail moved back and forth as it looked at him. Adam slowly walked out of the water its gills working hard.

The dog turned around then barked several times. The old man turned around adjusted his glasses. The bifocals were not made for seeing distance. All he saw was a blur. The dachshund bit and grabbed the old man's trouser leg. It pulled at him to move faster.

"What in God's name Georgie?"

The old man looked down at the dog searing its hackels up. The man squinted at the figure walking up to him. The dog barked then growled it moved towards the creature. It attacks Adam but it was futile. It would not be able to save its master today. A loud yelp filled the air as Adam sharp claws severed off the dogs head. Fear rushed through the old man. It shot through him like a jolt of lightning burning the message of danger to all his senses. The fear numbed his mind there was no way that, that thing in front of him was real.

The creature was now close enough for the old man's eyes to work. He kept on telling himself that there was no way it could be real. He saw the thing raise its clawed hand.

"What in God's name," he managed to get out the words as the sharp claws ripped open his throat.

The old man's eyes open wide. The impact sent the man's into the water. The water splashed out as his body hit the water. The water stained with his blood and entering where it had slashed the man's throat. The man moved his hands rapidly in an attempt to stay afloat. The man coughed water and blood as he tried not to drown. Blood filled the water like a red ink spreading. The creature entered after the man took the man into the depth of the water. It and the man vanished the water became calm moving as before. Meanwhile it pulled the victim down further and further into the abyss of the river. Adam took the man to a bridge that was two miles away. It climbed out of the water dragged the man underneath the Powell Bridge. It pulled the body onto the embankment next to the concrete incline. It dropped the body knelt down then began to devour the man's flesh. It thrash its head back and forth violently ripping flesh.

It ate cloth as well as the flesh moving faster ripping away the meat off the bones with its white porcelain jagged teeth. Human flesh dangled between its teeth. The red muscle tissue coming off in chunks. After a few minutes it had appeased its appetite. Adam left the body and returned into the arms of the river. Its head went under leaving a small ripple on the surface of the water. The old man's body lay sprawled out. A thing that had served its purpose and now was discarded. All one could see was the man's chest up to the head. From the waist down it was clean of all flesh. It was as if one were seeing through a plastic dummy that is used to describe the inter parts of the human anatomy. The lungs remained intact the intestines hung out of the stomach like coil slimy rope. The eyes open wide in a fear expression. A finger from one hand and two from the opposite hand remained.

It did not take the insects long to gather for the feast of the dead. The sound of vehicles passing over head above on the bridge filled the air. It was as if the body was all alone in a different dimension. The body alone and ignored only present to the insect world. Five hours pasted before a boater discovered the body and called it in. An hour later Pete looked out over the waters of the Willamett River. The police boat moved up under the Powell Bridge. Pete looked out over the water as they moved up to the bridge. It was amazing the small ripples of waves moving up to the shoreline as peaceful as the beginning of time. Peaceful but in this peace lay something ugly. There was a dead body the ugliest sight known to man. The officer on the boat steered then grabbed the lever to his right side next to the steering and pulled it back slowly. The boat speed reduced. It slowly crawled forward until it bumped onto ground. When the boat hit there was a slight force letting them know that they were now at the edge of ground. Everyone on the boat climbed off. They made their way underneath the bridge. The smell of the river water mix with the life it held instantly reached their noses. The forensic team was there already at work seeming to be on an automatic mode. The M.E. and Gary and the M.E.T., where busy sweeping the body for evidence getting it ready transport. Pete walked up to Jenny.

"That is what remains of the body," she says then faces Gary, "Put the excretion into a plastic bag and tag it."

Gary said under his breath in a whisper,

"Why? Why, did they have to wake me up at three thirty this morning? Why do I have to be so good at my job? And why did Jenny have to like me?"

With all the good and bad the one thing he did like was working with her. Hell, it was just too early and he was still half asleep his mind raced.

"Weird!" Gary said out loud then scratched his head.

"Yes, and I think it is going to get better as we go," Jenny replies back.

Pete kneels down next to the body. He stares at the half-eaten torso. Whatever had murdered and eaten him from the stomach down could not be human. The white bone protruded out like white ivory from under the hips with slight hints that flesh had been attached to the bones. Things seemed to be escalating for the worse. He had been told that it had been a cougar doing the killings. It was the blind leading the blind is what he thought. At this point he did not care if it was a cougar, lion, tiger, a fucking cat, or a small cat, or man he just wanted a clue that would send him in the right direction. But his intuition gnawed at him telling him it was not man and that worried him.

He had seen man and animals kill prey but leaving the kill behind did not make sense. It or he did not even attempt to hide the victim. One thing for certain it would kill again but where and when?

"Detective," a man from the forensic team called out to Pete.

"Yes," Pete answered back.

"We are done here. We have been under and over the bridge and the body even the embankment.

Nothing, not a damn piece of lint that is out of the ordinary. But there was the same excretion from all the other killings."

One of the officers approached, "detective the M.E.T., ready and needs help with the body."

"Get two officers load the body into the gurney tell them to take the body to the ambulance for the M.E.T. and leave two officers behind."

Pete, and Johnny watched as the body was hauled up to the street. It had taken them at least twenty minutes to make it up the incline.

"Well I guess where done here."

"Okay, we will see you back at the precinct," Pete told Jenny then turned around and headed for the boat.

Pete mind went into his fix a puzzle mode. They worked the embankment the body the surroundings area. That is what the forensic man had said. But they did not walk the shoreline to the north. Killers leave tail, tail signs. There has to be some kind of clue left behind. He knew animals came back for their kill.

"Tell Jake that I will be back Johnny."

He turned and began to walk down the shore line heading towards the Fremont Bridge. He kept his eyes along the shoreline. Pete stopped abruptly he thought he saw something. He waited for the water to move back out. Nothing. Pete kneeled down grabbed a hand full of dirt in his hand then siphoned it through his hand. He began to get a migraine. His mind raced on, no clue, impossible the thought ate away at him. He felt his acid reflux acting up. There was a victim the obvious. The mucus like substance found on all the dead.

Could it be a rabid animal? But how could it have gotten down here with the body without being seen? To boot with a grown man dragging behind it. And then the fact that there were no tracks. No footprints. Fucking impossible his thoughts bombarded his head with the question that how was it possible there was no clue. He stood walk several more yards up then again he thought he saw something. Perhaps his mind was playing tricks on him. He did want to find a clue. He took a second look as the water ran back out. It was a footprint. He scrutinized it again in his head he told himself it was a footprint. Pete rushed back to the boat.

"Johnny get forensic back up here a.s.a.p. tell them we have a footprint."

Moments later forensic and Gary, the M.E., where back on the scene. The forensic man knelt down studied the footprint as the water rolled back out.

"Make a dam around the print to keep water out," said the forensic man.

Gary knelt down made a mud dam around the print. It had taken another hour but they had managed to get a cast of the print. After they had left Johnny and Pete walked back up to the boat climbed aboard. Two officers pushed the boat back out into the water and quickly got in.

CHAPTER 31

Pete was abruptly awaken by the cells phone tone. He opened his eyes squinted trying to focus his sight. He lay still for another few seconds then rolled over on to his side. He reached for the cell phone on his night table. He moved the curser to the right and answered the phone.

"Hello," he said in a droggy tone.

"Pete I think they found the perpetrator to the murders," chief Golds tells him.

"Can't this wait?" Can I get at least a hello how are you doing."

"Not enough time for the sweet talk Pete." "Okay, so you are saying it is the killer? here?"

"They have it cornered up in the Beaverton area."

"Him or her."

"Neither, it is a bear," the chief replies. "You are fucking kidding me right?"

"No, Pete as absurd as it maybe we have to take all the leads that come in. And before you ask again if I am sure? Yes, it is a bear not a cougar. We have a bear so get your ass up and be ready for Johnny. He should be on his way."

"Pete Rodreqize detective I am." "Cut the crap and go investigate." "Trying to kiss up to the reporters?" "Quit with the smarts asshole."

"Take it easy chief I am new here." The phone went dead on the other end.

"Can you believe that not even a morning kiss or I love you," he says to himself.

Pete hated to go on a wild goose chase. It was a killer they were after and the bear was not in the picture. It was luck the chief had managed to get a hold of Johnny. Johnny had said something about going out with the woman of his life. Pete had not met Beverly as of yet. He did not know what spell she had on the young man. But if it kept the man happy it was a good thing for him.

Johnny was the youngest one of the brightest upcoming detectives. He was now the only friend he had in Portland. As the chief had said Johnny arrived in about twenty minutes. He was drinking the last sip of his coffee. He walked out close the door behind   h i m went to the car climbed in and they headed for Beaverton. At the sight Pete and Johnny climbed out walked about a yard looked up a tree. Pete and Johnny stared at the bear that was on a limb that seemed as if ready to break. The bear was frighten its claws dug into the tree trunk for dear life. It was a small brown bear it looked down at them. The zoo official took out the tranquilizer gun from the trucks back seat. He walked back aimed the gun as the other man looked on. He squeezed the trigger the dart went sailing out of the rifle hitting the bear on the flank. It took at most five minutes before the bear felt the effect of the drug. It began to sway back and forth. It looked at the ground as if it knew where it would be in a few seconds. Its grip let loose from the tree trunk. It swayed then fell like a bag of potatoes with a loud thump on to the ground. The two zoo officials quickly approached the bear to examine it.

"Seems okay Bill."

"We better get it on to the truck and put it in the cage like quick Jim. Before the drug wears off."

Johnny was about to move when Pete raised his hand to stop him.

"It is their expertise we do not know the first thing about bears. Or how to hand them. We will let them do their job."

Pete had something against things that could tear him apart limb by limb. Better yet swatting at him and killing him like a fly. It was not natural to go after an animal without armor he thought to himself. Pete respected the men they had to have a deep love for beast of the wild in general to do what they did. It was either that or they got paid a hell of a lot of money. He thought it but he knew it was not the case with these to men. They watched on as one of the men backed up the truck with the cage up to the bear. It stopped a few feet away. The driver rushed out of the truck then went to the back and let the tailgate down. The other man stood then walked up to the other side of the truck. He helped the other man push the cage to the edge of the truck. Away from everyones sight the bears claws opened and closed. It had been a miss calculation of the amount of sedative required to keep it sedated. The men moved up to the bear. Jim moved back quickly as the bear swung out with its powerful muscular arm. There had been no warning to the bears claws slashing out through the air. Jim had been lucky just avoiding the strike by a second. Bill fell backward then quickly he scrambled up to his feet. The bear turned its head looked around in a daze.

It charged at the first person it lay eyes on. Pete and Johnny were its next target. Pete knew by the look and the mannerism of the creature that they were the target. Pete scanned the surrounding quickly. The bear looked straight at them.

"The shed Johnny run now."

"Oh shit to hell," Johnny exclaimed out and ran following Pete.

Pete jumped on top of the trash can then onto the top of the roof of the small shed. The tin material making a metal sound with each of his steps. Johnny did as Pete. Pete reached out pull with all his might as he saw the bear swing its sharp claws. The claws catching Johnny's pant leg managing to rip the bottom part of the pants. Bill ran grabbed and reloaded the tranquilizer gun. He aimed paused for a split second then squeezed the trigger. He hit the bear at the right shoulder.

He reloaded aimed then paused for a second then fired hitting the bear on the center of the neck. He reloaded aimed fired hitting the bear on the side of the neck. The bear fell dropping on all fours. It was angry and scared. It turned and ran after the man. The man jumped into the front seat of the truck closed the door shut. His heart pounding fast. The bear lowered its head using it like a battering ram and rammed the door. It hit the driver's side hard knocking the man inside around in the cab. Pin ball Pete thinks as he sees the man bounce around inside. He pulled out his revolver he had the bear in his sight. From the corner of his eye he saw the other man shouting out from under the vehicle. Jim remained under the truck. All Pete had to do was pull the trigger and it was all she wrote. Just pull the trigger and kill the bear he told himself and slowly began to squeeze.

"Don't shout," shouted Jim.

Pete stared at the man thinking the man had gone nuts still he knew the man just wanted to contain the bear. Pete released the pressure on the trigger but stayed aiming at the bear. If the bear even flinched to attack he would end the charade. No more games his mind raced. The bear tilted its head to one side and let out a growl.

It was now confused by the drug. Bill climbed out of the vehicle and fired the tranquillizer gun again. The dart hit the bear in the chest.

The bear stood growled then drop onto all fours then charged. Bill ran with all he had Johnny held out his hand caught the man's hand and pulled. The sheds roof making the metal sound of urgency. The bears front paw slapped against the shed then it lost its grip and swayed. The bear swayed its eyes glazed over. It swayed again then dropped next to the trash can. Leaves and dust shot up from its weight as it hit the ground. There was no time to waste now. Pete, Johnny and Bill jumped off the shed. Jim crawled out from under the truck. Bill poked at the bear with his foot.

"This is the longest thirty-six hours we have been out for one of these animals," says Jim.

"What was that you said," Pete asked?

"I said it was the longest thirty-six hours I went through."

Pete had a puzzled look on his face then became pensive. Pete looked down at the bears foot noticing that it had one more digit than the killer. It was not the killer. It had been a waste of time. Pete watched the men as they lowered the tail hoist. They helped the two men roll the bear into the hoist then into the cage. The men closed the tail gate thanked them and drove off.

"Johnny lets head out."

Johnny looked at the bear then at his partner. "Next we will be told that it is an ape murdering innocent people. That is all we need a damn ape gone psycho running amuck."

"Stranger by the minute," Pete said.

Pete knew Johnny thought it had been a waste of time as well but he would play along.

"That bear wanted to tear some ass." "Yeah Johnny, angry it was."

"Well hells bells Pete wouldn't you be if you were stuck a few times with a needle?"

"You got a point Johnny."

"I am hungry as a bear," no pun intended.

"Let's go get something you know of a good place Jhonny?"

"Good thing you asked I have the place and I think you will love the food. Downright good Pete."

Moments later Johnny pulled up into Dianes a small restaurant off Foster.

"I am hungry and like my father use to say best food in town. My father was a character but like clockwork he would always bring us to eat here at this dinner. You know in a way it was funny. You see my dad didn't care to much for my mother's cooking."

"So I guess you and your folks ate out a lot."

"Good assumption Pete and yes we did." "So what is the best plate to order?"

"Order the chicken fried steak best anywhere and I am buying."

Pete smiled then got out of the car and they walked into the dinner.

"You buying most of had a hell of a night."

"Let's just say my Bev. loves her man.

" "Well if you are paying it works for me."

They both chuckles as they made their way to one of the tables.

CHAPTER 32

Jeff turned on to his side and watched as Mary got dress.

"Whats up Mary?" he asked then added, "why you up so early and on a Sunday. It's not even eight in the morning yet."

Mary put on a flannel shirt and blue jeans. She put on her pumps then picked up her purse from the dresser then replied back.

"If you must know Jeff I am going to tell my parents the good news about us."

"Well sense you are going to do all that today why don't you get me a tux while you are at it."

"I could just kill you," she says and jumps in bed and hugs him tightly.

"What else are you going to do today Mary?"

"I am going to go get fitted for the wedding gown. Then when we get married, I will collect on the insurance. But for now I just want to spend some time with my folks."

"Tell them I said hi and that I am sorry I did not go."

"I will Jeff," she says and walks out of the room.

Mary pulls up to a small house in Woodburn Or. The paint on the front of the house was peeling off. The house needed panting and the fence around the house needed repairs. She recalled back the first day she lay eyes on the house. Her dad had saved many years to pay it off in cash. At that time the paint was fresh and actually glimmered in the sun. As she stared at the house her father stepped out onto the porch.

"Papa," Mary shouted out happily.

"Connie look who came to visit us," her father said looking over his shoulder.

Mary felt the dig she could sense something was not quite right. But for the moment she would leave it alone.

"Mary," her mother called out as she stepped out onto the porch.

The screen door slammed shut behind her. Mary walked to the white picked fence opened the squeaky door. She walked up on to the porch. Her mother grabbed her by the hand and they walked inside the house.

"You got here just in time for breakfast."

Mary looks at her mother then ask, "is Papa mad at me?"

"Na, he is just like a big baby he has his feelings hurt because you forgot his birthday."

"Oh, my God mother that is right."

"Ah do not worry the old fart knows you have to work long hours being a doctor."

"Here sit-down Mary let me put the food on the table."

"Need help Ma?"

"No, just sit down," she tells Mary then returns with fresh coffee.

She puts the pot on the table on a coaster then returns back moments later with tortillas, bacon, beans, and eggs.

"Mom it smells good."

"Frank come and sit down," her mother shouts out to him.

He walks in sits down at the end of the table.

Mary quickly stood not being able to forgive herself for forgetting her father's day. She kissed him on the cheek then told him she was sorry over and over. Tears ran down her cheeks. Seeing the tears and the guilt of grief for not coming over on his birthday. He smiled for he was not really mad at her. How could he she was his baby. He just wanted to let her know that he missed her. And for just that one day out of the year he wanted her there beside him. He pats her softly on the back.

"Mary it is all right I know you have a very demanding Job. I know you did not do it on purpose. I know you love this broken down old man. Just do me one favor and do not ever forget my day. Okay!

"You have my word dad."

They ate and conversed about what was taking place. She told them she was getting married. She then asked about the paint on the house and fence.

"The paint can wait," he said then ads "the fence well we do not have a dog so why worry about the fence."

"You know your dad Mary always, mayana, mayana."

They all laughed out happily then continued to converse on the matters of the world.

CHAPTER 33

Jeff had just read the morning copy of the newspaper as Mary walked in. She had been in a good mood, happy. She placed her purse on the table walked up kissed Jeff on the cheek. The happy left it was destroyed as Jeff tossed the paper down. The headline caption read "Serial Murders continue."

"Adam," Mary says sadly.

"Yes, hon that is what it appears to be. It has taken the life of a child this time."

Jacob stumbled into the kitchen wiping the sleep from his eyes.

"You two look pretty gloomy."

"Adam, Adam has been seen and it has killed a child," I said then told Jacob and Mary to get a quick bite for we had a difficult task before us."

They got a bite to eat, and we got dressed and returned downstairs. I looked at my colleagues for a moment as I devised a plan then spoke.

"You and Jacob see if you can fine the other life organism at Salvie Island."

"Now, I am good Jeff but what am I suppose to do pull a rabbit out of my ass?"

Jeff broke a smile then said, "look it maybe the only chance of capturing what was created. So we need the other life form to lure it in. I say Salvie Island because that is where it attacked you. If we can find it we may have a chance."

"I see the family connection card," Mary quips. "I know it is a long shot, but it is possible."

"You know by now it is as well full grown and we do not know what D.N.A., it has taken Jeff."

"I thought of that Jacob but if my theory was right what genetic structure it has come in contact with it would become. We all agree on that. And if it is more dangerous, vicious, a being without a soul that kills. Then we are responsible and must find it. We are responsible for what Adam is."

"Not, entirely true Jeff. The final ingredient was human blood. And yes it appears it did get its intelligents but it has other D.N.A., as you mentioned. It would have become something without our help. Hopefully the human quality is what will give us a one chance in a million."

"I hope you are right Jacob." says the became pensive the ads, "you and Jacob comb the area at Salive Island. I will go up town to the bridge. Maybe I can find a clue. And I need to see the area with my own eyes."

Jacob and Mary headed off to Salvie Island. I took off to the bridge. An hour later I found myself down by the park. I crossed several streets and made my way up the Powell Bridge. I searched like a hawk for a worm. It did not take long for me to spotted the infants blood. It had become a brownish color with oxidation. I caught other droplets heading up the bridge heading north. I followed it momentarily then lost the trail then noticed something else. The feeling that came over me is indescribable. I became sick literally. I felt my stomach wrench I could taste my own sour bile in my mouth. I spit it out. Jesus, oh Jesus, I cried out then wanting to cry. I looked over the guard rail into the river below. I scanned the bank on the east side. Below I spotted the infants white and blue sneaker with only the foot remaining inside. Again, my blood curled. I rushed down the bridge and quickly climbed down the concrete incline to the edge of the water. I stopped and looked down at the sneaker. Blood stained the border of the shoe where one sips it on to the foot. As I looked at the sneaker and cried for forgiveness, I noticed form the corner of my eye the creature.

First, I saw it float to the top and its eyes staring at me. It then began to move its tail in slow movement pushing itself to where I was. It stopped for a moment then began to come up out of the water. Water rolled down its back. As I looked at it a rage entered me as none before. I stared at what it had in its hand. It held the skeleton of baby's right arm. I could not believe that this was all real. I could not believe that the arm was all that was left of the child. I was filled with sadness. I turned then became paralyzed at what I saw it pull from under the water. It looked at me then made gurgling sounds then lifted out of the water the remains of the child. I stood motionless it could have killed me with ease if it wanted but did not move. I believe it had been a warning for me to stop my pursuit and let it live free. It let out this loud squealing scream several times. It turned dragging the infant behind it like a rag doll. It returned to the depth of the water. I knew for certain now that this creature was intelligent. How the organism had crashed to earth who knew. Or was it deliberate? An intelligent being and any being that could control such a creature were no match for. And it could be that this life form we found was sent here to clean the weaker life. But why? Did these aliens that processed this organism think we were nothing more that a meal expendable. The ripples in the water vanished and I made up my mind to keep this encounter with Adam a secret for the time being from my colleagues.

CHAPTER 34

Pete looked at the clock hanging above the fridge both hands straight to high noon. He did not feel like making breakfast today. He reached into the cupboard and retrieved a cup of chicken noodle soup. He popped the lid put the soup into a bowl and put it into the microwave. Two minutes and it was ready. He shook his head thinking breakfast food for champions. Pete decided he would drink it so he placed the soup into a coffee cup and sip at it. He sat down at the table opened the newspaper. He lay it out flat on the table surface. The front page instantly caught his attention. It was as if the page stared at him saying look, look. The bold letter as well as the picture in the center half of the page stuck to him. The image penetrated to the back of his brain sending a numb feeling through it. It happened again it was as if time stood still. The horror of what was out there hit him like a wrecking ball. A wrecking ball crushing through his brain. He read the headline out loud.

"Baby vanishes in broad day light from the Powell bridge as mother stand nearby."

The woman was in her early twenty's it was her first child. She stood in the picture with an empty stroller with blood stains where the baby rested its head. The blood stained on cushion overpowered the page. The woman's hands outstretched with her mouth open in a scream. Pete read the article. The woman said that she had just turned away for a minute just to watch the passing ship go underneath the bridge. She said she saddle heard her son cry. She turned to see something carrying the baby away in its mouth. It stopped in the middle of the bridge with the baby firmly clamped in between its jaws. It look at her she recalls.

She then mentions that it squatted down and from a squatting position pushed off its hind legs and leap over the guard rail. It splashed into the water below it went under disappearing from sight.

It looked like a boy she insisted. She then said she noticed something odd. She related that it had a tail. It had a white tail with tints of black like shadows. It was like shades many shades and it walked up right. It walked on all fours then on its leg. Yes, it did stand up several time. And it's skin glistened as the sun reflected off its back. It was as if it were wet or sweating. The reports question was if she was sure and that people did wear strange clothe these days.

"No. It was not human clothed it was its skin. I am certain."

Pete put the paper down put the cup in the sink. He knew Johnny would be there soon. He opened the door and noticed the unmarked vehicle turning the corner. He knew he would be getting a call soon. No, sooner he began to close the door when his cell rang. As he talked the phone for the first time, he thought of it being of an unworldly origin. Pete felt his stomach churn. He would probably get ulcers. Fuck, fuck, fuck, the words ran through his mind.

CHAPTER 35

There was nothing more I could do. I needed to meet up with Mary and Jacob to see what they had achieved. Deep down I just hoped that they find the life form. Adam torment my mind I could not get it out of my mind. I continued on to Salive Island. I reached the turn off I then pulled off the highway. I slowly pulled into the small dirt road that would lead me to the Willamett River. I was surprised that it had not taken me long to find my colleagues. Mary came running towards me as I arrived where they are. No, sooner had I cut the edging off when Mary hit the window shield for me to open it up the side window. I rolled it down Mary was excited as she spoke.

"We saw it Jeff. We saw it just minutes before you got here." she exclaimed.

I opened the door climbed out put my hands on her shoulder.

"Take a deep breath Mary and repeat what you just said but slower," I said as I looked into her eyes.

"We saw it. We saw it and it was huge. But it was not like or Adam. This one was more like a giant frog, but it could stand erect like man as well."

"So, are friend was alive all along. It was just waiting for the right donor. A donor with blood, blood, the main factor."

"So, how do we explain the frog?" I ask.

"That is easy if you recall the men the goons. You seem puzzled Jeff," Jacob says. "A little," I replied.

"Remember one of the goons had been at the bank of the river."

"Yes."

"I recall looking down as he wiped something off his shoe. And as I pulled the air tank up I saw that it was a frog Jeff.

"Jeff this one is a female," Jacob tells him.

"Now how in the hell could you tell what it is without a close look at it?"

"Oh! I had a good look. It was not easy. But as far as seeing it I did. I saw the underbelly as it rolled over and presto boobies."

"Hum, I am beginning to think that we are meant as cattle."

"Why do you say that Jeff."

"Just make sense. It crashes kills the pilot. And escape the pod. The vials they kept them in a secured cell in a way. They were sealed with no air. This thing seemed to want to get into your mouth Jacob. I believe it wanted to impregnate you. And we better put are heads together and decipher the meaning of the words on the vial. And I think we need to do it quick."

"I concur," Jacob replied back.

Mary agreed. Jacob turned back around moved another foot into the tunnel.

"Looks like Jacob is up to his feet in mud literally."

Mary laughs and Jacob mumbles something like, " It wouldn't be funny if you were in here."

Jacob's body was now completely in the hole except his protruding feet. Jacob began to back out of the hole. He stood turned around sat sprawled legs out. He spread his hand out above his legs.

"Looks like you poked you head into a hole of sorts."

"Funny Jeff because that is exactly what I was doing," Jacob says then adds, "you heard the joke about wanting a little pussy but it's as big as a house. That isall I could think of in there. I do not know how many times I laughed out loud to myself."

"Did you see it."

"Yes, but when I grabbed at one of its feet, it move in deeper. And I have to say that is one big fucking tunnel. I as well was kind of scared in a way."

"What do you mean?" Mary asked.

"I had second thoughts going after it. I thought maybe I would be its dinner."

"I guess you would be scared nobody knows what an animal will do. But let's wrap it up and get you home so you can get cleaned up. We can figure out what kind of equipment we will need then come back to catch this thing."

As we walked to the vehicles my mind ran wild.

Adam this life form? What we helped create would be the most menacing creature ever recorded in human history. We want to believe in friendly alien. But Adam was not a friendly ET. It was the opposite side of the coin. Death reeked from its own name. We have a hunch that the government knows of other life forms that fall to earth. Some I believe that their intelligence surpasses ours by a mile. Why do I say this. Let's see they have spaceships that travel faster and run on sum kind of energy not known to us. Not to mention the weapons I saw in the ship and the technology that ran it. It did not matter the sender of this organism had anticipated what we would do if found. It began to rain as we drove back home. As we arrived, we saw three black limo's parked on the crescent driveway. I noticed the front double doors where wide open. Silva was holding one open. This man, this renowned Alientologist stood in the center of the double doors. He held up a jar. The grotesque life bobbed up and down in the brown solution. I almost ran up to the man. I was stopped immediately by his goons. I felt a rage against this man but held my tongue. I stared coldly at the man.

"You have no right to be in my house. Or to go down to my laboratory without my permission," I said feeling the veins in my head pulsating.

"Amazing doctor," Skyosky said as he was looking into the jar," he then looked at me then added, "so, doctor what do you call this one?"

"Quit with the bullshit. Just tell me what it is you want? I told you we did not find anything out there. Do you believe that we would still be looking if we had found something. Look at Jacob we were out there looking but still came up empty handed."

He handed me the jar then said, "We will be in touch doctor Mongroll."

Again I played it out I then kept my mouth shut. He studied my face for a hint, a twitch, of never indicating, I was lying. He pursed his lips then spoke.

"Yes, I guess if you had what I wanted those lab specimens would still be alive."

He waved his hand his hench men followed him to the vehicles and they drove off.

"Jacob go home get some clothes for about three days tops. We need to get the creature. If I am right that I know the doctor send a team out. He will try and find it. He and his goons will not find the creature before us. We know where it lives now. We have to move quick."

CHAPTER 36

Pete's mind remained in another world. He just stared at the pictures taped to the glass partition to his cubical. It was as if he hoped they would talk to him. As if they would tell him what the missing piece to the puzzle was. After several minutes of staring, he reached out brought in two of the pictures down then placed them down on his desk.

"I don't get this Johnny? Look at these photographs. Tell me what you see?"

He studied them then sat down. Pete walked up to the file cabinet pulled out a few more pictures then placed all the pictures together on the desk. One of the detectives on his way out of the building yelled out as he walked by.

"Trying to catch that big pussy doing the killing detective?"

Pete's anger rose but he stopped himself from telling the man to screw off. He did not know the man. He was new to the department. For now he needed to keep focus. It was bad enough to try to stay focus in a mad house as it was. Johnny looked at Pete. By the look on Johnny's face Pete knew he was not going to let that go. He yells out.

"Fuck you Herny."

The young and the quick Pete thought to himself. The phone rang. Pete listens the best he could. The people inside the building spoke out loud to each other. The room was a large white room from top to bottom, corner to corner. The furniture in the cubicles were a dull drab green as well as the partitions. Except for the top part that was thick glass. Pete brought his attention back to the pictures.

"What did you see in them Johnny?"

"The only thing I saw was that all the people were dead, slaughtered, stone cold dead."

"Funny Johnny."

"I noticed that all the people were getting devoured more as the attacks progress."

"Yes, so now it should be full grown and a hungry son of a bitch."

"I think I know what you are fetching for but that is far-fetched," Johnny says.

"Is it Johnny?"

"It is absurd you saying it might be a creature."

"No! I am saying just that John."

"I need you to make a believer out of me." Johnny interjected.

"Whatever stripped the flesh off these victims tore it off. But in the process, it was still able to keep the carcass intact. Most of the animals like cougars, bears, wolves, would have torn off the limbs snapping the bones right off."

Pete stood grabbed his coat. He put on his coat. Another, officers walked into the office.

"Another body found in the alley detective just a few blocks away from the precinct by Lauderman's Park."

"Thanks," he said to the man then turned faced Johnny, "Lead the way Johnny."

CHAPTER 37

He knew some of Portland but had not lived here long enough to know all of the city. It was by the River Walk. Pete and Johnny made their way through the crowd of people, cops, I.C.S., and other personal. The place seemed as if a hundred ants had swarmed around a piece of candy. Candy that had been left for the taking. But these where not ants they were human's just attending to business.

In this case the candy was a dead human. Another clue to the puzzle. A part of the on going death that could not be explained as of yet. Forensic dusted the area. Everything, from the dumpster, corpse, and the buildings walls. Cops moved about searching with lights under debris. Johnny walked up to the dead body. His heart dropped. It was his good friend Kwok. Cho smoked away at a cigarette like a freight train. Johnny looked down at Kwok. Kwok was not looking very well or living in the land of the alive Johnny thought to himself. He could see that Cho was in deep sadness. It was reasonable they had been friends from the six grade. Johnny opened up a small note pad. He flipped several pages over and began to write down the date and time.

"Cho," Johnny says but before he could ask his question he was cut off.

"He was fine when I left him Johnny."

"I know it was not you Cho. Can you tell me anything more than he is dead and in a dumpster? Anything that lead up to his death."

"It was three days ago Johnny. The same day you came to the club to meet Beverly. I was outside here talking to Kwok and it was my shift to cook. He was getting ready to go home. I came outside to smoke while he threw away the trash before he punched out. I still had several minutes before I took over. We conversed for a moment then I said I was going back inside. He put down the trash can, pulled out a smoke. They called my name I took the cue and went inside. It was the last time I saw him."

"Cho I am going to do all that I can to catch this sick fuck. But I need you to say if you are asked that if I know you to say no. If you say yes it will be a conflict of interest and I will be pulled off the case."

"I understand Johnny."

Pete walked up to the corpse. Johnny turned closed the note pad and walk up to Pete.

"How long has this man been hanging around here?" Pete quipped.

"Sick Pete," the M.E. says as she walks up.

The E.M.T., pushed the gurney up next to the dumpster.

"Tell me when you are done Jenny."

"Oh, the answer to your quip there Pete is by the stink I will have to say three of four days tops at least."

"The whole city is in a frantic frenzy. These days everything, they see is a damn stalker. I hate when that happens. Do you know what it does to the telephone lines not to mention the false reports?"

"So, Jenny I gather you are having an exceptional day."

"That is right on the money Pete."

Pete got closer to the corpse then took a pen out of his breast pocket. He took the tail end of the pin and poked it into the man's eyes.

"Look mom no eyes."

Jenny smirked at Pete's humor as she faced the body.

"Blondie how about a cup of coffee."

 "First off Pete I would like you to call me by my name."

"Okay, your wish is my command but only if you agree to take me out."

"A real Texas gentleman I see," she says then gives a slight smile.

"My girl this is 2011. 1984 chilvary died and is gone. It is and equality era."

Pete waited for a reply. He knew she like him she knew Pete like her as well. She looks at him for a second knowing that it would not be long before he called her Blondie again. It was his nickname for her now. And Texans do love to give people nicknames she thought to herself. And it did not help matter hearing Johnny call her Blondie. She asked Johnny why he called her that.

He had said that she reminded him of the character in the comic. What an honor ran through her head. For some unknown reason she did not mind when Pete called her that. Oh, shit she was falling for the guy.

"Anything?" Pete asked knowing the answer to his question.

"With what we are dealing with so far, I have to say that it is an animal, and not human. It still points to the cougars Pete. Probably the same cat that killed the cow in Medford."

Jenny walked around the corpse as she took off the plastic latex gloves. Pete grabbed her arm. She stopped and looked at him.

"You think it could have traveled that far its habitat Jen."

"Pete their habitat is where they can find food and as far as distance goes they can make tracks especially if they are hungry."

She turned around and caught a flash from the photographer's camera. She told the man to take pictures of the corpse before the body had to be placed onto the gurney. He took several more pictures then took several of the dumpster then the wall of the building. He turned around the closed the lid to the camera and left. I.D.S., had done their job the only thing left to do was to transport the body to the morgue and to barricade the place off. Jenny put the name tag on the victim's right toe. At least they had a name she thought to herself. Two men transported the body to the ambulance.

"Okay, Johnny sense you have been waiting so patiently tell me what you have."

"Cho the man over their said he talked to the dead man about three days ago. He said it was his shift to be the cook. Cho was about to begin his shift. He said that Kwok decided to stay outside to take another smoke and throw the trash.

"I guess smoking kills," Jenny says joking. "Should we put Cho down for a suspect."

"Everyone is a suspect Pete. But he said that they had been good friends since grade school."

"Friends do friend in Johnny," Jenny says as she takes off her gloves.

"I guess he is a suspect until we can find the real corporate," Johnny agrees.

"Pete this man must have been the second person murdered."

"Why do say that Jen?"

"The paw prints are small like the ones found next to the first victim Betty."

"I hope it does not become another scare panic like the one in California. Maybe where are searching up the wrong tree as they say."

"Perhaps Pete. I said it was possible that it could be a large cat but there was never any fur hairs to be found on the victims. We did find fish excretion but I personally do not think a fish is the perp."

"Cat could have eaten a fish before killing the victim."

"I would agree with you Jenny but. When a cougar, lion, wolf, etc., kills it takes its kill.

It drags the body off to a safe place. One more thing whatever it is that kill this man was quick. There should have been more blood."

"It was hungry," Johnny says.

"All I can say for now is that I am baffled.

There should be more blood splatters no matter how fast it ate.

"Jenny I believe in is of an unknow origin."

"Monsters, spiders, and snakes Pete. What they follow you," she tells him jokingly.

Pete smiled and remained silent then said, "it is a curse my dear lady."

Pete looked down the alley he knew then that it was another nightmare. He knew it was not human or cat. There was no way this thing was a killing machine.

CHAPTER 38

Jacob grabbed a couple of shirts from the dresser and other garments enough for the three days. He packed his suitcase shut then walked out of his room. He knocked on his brother's door.

"Come in," Angle said.

Jacob open the door entered the room. Angle quickly noticed the suitcase in his hand. He sat straight up in bed.

"What is up Jacob?"

"I need you to take care of things around here for a couple of days. Look after mom, and pops."

"What is wrong?"

"I will be busy I just need you to take care of them while I am gone."

"I can do a couple of days Jacob," Angle replies back.

"Good. And there is one more thing before I leave. There is a visa card and a check book in my dresser. There is enough money in these accounts just in case I get hurt or worse. Do not ask me any questions Angle. Just do as I say."

Angle hugged him. Jacob smiled then turned around then went into the living room where his parents sat looking at the T.V. He walked up kissed his mother gently on the forehead. He then hugged his dad and said goodbye. It was as if he knew his death was preordained.

"Where are you going Jacob," his father asked.

"We have a lot of work dad so I am staying at Jeff's for a couple of days. We need to catch up on or work."

"To much work makes Jack a dull boy."

"I know dad," Jacob says then ads, "I am going now."

"You know Jacob I like to talk a while. We do not do that enough anymore."

"When I get back dad. We will talk up a storm."

"You know if you do not want to talk to us old folk then get a girlfriend."

"No, time dad."

"Leave Jacob alone Lou there is plenty of time for a grandkid."

"You always on the boy's side Mia."

His dad lean back in his recliner and became quite. Mia nodded her head giving Jacob the cue to make the escape.

"Love you mom," Jacob whispered then left quickly.

Four a.m., the next morning the vehicle was loaded and ready to go. Mary, Jacob and I arrived at the Salvie Island. Thirty minutes later we climbed out of the van. We prepared the equipment. We then went off to search for the creature. We combed the area with a fine-tooth comb as they say. We moved along the landscape as if hunting for a needle in a haystack literally. We searched every imaginable place.

We set up special traps with nets in hope of catching the creature. We waited like rats waiting for the human to leave before springing into action. The traps had trip wire and when it tripped the wire we would snare it in the nets. I had a tranquilizer gun in hand at the ready. Night came upon us without a sign. It crept up slow and easily undetected. The witching hour approached my thoughts where what could go wrong now. The trip wire alarm echoed out. Our adrenaline shot through are veins like a jolt of electricity. We hurried towards the trap. We shone our light at the net. It had been a false alarm. It had been a small rabbit that got caught up squealing frantically with fear. I grabbed the rabbit went back to the camp site. I looked at my colleagues with the rabbit in my hand.

"Breakfast will be done in about thirty minutes," I tell them.

I cut a long branch from one of the trees sharpened a point at one of the ends. I skinned and gutted the rabbit. I then shoved the branch form one end to the other. I placed it above the fire for slow cooking. As we began to whine down from the excitement, I saw something big jump into the river. The object jumped several time above the water. Its large frame protruded above the water like a huge log. It then began to swim forward toward us to the embankment.

"Look," I said out loud for my colleagues to come and see.

It reached the shoreline it began to climb on to dry land. We look on in disbelief. The hunted was now the hunter, and it was coming for us we thought. It continues to get closer. It stood about two yards away from us. It studied us then the fire. It was like seeing an infant intruded with the humans and the glow of the fire. It appeared this one was not as smart as Adam.

"Jacob distracts it," I said then grabbed the tranquilizer gun.

I placed the dart into the chamber aimed. Jacob began to talk to it as one would to a baby. Short from the cooing. I squeezed the trigger out went the dart flying. The dart hit it in the back at the base of the skull. I loaded up again and fire another shot hitting just a fraction of an inch below the first dart. At first it stared coldly at us. I thought the dosage had not been enough for its bulk. But suddenly it wobbled like a drunken man. It torso seemed to make a circle from the hips. Its head made the same circle then it fell hard with its mouth open wide to the ground. I ran to the back of the van grabbed the camera and its carrying case. I returned back took several pictures for proof. Mary was in awe looking down at the creature's mouth. I focused the camera. Mary squatted down and pushed its lips back. She looked at the camera.

"Look mom no teeth," she quipped.

Jacob laughed for a brief moment with relief. Jeff handed the camera to Mary. He kneeled on one knee put his hand on its head. Mary took the picture. Jacob took another picture with him laying down next to it. It was for one to see the bulk and size of the creature. He stood then continued to stared at the alien life form.

"I bet that thing weighs at least a ton."

"I am saying more like five hundred pounds Jacob," Jeff says.

"Yep, like five hundred pounds and more," Mary interjects.

To be honest I do not know how in the world we managed to pick it up between us. Maybe it had been pure determination. Or maybe it had been desperation. I wonder just the same. We returned to the laboratory with our new find. We placed it in Adam's fish tank. We filled it with clean water. It at first did as Adam had done when we had placed him in the first fish tank. It just laid there motionless. We fed it raw flesh, but it just remained motionless. We then fed it worms, fish food, food that we thought a huge frog would eat. It ate the food but for some unapparent reason it died. Maybe its size was too much for confinement. It had lost its freedom the wide void of the Willamette

River. I dreaded the fact that it was dead. But perhaps I could still use it to lure Adam in to kill it. I wish I could turn back the hands of time. I emptied the water from the tank then filled it with formaldehyde. The huge bulk of the creature moved up and down in suspended animation in the liquid. Inside I knew Adam would come for it they were siblings. Adam had felt the demise of its sibling. It was like twins that can feel the others hurt. Adam would kill this I knew. I knew it would come to kill anyone that got in its way. And we would be prepared for it. We ready all the material on Adams make up. Now it was time to study its sibling to find a weak point there had to be one. It had been three days and time was running out. In the laboratory I looked at it floating in the formaldehyde. I went to the far wall took a crowbar off the hook that held it. I returned to the container my colleague's studying my actions.

"It is time we must do the autopsy today."

I struck at the glass three times before it broke shattering the glass sending the liquid onto the floor. The creature's body just slid along the floor then stopped as the water left. I then ask Jacob and Mary to give me a hand in placing the body onto the metal table. We then cleaned the broken glass and formaldehyde off the floor. We were now ready to begin. Mary stood next to me Jacob across from me across the table from us. I took the surgical knife in to my hand. I cut from the throat down to the pelvic area. A hot steam a mist of gas hissed out of the cavity as the flesh spread open. The creature looked up at us with a lifeless stare. Its body was still slightly warm. What I saw next was astonishing. Inside were parts that of a human but how. Had it come in contact with a human? Now its skeletal frame made some alterations. The bones where thicker stronger and branched off covering protecting the vital organs. I studied it up and down. I noticed that there was a way to kill it. I just hope by a slight chance Adams was identical. At an angle at the temple plate. I looked at my watch it was nine p.m. I remembered the time for that is when I heard the scraping sound along the hard asphalt road behind the laboratory. It was at the back entrance an entrance that was not used often. It took hold of the metal door tore it off its hinges. It had been as easy as if it had been cardboard. Mary screamed at the top of her lungs but it did not want to kill her. It just wanted what was his. And that was its sibling. It snarled its lips turning up to let us know that we should give it room and not move.

It walked up to its sibling then placed the dead creatures hand on to its forehead. It lifted the hand and released it. The lifeless arm slapped the top of its head. He repeated this several times then it looked at us. I could see the hate. The arm fell limply to the table. Half of its arm hanging over the table. Adam tilted its head back and let out a horrible screaming noise. It then took it by its hand turned and dragged the corpse off the table. The body hit the floor with a wet thud. Adam did not look back. We did not try to stop it. We knew if we had or had attempted to stop it. It would have killed us without mercy. We watched as it moved away out of sight through the tall fir trees.

CHAPTER 39

Pete shuffled through the pictures that he had received from forensics the following day. Maybe he would find something to use though he did not think he would. He scrutinized every inch of the pictures. All he could see were half eaten corpse. Cause of death creature. What in God's name was it? Pete had a good ideal but he would wait until Jen had an ideal of what it could be.

"Here you go boss," Johnny says then hands him a hot cup of coffee.

"Thanks Mr. Juanito."

"Fuck, don't get mushy on me Pete."

"It is your name in your native language."

"I know mom called me that when she was mad. But as for native language. I am from Portland Pete."

Pete placed the cup of coffee to his right on the desk. He looked at the pictures once again.

"Johnny I think we are going to be surprised. And this dead man? I know there is something different."

"Look Pete what is there to figure out the old man is stone cold dead."

"Cute Johnny that is really helpful."

Johnny pulled up a chair grabbed one of the pictures. He sat down studied it for a moment. He looked up at his partner.

"What you want to say is that this is going to be real bad. I know you have been contemplating that it is something of the unknown. You can see it in your face Pete."

"Tape it to the wall with the others Johnny."

Johnny stood goes to the glass part of the partition taped the picture to it with the others.

"It is bothering you that bad?"

"I just have a problem with all the flesh that has been eaten and the discard. What animal does that Johnny?"

"Maybe the son of a bitch is just real hungry Pete. Or maybe just plain mean."

"Could be," Pete says then stand up and says, "I am going to go get a drink or two is what I am thinking."

"Want me to tag along."

"No, I have a date let's say I don't want you cock blocking me."

Johnny laughed then said, "Do I know the lady?"

"Yes, but do not ask who it is."

"Well, I better go it's beginning to get dark outside. I will see you in the morning Johnny."

"Okay, boss."

Pete left for his date the date with Jenny went well. It had been a while since he had a date with a women after his wife's death and Nancy. Nancy could not take remembering the demon Two Souls.

The fact that it was him that the monster wanted. He was the Eagle Warrior protector of the ancient one. It felt good and he enjoyed the company of a woman. He enjoyed Jenny's company and her his.

They had hit it off they had wound up at his apartment. Morning it had come to fast for Pete. He looked up at the ceiling looked at Jenny laying next to him. He smiled he felt a sense of feeling content. He wondered if she would turn and run like Nancy after this investigation. All Pete knew was he like her from the moment he had lay eyes on her. Soul mate he thought. Only time would tell his mind raced pleased. He turned kissed her softly on the cheek. He rolled out of bed then got dressed. He returned to the side of the bed bent down kissed her on the lips. OH, she moaned softly then wrapped her hands around his neck returning his kiss. Pete wondered how she could do that without opening her eyes. Had to be a woman thing he thinks to himself and smiles. It was too good to be true he felt.

"No, time for the good stuff today honey. Besides I need to save my strength."

Jenny threw the sheets to one side then called out.

"Pete breakfast of champions."

"You know you have to be somewhere as well."

"The cadavers can wait a few minutes, but I can't."

"You are awesome," Pete says as he unbuttons his shirt.

He climbed back into bed. She threw her hands around him and kiss him. Twenty minutes later Pete stood before the mirror. He put his tie and clothes back on. The doorbell rang.

"You expecting someone Pete?"

"No, not really. Get up get dress and after I see who it is I will start up some coffee for you."

"I'll go and answer the door Pete." "No, I'll do it."

"What you don't want anyone to get a look Pete."

"Funny Jen but I will take care of it," Pete said and walked out the room.

Pete walked into the kitchen opened one of the cabinets. He grab a bag of instant coffee. He went to the door opened it. Johnny stood there leaning against the side of the door with a toothpick in his mouth. He was whistling.

"Up in the morning and off to school." Johnny kept his eyes on Pete then spoke.

"Hum, your date seems to do wonders for you disposition"

"No, I am not telling you who she is Johnny. So blow it out of your ass."

"Ah, that is the Pete I know he's back."

"Tell me what was so important you could not wait for me to get to the office?"

"Oh, I knew I came up for a reason." "So."

"Another body at the Sandy River right where it runs back into the Columbia River. Close to where the previous body was found. Body was next to the water."

"We need to change are mind set. I do not believe a cougar is the corporate. It might be a hungry animal, but it would be hunting up in the woods for game. Feline family or not. It hunts prey on land. Now a bear it hunts for its favorite food in water. But it is the Salmon, Coho, Jack, and it tries to stay away from humans."

"Pete it could be anything right about now.

Hell, I would say it is Jaws. But fish do not climb out of the water," Johnny says.

"Johnny hold up a minute I will be right back."

Pete returned to his bedroom and was about to tell Jenny about the crime scene. He opened his mouth to speak. Jen put out her hand to quite him. She talked to the person on the other end then hung up the cell phone. She told him she had just finished talking to the chief and that she would be right behind him. And that she would meet him at the scene. Johnny waited patiently in the car. Pete climbed in Johnny put the car in reverse and pulled out.

"Was she worth it Pete," Johnny says.

"Who? Pete said acting dumb.

"Your date. You do not have to tell me who. I am just asking."

"You are right it is none of your business."

"Come on what is her name?"

"I will tell you when it is time Johnny."

"I know it is one of them secret connections. It's not a hooker you fallen in love with is it."

They reached their destination. They climbed out of the car walked up to the scene of the crime next to the eaten corpse. The body lay about five yards away from the river. Forensics was on the search mode dusting and searching for the missing clue.

"Jesus all mighty," Johnny exclaimed.

The photographer took overlapping pictures. It was a procedure they did to protect evidence. A few minutes later Jenny arrived. She got out of the medical examiners van. She walked up to them, and the M.E.T. Pete faced her as she approached them.

"Blondie," Pete greeted then paused. "I mean Jenny."

"Same as the others." "I am afraid so."

Jenny looks down at the corpse then says, " looks like it is getting a lot hungrier Pete."

"No, I believe it has grown its full size. It now has to consume more protein," Gary says as he stands up.

Gary grabbed something from a black suitcase then walked back knelt down next to the corpse. He lay his hand on the corpse hip bone.

"Pete you know they have a search party in progress for another cougar spotted back up in Damascus?" Jenny asked.

"So, they will be hunting for a needle in a haystack?" Johnny quips.

"I believe that sums it up. I know the slaughtering death are more frequent now. People are beginning to panic," Jenny says.

"Johnny, see if you can find a trail leading to the road."

"Pete you and I both know it will lead to the river somehow."

"Pete lets me and you take a walk. I have something to tell you," Jenny says suspiciously.

"Don't tell me your pregnant already we just slept together last night."

"Real funny real funny Pete."

Pete laughed then said, "What is the secrecy all about Jenny?"

They walked up a little farther away from ear reach next to the riverbank.

"Pete," she says then looks out at the river then continues, "the horrendous acts of murder seem to have escalated and our perp Pete has four finger large ones at that. When we were first called out on the first murder I figured it was a rabid dog or cat. Now the man in the alley perhaps he was caught off guard. And the others signifies that the creature might have been growing. But these wounds on this dead body are centered in the stomach area and back. It brought this man down hard. Cougar or demon it does not matter it does not tear the flesh away like a cat. It eats away at the flesh. I have to say like a machine. Oh, but do not get me wrong Pete it is without a doubt a predator."

The trail lead to the river just as Johnny thought. He caught a glimpse of something shinning, twinkling, on occasion as the sun rays hit it. He knelt down on one knee. He ran his hand along the center of the glob of liquid.

"Sick, fucking vomit," he says to himself then ran the slime between his fingers.

Gary approached his side, "It seems that way Johnny but whatever is leaving this behind is made by it."

"Tell me you are not trying to say it is something else besides cat or human."

"Maybe the fish had a cat for dinner." "Now what does that supposed to mean Gary?" "Nothing Johnny nothing."

"By you being here I guess the trail lead back here to the river," Pete says.

"It did boss it runs into the water. Pete follow me," he says and begins to walk along the bank of the river.

Pete's eyes quickly spots another footprint.

He stopped waited for a moment until the water rolled back away from the bank. That made two prints one on land and the other returning to the water. Whatever it is came out of the water just as he had figured Pete mind raced. But why? And what could walk out of water like man then return to the water like an amphibian. There was no such creature except for an alligator or crock.

"Good eye Johnny," Pete says then faces Jenny," you seeing this Jen?"

Jenny sees the print just seconds before the water rolls in covering up the print. Gary had left for a moment. Jenny looked for him then noticed he was carrying a bucket of water and a bag of plaster. As he rushed to them he yelled out for them to build a dam around the print so he could get a print.

"How and with what?" Johnny asked.

"Use the mud build it about four inches high around the footprint that will be enough."

Pete and Johnny wasted no time they knelt down and they began to build the dam. Jenny went to help Gary with the equipment. Gary walked up to the river edge filled the small bucket he carried with water. He then knelt down next to the dam area Pete and Johnny had constructed. He poured the white substance from the bag into the bucket stirred it into a glob substance. He then poured it into the cavity of the footprint left behind. They waited for the plaster to set. Gary then reach down carefully withdrew the footprint from the cast mold.

"Presto change-o," he exclaimed.

He walked back to the equipment and the crew. He retrieved a plastic bag a pen from his brief case on the ground. He tagged it gave it a number. He felt everyone's eyes on him. Gary knew they need to hear something new on the investigation. I guess it was closure they wanted. Pete finally spoke.

"What do we have Gary?"

"I will say in a guess that out of an equivalent of one hundred. I will be ninety-nine-point five percent right."

Genius why do they always have to go all the way around things? Why can't they just get to the point in laymen terms Pete thought to himself.

"By looking at the print saying that it is the front paw and not the hind leg."

"Get to the point," Johnny interjected.

"That is exactly what I am telling you detective. But sense you have your panties up in a bunch. I do not think that this print belongs to any of the feline groups. I believe that this creature is not in any of our book or know to man."

"That is fucking absurd," Johnny bellowed out then ads, "maybe it is an alien."

"Skepticism killed the cat detective," Gary says then handed Johnny the print.

Johnny stared down at the footprint in his hand.

"Now take a good look at it then tell me what you see detective?"

"Okay it has mighty big claws for a cat." "Good, now tell me what else catches your eye."

"Looks like webbing between the digits and scales at the bottom of its foot. Like that on a fishes underbelly perhaps. Or that of an alligator," Johnny says uncertain at what Gary was getting at.

"Perhaps Johnny they do have reports of one being loose somewhere out here, "Jenny says then looks at Pete and ads, "did I mention that this kid is a genius."

Jenny noticed that Pete's mind was in another world racing as he was putting the puzzle together in his head.

"Water again," he said then added, "water is the element the main factor to all of these murders."

Gary really did not know Pete but he had a good inclination that Pete had a good picture in his head of what they were dealing with. He knew of the story of the Eagle Warrior. Of the man that had dealt with the unhuman of a being of the underworld.

"Pete I and Gary will do a rush job on this. We needed solid evidence. It couldn't be better than this," Jenny tells him.

"Shit, shit. There must be a million bugs out here. And they are trying to feast on my flesh," Gary quips half joking as he swats at a mosquito then says, "how is it that these bugs know when death is around. Detective before you walk away you are right about one thing. It may just be from the water. It is like nothing we have encountered before. I can tell you that it is at least seven feet tall by the footprint," Gary ads.

"Now we know how tall it is and that it does walks up right on its hind legs as well Pete," Jenny mentions then ads, "we have the right foot Pete. And it is a good one. Let's see if we can find the other print in the water. It should rest on the ground about a foot and a half away from this one by its stride."

It took them about twenty minutes to find the left footprint. Studying the objects Pete spoke.

"We will go back to the tooth found, the claw, and claw marks, the prints, the jumping off the bridge. We know as well that it is an amphibious creature now and that it has the ability to kill. A fish man."

"What?" Johnny snapped and look at Pete. "Questionable huh Johnny?" Pete says then says,

"I believe that it is half man half fish. What do you think Jenny?"

"I am believing the same Pete." "Gary what do you say,"

"I am right with you detective. I believe fishman as well. I know you have thought this for a while Pete."

"Yes I have been heading in that direction.

But there is still that one thing we need and that is to see it with our own eyes," Pete says. Pete could see in their eyes the concern. Yes this thing this fishman was real. Death would continue on until it was captured or killed. Later that afternoon Jenny walked into Pete's cubical.

She looked at Johnny then at Pete. "Ready for it?" Jenny asked.

"Let me have it. Do not leave anything out.

Give me both barrels," Pete replies.

"Okay here it goes. It is possible that its origin is from another world."

"What?" Johnny questioned.

"Not from mother earth. Oh it gets better. We were right. It is part fish, part man, part rat, and alien of an unknow origin."

"Absurd," Johnny says.

"Still not a believer. But the facts Johnny say that what I have said is true. I wanted to be wrong. You do not know how many test, I ran just to make sure. Gary is on cloud nine right now. It is a dream come true a find of a century."

"Come on Johnny we have known that it was an unknown species to our world," Pete tell him.

Pete thoughts run wild. Perhaps it is a Chupas Chabras he thinks to himself. He kept from saying it out loud.

"I have a gut feeling it is going to get worse before we catch this thing," Pete says and taps his pen on the desk top several times then ads, "I am going to let you brains figure it all out."

Jenny looks at Pete smile then walks out of the cubical. Pete watched here well developed ass as she saunter out and down the corridor. There has to be a law to outlaw dresses to women with big butts. Jenny turns back around and smiles again at Pete. Johnny face remained blank just staring into space. Pete was glad that Johnny did not catch the obvious between him and Jenny.

"Well what's your mind saying?"

"It is telling me that I hope we do not wind up being fucking fish food." Johnny quipped.

Pete chuckled at the remark then grabbed his coat and put his Springfield into its holster.

"Let's get a cup of coffee Johnny.'

"Hey Pete why don't you leave you weapon in its holster. Wouldn't that be, easier."

"I like to have it where I can see it. And it is my good luck piece."

"I have to say that is weird."

"Let's get that cup of coffee," Pete says and they walk out of the cubical.

CHAPTER 40

Fog ascended up like tiny gray plume fingers from the Columbian River. Jimmy and his grandfather climbed out of the truck early that morning at the river. A morning that would be imprinted into their minds locked away like a burning page a vestige in time. Jimmy's grandfather walked slowly as if he needed oil in the hinges of his knees. He unhooked the boat let it slide back a few inches into the water then tied the end of the rope to the boat dock.

"Jimmy," he called out then said, "quit dragging your feet. Climb into the boat start it up while I go back and park the truck and trailer. "Okay, Gramps will do."

Jimmy started the ninety-horse powered engine up for the Whaler. Jimmy then waited and watched his grandfather untie the rope to the ramp then climbed in.

"Well boy what you waiting for take us out into the deep."

Jimmy was excited he moved the lever down slowly edging the boat out hitting the ramp kind of hard. It was a good thing that his grandfather rigged up the boat with bumpers just for that one reason to keep the boat safe.

"Careful boy," his grandfather tells him.

"I have it gramps," Jimmy replied then moved out far enough to begin to turn the boat around in the direction that they needed to head off in, "steady as she goes," he exclaimed.

"Captain to the fishing hole." "Okay, gramps."

It had not taken them long it had taken about twenty minutes to reach his grandfather's favorite fishing hole. His grandpa felt the boat slow as Jimmy moved the lever back. They stopped Jimmy threw the anchor overboard and waited for it to hit bottom. He let several yards of rope to be taken then tied it to the rig hook. He then retrieved a fishing pole. He rigged it up for the sturgeons. He was now ready for his cast.

"Throw it up there right where the water is circling in the eddy."

"Okay, grandpa," he replied then cast out his line.

"Good cast Jimmy." "Taught by the best."

"Why yes you were," his grandfather replies," then cast his line out a few feet apart in almost the same place as Jimmy's.

"Grandpa did you see that it was huge."

"Better get some muscles on them bones Jim if you wish to reel that sucker in."

"Funny grandpa I have plenty of muscles see," he tells his grandfather as he shows him his bicep.

"I guess I was wrong boy. Them is some big guns."

"I know grandpa," Jimmy replies back proudly.

They sat quietly for a while then suddenly Jimmy's pole line began to make his pole tip twitch. They both stood up excited as Jimmy reached for his pole.

"Okay Jim real it in a bit at a time. Keep tension on the line the way I taught you. Make sure that the drag is set.

"It is Grampa."

"Set the hook in then repeat to set the hook in firmly in its lip."

The tug came and Jimmy was ready he pulled back on the pole setting in the hook.

"Okay, gramps time me."

His grandfather looked at his watch. On occasions he looked up to see his grandson. It was a gift he thought to watch his grandson having so much fun. After eighteen minutes with what was on the other end the line became slack. The Oldman could see the look of disappointment on Jimmy's face.

"It is okay boy they do that sometimes it is still there just have to throw in the line again. You'll get the fish."

Jimmy reeled in the fishing line then cast out again. It had only taken a few minutes and the fight was on again. It had taken him ten minutes to bring up the fish. Jimmy brought the fish up along the edge of the boat. His grandfather quickly grabbed the gaff from the floor of the boat. The sturgeon popped its head out of the water. Suddenly seeing the sturgeon both of them did not know what to think. They were both bewilder as they stared at a fish with the bottom half gone. Abruptly as if they had hit something the boat jarred. It was hit from underneath causing the boat to sway violently. Jimmy and his grandfather lost their footing falling. They caught themselves on the edge of the boat. Another hit.

They fell on to their knees.

"Grandpa," Jimmy called out in concern and fear.

His grandpa stood up again the boat was hit from underneath.

This time the old man missed the edge of the boat and fell overboard into the cold water. Suddenly in a matter of seconds from falling in he felt something grab him. He knew immediate that it was something else beside a fish. He felt the sharp digits with razor sharp nail dig into his calves. In a few second longer the water turned red with his blood. Jimmy watched as the water churned as if boiling then became calm. He leaned on to the edge of the boat calling out to his grandfather desperately as the fear grew with in him.

"Grandpa, grandpa, grandpa," Jimmy called out in despair.

"Nothing! It seemed as if the world had died and gone into a complete stand still. The wind picked up slightly as it did everyday about noon time at the Columbia River. It was like a ritual between the river and Mother Nature. Jimmy continued to call out but there was no answer.

Scared along the panic begin to set in deeper. But there was no time for the panic to completely take hold. Like a torpedo the creature shot out of the water. Jimmy's eyes bugged out opening wide with disbelief at what his eyes saw. Adam's cold eyes sent the fear of death like a telegraph into Jimmy's brain. In a matter of seconds it grabbed him by the shoulder pulled him into the depth of the water. It drugs him behind deeper and deeper into the river. The water calmed. The grandfather and grandson on the boat a shadow a vestige in time vanishing leaving the boat vacant. The boat swayed back and forth desolated in the water like a boat hanging in a picture frame in a vast ocean. A ghost boat.

CHAPTER 41

It had been three days since Jimmy and his grandfather went missing. A man and his friend moved along the river in their boat.

"Josh look up there," Ben called out spotting the bodies.

"Josh, over there looks like an old man against the riverbank."

They maneuvered the boat in that directions. As they got a bit closer they both noticed that from the hips down there was nothing but bone.

"Do not drop the anchor, Ben. We need to go to the authorities and report this immediately. They will take care of it."

Josh turned the boat heading up stream then pushed the lever down. The tip of the boat lifted as they sped away. Two hours later Pete, Johnny, and several officers on the police boat made their way to the bank of the river. The Columbia was treacherous on its own but certain areas of the river just dropped off a foot away from the bank and this was one of them.

"We will have to get a flat boat out here. It will need to hold forensic and the M.E., as they do their work."

"What about us Pete?"

"Johnny we will have to wait until Jen gets the bodies to the morgue."

It was not a normal thing to do but this was not a normal case. Pete knew what killed then as did Johnny but procedures where protocol.

CHAPTER 42

Mary looked around the laboratory then pushed down on one of the buttons on the computers keyboard. She stood up lean back stretched her back. She then went to the stair she began to climb up out of the lab. She walked up to the front double doors knowing the newspaper boy should have already delivered the paper. She opened the door reached down for the newspaper. It laid just a few inches to the right. The thought of how the paperboy's accuracy in delivering the paper to the same spot was amazing. She rolled the rubber band that secured the paper from unrolling back and to the end. She wrapped the rubber band around her wrist. She opened the newspaper. What looked back at her from the front page in big black letters hit her brain hard. Her mind froze numbness flushed through her like a tidal wave. She quickly closed the doors.

"Jeff," she called out twice in a loud tone. "Yes," he shouted back.

"You need to come and see what is in the newspaper."

"Be right there."

Jeff made his way into the kitchen where Mary was. She was just staring at the headlines reading it over and over to herself. Mary placed a cup of coffee on the table for Jeff then sat down with a cup of coffee for herself. Jeff sat down then Mary handed him the paper. He took a sip of coffee as he read the headline. It jumped out at him instantly. Jeff coughed caught in his throat making him gag.

"Grandfather and Grandson found on the Columbia River half eaten."

He was to make a human superior than any other. He dealt with the taking of lives to experiment but to have a child murdered. It pained his soul.

Mary wiped away her tears. The phone rang Mary reached for the wall phone.

"Hello."

"Mary did you see the paper?" "Jacob he just saw it."

"I will be right over. I am just a few minutes away from you."

"Where are you? There is a lot of noise."

"I stopped at the seven eleven. I could not call from home. I got a cup of java. I will be there in ten."

Mary hung up the phone. Jeff tossed the paper down spilling his coffee. Mary was about to get some paper towels to clean up the mess.

"No miss Mary I will take care of it you two go do what you have to," Silva says and begins to clean up the spill.

Jacob arrived the doorbell rang. Silva opened the door before Jacob could say something she pointed to the laboratory. Entering the lab he could see them debating on something. It was probably a theory on how to kill Adam. Seeing Jacob as he put on his lab apron Jeff said.

"Ah good we are all here. So now we figure out what we are going to do next."

"Let's include that it is full grown. We know it lives in the Willamette. But why did it venture to the Columbia to kill?" Jeff ask out loud to his colleges.

"It lives in the Willamette Jacob home is where you lay your head," Mary interjects.

"Get the equipment ready Jacob. Mary run more data on how to kill Adam," Jeff says and stands up from the stood he was sitting on.

"Do I grab the air tanks?"

"Everything just in case," Jeff says then begins to help Jacob with the equipment.

Night came quick. We took the large battery powered flashlights with us. It was darker this night than the others. We searched for Adam. The orbs of our lights moved along the body of water near and far like fireflies. As it is ordained by the higher power Adam stands popping its head out of the water. Its torso, legs, dripping water.

Mary shone her light on its face. Adam lips moved back in a scowl in its displeasure of the light in its eyes. The lips went back farther. It showed its jagged porcelain sharp teeth. Its appearance was as if it knew we would be there on this day.

Mary looked at Jacob and me. Our lights shinning on it as it began to walk forward. It stopped halfway then a deep gurgling sound resonated from within it. I felt a chill run down my spine. Mary and Jacob felt the same chill run down their arms and spine as well. There was nothing we could do. It knew why we were there. The only reason we were still alive was that I was its father by blood. It let out another sound similar to that of a dolphin. But Adam was not a dolphin it was not a friendly fish. Adam was created. It could devour a human up in a matter of seconds and still have room for Jell-o. It was strong and vicious. I had a tranquilizer gun as did Jacob. But we did not even attempt to lift them up into position. Not once did we even try, we just stood there mesmerized. It turned and in a slow gate it returned back into the river then vanished from sight. It had been the second time I had seen Adam face to face. I would keep my secret of seeing it to myself. It would be back that I was certain of. I walked to the van Mary and Jacob followed. We put the equipment in to the van. I had been right three days later. "We need to head to the Willamette River." "What about the sibling?" ask Jacob.

"We need to kill Adam."

"Why the Willamette?" Mary asked.

"Food there will be plenty tomorrow."

"Food it can get," Jeff says as he closes the double back doors to the van.

"Food. People will be wading they will be plentiful tomorrow, swimming, jumping, doing everything fish like."

Jeff ran his hand through his hair, "fuck, fuck, fuck," he says aggravated.

"I guess we camp out at the river tonight," Jeff says.

Jacob looked at him for a moment then nodded his head and followed Jeff. They arrived at the park. They pulled the gear back out laid it on the ground by the van. Mary checked the tranquilizer guns making sure they were loaded and ready. She then took out a forty-five revolver. Jeff and Jacob looked at her. The thought dirty Molly crossed their minds.

"Just in case it gets to close."

They then returned to what they were doing. Morning came around the rays of the sunrise broke through. Morning would show in a few hours. Out of all the times the weather man had been wrong by saying it was going to be a nice day and the next day it would rain as if on cue. Over the years why did he have to be right this day? The weather man announced that it would be a nice sunny day and it was. The park thrives with families, friends, and their pets. They all came ready to hit the water in their colorful swimsuits. Some suits more revealing than others. Boys and girls ran to the water with small wind surfboards under their arms laughing joyfully. As they got out to the middle of the river they lifted the small sail in the middle of the board. The sail would catch the wind and move them as if they were surfing. The noise picked up as they continued to arrive. Laughter filled the air as several of the women called out to the smaller children to not go in to deep. In the distance several teenagers called out to one another as they hurried to catch a gust of wind.

Parents mostly called out as they sat on the sandy area as their children swam in the river. Lounge chairs, coolers filled with soda, food, and towels of a variety of colors spotted the area. Three teens with water goggles and snorkels dove underwater at the same time to explore the depth of the water. The water was murky but still one was able to see a few feet in front of them with the goggles. The water splashed as another kid dove under then popped back up then slapped the water hard with his hand.

"I will be back in a bit," he told one of the boys as he move deeper into the water.

As he dove into the water, water, entered into the snorkel making him to rapidly jump out of the water. He spat water coughed as the muscles in his throat contracted. He felt as if he were going to die as he gasped for air.

"You all right Bill," Janie a blonde with blue eyes called out to him.

At first all she heard was him gasping then his throat muscle relax a bit.

"I am fine," he relied in a constricted voice then tried to play as if he had not been scared.

"You sure?"

"Yep just swallowed some water unexpectedly. I hope I do not wind up I "Monster inside me.""

"You are funny Bill," she told him then thought if she should ask if he would like to be boyfriend and girlfriend then thought not to.

"I see you in a bit I am going under."

He swam as if he were heading for deeper water then made a bee line back to the group. He swam around until he saw one of the girl's legs. He did not care who's at that moment. He got closer then reached out pinched the girl softly then swam away. As far as he could before popping back up out of the water. As he moved his hand he felt something. He stopped and did not move his mask. He continued to breath calmly through the snorkel. He dove into the water to examine what it could be thinking it was one of the other boys. He searched the water a few seconds passed then it appeared. Adam stared deep into Bill's eyes penetrating deep horror into him. Frighten he gasped for air forgetting he was in the water. Air bubbles escaped within the mask. He quickly made his way to the surface and stood up. His legs shot him up as if they had been coiled springs. Water sprayed in all directions as he tore the goggles off as gasped for air in between his screams. Frantically he shouted to warn the others of the lurking danger, but it was futile. He continued to jump up and down screaming. He felt the sharp claws of the creature rip through the flesh of his back. The hot searing agonizing pain at the base of his neck and back felt like fire. Blood pooled like ink from an octopus circling him. His mind became blank as life left his limbs. Like a cork or a bobber on a fish line the boy was yanked under water. The water churned as if boiling as the creature thrash and rolled to devoured the flesh.

"Quit playing Bill we know it is one of your paint pellets," said one of the girls as the group of kids looked on.

After a few minutes they saw that Bill did not surface. Fear begin to set in. A body surfaced it lay motionless on the surface of the water. It lay on top of the water like a crocodile suspended watching and waiting to attack. It searched for its next victim. Freddy a tan pimple face boy sensed a wave of panic surge through him. He froze in fear staring into the creature's eyes. He turned to face towards shore. He moved his legs as fast as he could. But it was like walking in slow motion with the weight of the water pushing back.

Instinct took over he began to yell for dear life. Adam stood out of the water. The water rushed off its body glistening shinning like glass sparkling as the sun rays hit its body. The girl next to the creature wasted no time she dove but Adam a true predator anticipated her move. There was no chase or freedom for the girl. Adam was up upon her in an instant it had her in its grasp. Blood filled the water as it rushed out of the flesh wounds its deadly teeth made. It sunk its piranha like teeth into her flesh over and over again. It began its deadly roll causing the water to churn. The girl managed to escape for a second she managed to get a few feet away. A huge chunk of flesh gone from her thigh. The fear penetrated in her face and eyes. The disbelief shone like an aura over her. Hearing the cries for help Mary, Jacob, and Jeff scrambled out of the van. They ran to the edge of the river. There in the water it floated on top looking at the girl. It gave her hope that she could make it to land. Then like a whip being snapped it switched its tail. It shot forward like a missile. It hit the girl's legs striking out with its claws it grasped her firmly in its clutches. Its claws sunk in two inches deep into her flesh like a backhoe.

It pulled the girl under turned and made its way into the depth of the Columbia. Underwater the girl's eyes bugged out from lack of oxygen. She knew her fate would be death at the hands of this creature. The only good was that she would not be alive to feel the pain of being eaten. Life left the girl worries of being eaten vanished as well as her fear. I Jeffrey Mongroll could do nothing but look on like a tree in the wind. I the creator of this devil of this monster. I wanted life to be of new. I wanted humans to live in harmony. But instead, I brought something into this world that could eliminate all humans from this world. The cries and moans brought Jeff's attention back to what was taking place. Again all he could do was to remain silent and just watch. This feeling of helplessness was devastating. It ate away at him like termites in his intestines. It had not taken long for the sound of the sirens in the air to reach them. This was one day that the paramedic's would not be saving anyone. I then noticed for the first time the unmarked police car. It was the first time I had the pleasure of meeting the detective and his partner. I then saw several other cop cars, the M.E. vehicle, and the M.E.T's, truck that resembled the ambulance that had arrive just minutes ago. The detective and Johnny asked the typical question. Did you see anything out of the ordinary? What was it. Or what did it look like? Was it or he alone? I could see the detective looking our way. I knew he would make his up to us soon. The people in this park were more than willing to describe what they thought they saw. Several of the mother claimed it had be an alligator. The told the detective it seemed deformed. Johnny flipped a page over on his small notepad and continued to write everything down.

"You did say alligator?" Johnny asked one of the mothers that barely was able to stand on her own legs.

Lay off the taco's, loose weight feel great Johnny's mind ran on.

"Yes!" The woman said as she tried to wrap a beach towel around her midsection.

By a bigger towel Johnny thought to himself and kept from laughing. Johnny pushed the thoughts away. He asked the other women that was standing by the lady.

"I do not know what it was detective. All I know is I have never seen the water churn like that. I am just glad my kid got away."

Jenny and Gary walked up and stood silent a few feet away from the bank as they looked around. Jenny held on to a large black medical bag that held her tools.

"Where do we start?" she asked noticing that nothing seemed out of place. Everything had taken place in the water.

"I guess you have to go swimming Jenny," Pete quipped.

"I know you are kidding Pete."

"I guess this is one scene you have no work at."

I noticed the detective looking my way. I knew he would come to speak to me and my colleagues now. Pete made his way up to Dr. Jeff Mongrol II. He stopped then looked at his colleagues. Pete asked himself why are these people doing here? What is it they are after?

"You seem pretty calm what did you see here mister," Pete says.

"My name is Jeff Mongroll II. What I saw was not much."

"You seem out of place here. What is your interest in all of this?"

"And may I ask who are you," I ask knowing he was a detective.

"I am detective Rodriquez now how about an answer to my question.

"I am a Geneticist."

"So what is so special about this river? Or is it what is in it?"

"Like I said detective I am a Geneticist and my interested is aqua life. That is why I am here for detective."

"So, what do you think could have done this terrible, act?"

"I cannot tell you until I see what did this detective."

"Hum, well if you think of anything of value you will let us know as soon as possible won't you doctor Mongroll," Pete says looking the man straight in the eyes.

"I will a.s.a.p.," I said knowing that I would not.

What was I going to tell him? I created the monster that kill the kids. I turned around then headed back to the van where Mary and Jacob waited. Pete stared at the van as it pulled away on to the road. The thought of why the Geneticist was so interested in the Willamette River. What was it? Maybe it was just by chance him and his team where there. Perhaps, perhaps that scientist was just there. No, there was something more Pete just knew it. His intestines were telling him that there was something not quite right. The suspicion that they would be involve somehow and that they would bump heads again ran though his head. Johnny walks up to Pete. He looks at him.

"Well tell me what you have Johnny?" Pete asked him not wanting to reply to any question at that moment.

"I do not have a thing. But we got another call, another body at Roster Rock. Jenny is already on her way there as well as forensic."

"Another body?" Pete scratched his head then thought for a moment.

This murdering bastard, thing, was working overtime. What are you Pete's mind raced on.

"Pete."

"Johnny you are driving so let's go take a look at this other body," Pete said and tossed him the key.

Pete was trying to figure out the puzzle of death and did not feel like driving. Besides he was getting a migraine. They turned into Roster Rock Park. Pete feared most for the people in the water. It was just a gut call but he knew that evil would have a hand in what was to come. From one great river to the other in one day. We stopped at the pay booth a small shack with a girl in her teens smiling back at them. She then greeted them. I showed her my badge. I ask where the body was. She pointed south then mentioned it was at the boat ramp. She said just take a left at the stop sign go straight and that we could not miss it. She was right there was no way we could have missed it for the road ended at the boat ramp.

We climbed out of the vehicle walked straight to the body. The body was sprawled out on the boat ramp. To Pete it reminded him of a baked potato. All the flesh from the bottom lip to the neck gone. Seeing Pete, Jenny stood walk up to him and began to tell him the details. She told him that the body the clue where the same as the other.

"Pete it left the slime behind. But the attack seemed more vicious. It tore the man up."

"Question is why had it brought the body here.

It had brought it form somewhere else. It had placed the body on the boat ramp just to eat its feel. But why? What was the reason Jenny? It is a predator and predators return to the scene of the crime Pete thought to himself.

Perhaps by chance they would get some kind of lead. "What are you thinking of Eagle, "Warrior."

"I am thinking we will camp out here tonight." Good come back Johnny thought.

"Pack it up Gary," Jenny says then begins to make her way to the van.

She stopped and waited for Gary to approach then continued to the vehicle.

CHAPTER 43

The next morning it seemed that it was the beginning of a nice calm day. The first sign of life walked across the lawn of the Portland State University professor Giles rushed with her hands full of paperwork. Papers she graded for this day's classes. She awakened early she blamed anxiety to be the corporate to her restless night. Maybe it was the moon hovering in the sky like a giant light bulb. Its unearthly rays radiating over the earth making her feel strange. Then suddenly from the corner of her eye she thought she saw something. A shadow of something but what? Shit! I am seeing things her thoughts giving her and uneasy feeling. I hope it is just the lack of sleep. She shifts all the papers on to her left arm then begins to walk faster. Hell, I could use some strong coffee she whispers to herself. The shadow shot across the lawn again just feet away from her catching her off guard. Looked as if it had a tail she thinks then ignores it and continues on her way. She picks up her pace rushing to the building. The papers in her arm worked themselves free falling to the ground scattering on the ground. The wind picked them up lifting some of the papers off the ground as it they were huge white leaves in the wind. I just might make it through this day yet she says as she bends down to pick up the students homework. She stood looked around.

"What else can go wrong?"

She closed her eyes for a brief moment. Abruptly she heard the snapping of a twig the rustling of the leaves. She looked around then the shadow appeared. It was not her imagination. It could not be for the shadow now took shape and it was running straight for her. At first glance she thought it was a young man but then she noticed something different. She noticed its arms were elongated. Its torso as well. Her eyes focused on the creature's face. Subhuman, its mouth was full of jagged teeth. Fear entered her without a warning to her brain. She dropped the paper shifted direction to the other entrance of the building. She looked back to see if it was still coming or to see how close it was to her. From the corner of her left eye she saw it charging on all fours. The grass kicking back from its hands and legs as it moved on its onslaught. Distance between it and her disappeared quickly. She looked back again she stumbled. She fell trying quickly to scramble to her feet. She clawed at the ground desperately finally she managed to get up.

"Run, run," she says to herself, "one foot in front of the other."

The stair where just three yards away. She just had to make it to the double doors and shut them behind her. She took one last glance. As she looked back it leaped off the ground. It sailed through the air. She bent down Adam shot over her head like a missile. Its claws caressing her hair softly. Adam landed on the steps rolled into the double doors. Its claws scraping franticly at the concrete then like a spring it lunged forward. One clawed hand landed on her shoulder the other on her face. She screamed out from the searing pain. She dropped to her knees her hand came up to her face. Blood quickly stained them. She looked at her hands as she did Adam attacked again tearing away at her flesh. It sunk its claws into her shoulder bringing her down. She gasp her last breath of life. It ripped her throat out then moved down to her buttocks the softer meat. Adam had grown a taste for it. It was sweeter less muscle and more human fat. Adams ears caught a sound. It heard purring it lifted its head. Blood dripped flesh dangled from its teeth. It snarled at the cougar that held its spot. It knew the creature was not man and that it could kill it. It lay down would wait patiently. Adam felt no threat it continues to eat away at the flesh. Gorging its fill of the woman Adam slowly walked down the steps then vanished. The cougar waited until it could not see the creature then slowly moved inching its way up to the redhead. It purred softly then began to eat at the woman's flesh. Jamie the custodian opened the double doors. He saw the cougar and Miss Giles dead. Seeing the cougar eating away at her flesh made his stomach lurch in. He dispelled his breakfast. He composed himself the best he could. He call 911. Moments later they had arrived. The M.E., forensics, Pete, Johnny and P.P.D. Four of the offices redirected the students showing up for classes. Pete, Johnny, and several of the offices surrounded the cougar with their guns at the ready. The cougar turned growled then stood on all fours. It was confused in which way to escape. It moved back and forth like a caged animal. Johnny saw the cougar crouch down on its front legs. Johnny aimed squeezed the trigger. Bang, bang, a flash of light from the muzzle of his gun. The bullets lodged just behind the cat's right eye. Pete's was not fast enough to see the cat leaped. All he heard was a bang, bang. He looked at Johnny.

"The animal activist group is going to get a whiff on this," Johnny says out loud.

"Things just happen sometimes Johnny. You did what you had to and it was a good thing for me."

"Is that a thanks partner, good job, that a boy."

"Do not push it Johnny my gun was caught." "Yeah, it did," Johnny says.

Johnny twirls his forty-five then rebolsters it. Pete tells one of the officers to block off the area.

"Where are you going?"

"Going to tell the dean that there is no school today."

Pete hears Jenny's voice.

"Looks nasty what's wrong cat got your tongue." "Bad pun Jenny."

"Yes, I guess. I could have waited for a better time. I hope it is the perp."

"You don't sound sure Jen."

Jenny knew that it was not the cougar as did Pete. Pete makes his way down the stairs.

"Will catch you at the morgue," Pete calls out then makes his way to the vehicle.

CHAPTER 44

At the precinct Jenny tapped on the pain glass partition that made Pete's office. Each cubical office was the same as the others in the building.

She walked in and as she did she pretended to open a door an invisible door that was not there. She entered sat down. Pete and Johnny just looked at her wondering what she would do next. There was a silence for a moment then she spoke. She crossed her legs and arms looking straight at Pete. Pete followed the curvature to her well structured legs. His eyes following up and down. She was a pistol, pretty tall and well built. Blonde and had deep blue eyes that melted his heart at that moment.

Pete knew he was hers like butter to toast. Suddenly the thought of why such a good looking lady would choose her profession ran through his head. Jenny wore a red skirt with a white blouse. The blouse holding in the well developed flesh inside. He brought his thoughts back to the more serious matter at hand. He would see her that night he could tell her how pretty she looked in her outfit. She smile as if to read his mind.

Leaning against the far wall Johnny looked at them. He felt something was up between the two. He could just not figure it out. It just did not register in his head that she was Pete's date.

"So Jenny what do you have for us?"

"I have a feeling you will not like this Pete." "Shoot!"

"How does fish strike you?" "Fish!" exclaims Johnny. "Fish!" Pete repeats.

"That is it. Fish that is all just fish."

"With all the fancy words you use and the fancy equipment in your lab and all you come up with is fish," Pete interjects then adds, "What the fuck does fish mean?"

Pete walked around the desk and sat down on the edge of the desk. He knew where it was going and he did not want to hear it.

"Fish, fish, period there is nothing more I can tell you because that is all I have. I did the test the autopsy on the cougar shot at Rhododendron. The one shot at the school. Which I believe was the mother of this one in the morgue. I must have been hungry to show itself. I know this one was caught in the act of eating but it had very little human flesh in its stomach. Blood yes. Remember the calf?"

"Yes," Pete replies.

"Remember the mucus like substance." "Yes."

"Well the amount that the cougar had in its belly was a good amount. What I am getting at is that whatever killed the woman was not the cougar. What killed her was the same thing that killed the calf, the Oldman, the kid, and Betty and all the rest. The cougar let's say was just a scavenger feasting on the kill of a more vicious predator."

"Okay, the cat sucked up some fish excretion that you believe belongs to the killer," Johnny says.

"Let's go back again. Remember the boy found with half his side missing? But before I go any further let me explain about the excretion found. Well make things more interesting. Now I found the same thing on the boy. I found scales on the grandfather and the boy. I found a tooth in the boy's flesh. I have never seen a tooth like it."

"This is getting better," Johnny said amused.

"I ran comparison with hundreds of fish. I ran it through computer. I compared it with a shark's tooth, barracuda, whale, and a piranha's. I ran the information on the shape size the jaggedness to the tooth edges. Guess which one it matched."

"Shark!" Johnny exclaimed.

Jenny shook her head then looked at Pete. Pete stood and thought for a moment.

"I know I am going to hate myself for this but I have to say Piranha."

"Correct Pete you win the prize," she quipped then added, "Piranha is right but it still gets better. The print we found well it winds up being the front paw of the creature. Notice I said creature," she looked at both then continued, "the front paw of what belongs to a very large Rattus in resemblance. And the scales belong to the snake family not the fish. And the excretion on the bodies."

"Let me see could it be a fish," Pete says sarcastically then softly says, "hands of a rat, scales of a snake, and fish spit. And maybe it is just plain and simple. Let's say that it was just a fish eating the decaying bodies."

Pete felt the inside of his stomach tighten. Fish, rat claw marks, snake scales, he ran it in his head. Pete knew it was not human he had known for a while. He had dealt with the unnatural.

"So you want us to believe that something of the abnormal is out there stalking people for dinner?" Johnny questioned.

Pete knew she knew what it could be. Inside he wanted it to be the cougar. He had dealt with the unknown and did not want to repeat it. Pete placed his hands behind his head and leaned back stretching.

"Though I believe you Jenny. All I have is bodies, dead bodies, eaten bodies, shit I need concrete evidence like a sighting."

"He will be all right Jen he just afraid he is going if for another unworldly experience like before. He does not want it to tie up to him being an Eagle Warrior and all."

"Drop it Johnny," Pete says and watches Jenny walk out the cubical.

"By the way see you to night," she says as she turns around.

Pete smile as she stepped out of the cubical then watch as her head moved up and down over the partition top as she made her way to the elevator. Pete sat down in his chair it squeaked. Pete looked at the ceiling. What was out there? What? What in god's name could it be? He had a picture in his head. But he knew when they met it would be more hideous. His thought ran wild on the possibility of the creature. He had a good picture in his head and it gave him chills. Goose bumps ran up his arms. How long was his luck going to hold? And why did it have to be him? The "Ancient Ones" called it a gift. Pete called it a curse.

Johnny looked at Pete for a long moment and was about to say something but Pete cut him off.

"Yes, Jenny is the mystery girl. And yes she is my girl. Now you know now we can focus on this creature Johnny."

"Yes, sir."

"Let's go to the Powell Bridge Johnny I want to take a look at something.

The clouds blanketed over the sun. The wind blew softly a typical day in Portland. The wind picked up slightly right about eleven that morning. The 4th of February. Winter was at its best. The forecast for the next few days ahead had a possible chance of sleet mixed in with snow. Pete longed for the good old state of Texas. He hated the cold and it was an everyday occurrence in Portland.

Every day the temperature dropped a few degrees. He wondered if it was some kind of punishment of sorts thrown his way. The cold was different than Texas weather. You could feel the moisture in the air and that made it even colder. Yep snow definitely snow he thought to himself. Pete put on the flasher parked the unmarked vehicle. He climbed out of the vehicle on to the Powell Bridge. He looked out over the Willamette River. Johnny climbed out then walked to the other side of the bridge crossing traffic. Pete shrugged from the cold then put his hands into his Pocket. That's all he needed the thought stuck in his head.

"What are you thinking about big guy?" Johnny shouted.

"It is out there Johnny."

"So you think maybe the prep lives in these waters?"

"I believe I am right Johnny."

"If, if it lives in these waters Pete it is frozen by now."

There was a half inch blanket of ice over the water. It was one of the colder years in Portland Pete. On the bridge vehicles crawled slowly over the icy bridge. The street like a skating ring.

Johnny walked off the sidewalk making his way back to the car to answer the call over the two-way radio. Johnny reached for the driver's door and from the corner of his eyes he saw a motorist spin out of control. The vehicle swerved Johnny jumped on to the hood of the car. The vehicle missed Johnny by inches.

"Jesus all mighty," he exclaimed loudly as the adrenalin in his blood shot through his veins.

The car made a 380 up ahead then hit the curve bounced back turning the other way. It came to a halt in the middle of the two lanes. The other vehicle continue in a crawl. Pete chuckled for it reminded him of bumper cars like the ones in the carnival. It reminded him so much he said it out loud.

"Bumper cars."

He could picture children and their parents laughing having a good time. Then as soon as the thought of happiness had popped into his brain another shot in. This thought was that humans had a special quality to them. But underneath their facade lay something that not even doctors could figure out. Pete called it the ugly side to humanity. For some reason he recalled the beating of a nun by two men. He could see the nun in his mind crying begging out for mercy. Her assailants laughing as they committed horrendous act. He recalled another incident where a woman jumped to her death off a building with her daughter at her side. How could one do such a terrible act? How could one be so selfish to one's own need thinking that things revolve around them? It was one thing to commit suicide and plummet to your own death.

But it was another thing to take the daughter along for the ride. Senseless acts. The world was going mad heading to the dark side instead of believing in the one savior an that was God. If one only believed in the power of the mustard seed. Then all things could change in one's soul. Johnny finally climbed off the hood of the car he brushed himself off. Then stared at the car. The thought of the woman not giving her child the chance to live bothered Pete the most.

"Shit did you see that? I think I shit in my pants. That was just to fucking close," Johnny says then notices the look on Pete's face then ads, "Did you see that?"

"Yes, he said then said, "watch out for that car."

"Funny," Johnny says then smiles.

It was from one of the cartoons on Saturday had some girl in a car Johnny recalls.

"Now you are a comedian."

Pete ignored the remark turned back around looked back over the Willamette River.

"There has not been a killing in a month Pete."

"Yes, Johnny it seems that way. It gets cold the killings stop."

"Maybe it left to a different state."

"Now how in the hell does that make it good Johnny? If we do not catch the killer that means the killings will continue. The slaughter of the innocent," Pete interjects.

He leaned forward resting his elbows on the bridges guard rail. He stares at the water rush under the bridge making its way south.

"Pete I believe that it is still the cougar."

"John," Pete says then ads, "cougars, tigers and lions all cover there meal up for further consumption for a later time. You know as well as I that it is of the unlordly kind," Pete stands erect.

"It is just hard to accept that a Fishman is the Perp."

"It all does not add up. I believe that it is here in these waters. It climbs out to kill."

"I do not think animals are capable or that they are smart enough that they plot their kill at the element of surprise. They just attack what they catch sight of."

"But these killings are thought out Johnny." "I know what you are saying Pete."

"This creature has been ahead of us. It has evaded us in every way. Then it shows itself as if to say catch me if you can."

Johnny looks at Pete contemplates what he said then nods his head in agreement. It rained for the next couple of days. It rained constantly another unusual pattern to the weather. It had been the first time in over ten years that the flood warning had been given. The news reporter repeated the danger of the flood water to come. In Oregon city people moved quickly to fill sandbags preparing for the worst. Pete felt something was not right. It was out there and it would attack soon. Pete burned the midnight oil that night. He studied the pictures on the glass partition. He studied the water the land. Columbia, and Willamette River.

It was in the waters. It was hunting along these two rivers. He also noticed that the first victim Betty the claw marks were small perhaps like a possum. And as the murders continued the claw marks grew in size. That meant it was growing his mind raced. Now the question he asked himself was how was it able to rip the flesh off the bones so cleanly? It had scales, and mucus like substance. Pete pictured the teeth on this killing machine.

Life from another world or another dimension. The horror of such an ideal resonated in his every being. How strong was this creature really he ask himself? He took a moment to think back. Why had the doctor that he talked to at the Willamette say that he was studying fish? What was his real purpose? A doctor of genetics how was he involved. Why had he been at three of the crime sights. How was it possible for him to know before we did? How? Unless he knew before hand? Fish why does the word fish come to my thoughts. Pete ran information through his mind then it hit him like a flash of light. The doctor had said fish then corrected himself then said piranha. Piranha, piranha, that explains the way the flesh was stripped away. It was something he had created and it had gotten lose. Pete stood then put on his shoulder holster and his coat. He placed the picture in his hand back into a folder on his desk. Jenny had said the mucus was from aquatic life and that the teeth matched the piranha but bigger.

CHAPTER 45

Pete look at the victim's pictures he had pinned on the wall. He stared for a good while. He scratched his head. Where are you going to strike next.

"Do you mind," Pete says as he waits for Johnny to move out of his way.

"Did not mean to get in the way of progress boss."

"Knock the boss crap off. I could not get by." "Gaining weight here in Portland big guy."

Pete laughed then said, "up yours Johnny," he then returned to his desk. He wrote down some notes on his note pad then looked up.

"Okay Johnny let's see what you can tell me. Look at the pictures then tell me what you see."

"Victim one Betty a woman in her thirties taking out the trash. Second victim Kwok a cook taking out the trash. Three babies taken from its stroller right in front of the mother. Four kid at the Willamette Park vanishes and a doctor that studies fish. Five and six Grandson and Grandfather fishing. We have been over this before Pete."

"We need to see this creature eye to eye Johnny. We need to think like it. Then maybe we can figure out where it will strike."

Officer Bell walked in and tells them that they need to head out to Rooster Rock again.

"So big guy how's the love connection?" "Love connection."

"You know the thing between you and the M.E." "That is going pretty damn good Johnny?" Pete walks to the coat rack puts on his coat.

"We need to get a warrant for the doctors abode."

"You bring it up to the chief," Johnny says.

"Na, you can do it. You like getting your ass chewed out," Pete says joking.

They made a quick stop at Golds office. They explained what they needed. Golds told them the warrant would be ready for them in a couple of hours. By the time they had entered the medical examiner's office another call came in. Another dead body at Rooster Rock Park.

By the time they arrived forensics people were already busy like ants in an ant farm. Jenny had beaten them there and was opening up her black bag. Pete smile he did not know why he found it so amusing. He imagined a presto change-o and a rabbit would appear out of her bag. She carefully collected the tissue samples, saliva, on to the tip of a swab. She placed it into a plastic baggie tagged it with date, time, and what sample it was and from what cadaver. She tagged it John Doe 2. She repeated the procedure for all the samples she took. Meanwhile forensic took pictures, overlapping pictures, of the crime scene. The half, eaten cadavers, purplish in color from lack of oxygen. The flies fling around like tiny b-52 shooting down onto the corpse taking a meal then taking flight again. Some beetles, and worms, moved around underneath. Pete knelt down next to the M.E., then ask her what they had.

"Same thing just a different day Pete," she said in dismayed.

"We have a serial case Jenny. Things are not going to get better not until we kill this man creature."

The M.E., bobbed her head up and down in agreement. The Park Rangers moved back and forth talking to several of the pedestrians moving about near the scene.

"Who found the body Jenny?"

"Park Ranger said that they came to check out the park early this morning before the people began to arrive. As they made their rounds they came across the bodies. Said the bodies whereas it fills of flesh Pete. The Park Ranger over there halfway in the water and half way out. Legs above water were it took it's the one that looks like the wrestler Randy Savage said he saw something big move into the water. He said it looked like a crocodile swimming away."

Pete walked up to the Park Ranger. He asked him if the park could be closed down. The Ranger said it could but on what grounds. Pete told him death. The man told him that the fish like sturgeons grew quite gigantic. And as for crocodiles impossible. They needed more to go on.

"This thing just came in for a snack then swam away. Placed the corpse face down into the water then ate the other half from the hips down. Now what are the chances of it coming back here?"

"Don't know Pete," Jenny says then ads, "but we will hear about it again."

"No, we will be back bright and early ready for it. Maybe we can manage to save a life perhaps."

"What makes you think it will strike here again?"

"People, a smoregisborge of flesh for the taking. It has become like a rabid animal tasting blood and liking it. It is imprinted in its brain. And for the love of blood it will come back. Maybe this will be its expiry."

Jeff, Mary, and Jacob, arrived at Rooster Rock early the next morning before everyone had begun to arrive. They set up tent. Jeff noticed the growing crowd arriving. People moved out to the sandy area. I guess in a way it was a small beach for Portlanders. It was a sandy area that ran a few blocks. The water rolled in and back out like it would at an ocean beach. The warning of the possibility of a Piranha infestation was dismissed quickly.

Safety was not at the top of the list it seemed. Jacob brought out the tranquilizer guns in the black briefcase to keep the weapon away from human eyes. Jacob laid the briefcase down then moved to the top of stairs next to a concession stand. I took the second set of stairs leading down to the wading area. The sun climbed rapid as well as the people. By ten a.m., the swarm of people moved about like busy little ants. Some sported their new swim wear strutting about hoping to catch someone's eye. Others sunbathe getting a tan for the year. Others patronized the water some swam others jet skied in the distance. Others just played in the water. Several boats bobbed up and down at the far range of eyesight. I caught sight of Jacob as he pulled out the tranquilizer gun from the briefcase. He ran down the stairs. He glanced back at me then pointed. It was my cue to grab the other gun. I knew he had seen something. Adam I said to myself. I looked out over the water. I saw a figure just laying on top of the water. It was Adam. Jacob's voice echoed out as if it was coming out of a bull horn.

"Get out of the water. Get out of the water," he shouted at the top of his lungs.

Jacob ran into the water and I followed. Mary came running toward us from the third set of steps south of us. The screams of women, children, and a father's panic screamed emanated through the air.

I figure it was the fact that Jacob had the tranquilizer gun in his hands and was running in their direction was the cause. The screams reached the Rangers ear. I caught sight of them running down the stairs next to the concession stand. They shot straight for us like a pack of wild dogs on the track of a coon. I really do not recall how they had reached us so fast. Before I knew it I was hit square in the jaw. I felt my knees buckle. I felt like a tree toppling over after being cut down. Jacob fell to the ground as the other Ranger blindsided him. Clothed lined him from the back.

Two hundred and twenty pounds of flesh behind the muscles in the man's arm would have knocked anyone down.

"No," Mary cried out.

Mary ran as fast as she could stumbling and standing back up a couple of times before she reached us.

"They are scientist they have tranquilizer guns there tranquilizer guns" she shouted out.

They looked at us then at the weapons we held paused then said, "drop the guns either way."

I let go of the weapon as did Jacob. The Ranger lifted Jacob by the shoulder. I pushed off my right leg stood as the other Ranger held on to my shoulder.

"Look the danger is not us it is that," Mary told them and pointed at the creature.

"What on earth," the heavier Ranger says in disbelief.

"Crock, we have no crocks out here," said the other at Jacob's side.

Adam's back lay on top of the water its tail switched back and forth slowly. It laid still for a moment then it violently switched its tail.

In a matter of seconds before anyone could move it hit a kid snorkeling. It hit him like a torpedo. The kid went under staying submerged for a minute.

Then like a bobber he popped out on the water. He clawed at the water his eyes open wide with fear. He rolled over onto his back as he held his stomach. But it was to no avail. His intestines floated on the water like string noodles. Adam reached out grabbed the kid by the hair. It then began to move back into the depth of the water.

There was a splash and it and the kid went under. His intestines trail behind like ribbons blowing in the wind. Before they could tell the people to get out Adam popped up out of the water again. It scanned the area for its next prey. A family three yards out that were attempting to get to back to land. Adam switched its tail shot forward the water parting as it sped toward its kill. Jacob reached for tranquilizer gun. The Park Ranger pulled his revolver out of the holster. I ran to help the people to get out of the water. The next thing happen so rapidly that it could not be prevented. As the boy reached out his hand in that one split second. The boy was pulled out through the center of the inner tube into the water. Several yards out the boy popped back out of the water screaming clawing at the water.

"Oh Jesus, no," he cried out in agonizing pain as he felt the sharp claws of the creature dig deep in him.

I Jeff Mongroll knew there was nothing that I could do. To avert the horror of the boy's death. But hopefully he could help the rest of the family.

I grabbed hold of the mother, daughter, and rushed them to the shore. I looked over my shoulder. I could see the water turning red with the boy's blood. The water churned for what seemed forever. But in reality it had only been a minute maybe two. The boy's body popped up as it discarded his carcass. It had taken two more lives that day in less than an hour. I moved back into the water and made my way to the boy's half eaten torso. The bleached white bones left on the lower half dangling. I felt something brush against my leg.

Chill ran up my spine for I knew it had been Adam. It circled my legs several times then vanished. I stared down at the boy's carcass. I heard the ambulances siren. The detective arrived and ran down the stairs. I made my way back to the shore stood there until the paramedics came for the body. In the back ground with all the dismay I could hear the boy's mother sobbing hysterically with sadness. First forensic then the M.E. arrived then Pete and

Johnny. Jenny took off her latex gloves toss them on the skeletal remains of the boy. The paramedics lifted the boy put him on a gurney. Pete made his way down to the wading area just as one of the Rangers placed the handcuffs on the doctor. Pete walked up to the Ranger.

"I'll take it from here."

The Ranger stared at Pete. Pete could see he was about to be challenged. He moved his coat lapel to the side showing the man the badge.

"They had tranquilizers."

"Gun or not they were guns and guns on the beach. I know."

I'll take full responsibility besides he will be released in an hour or two after he is booked. And with a good lawyer."

"Okay detective he's all yours," he said and removes the cuffs.

Pete watched as the two Park Ranger walk up the steps.

"Now doctor tell me what you have to do with all of this. You know the piranha, fish. The kind from the Amazon."

"Correct detective."

"Come on doctor there is more and sooner or later you are going to have to spill the beans as they say."

"There is nothing more detective I was just looking for the piranha's that someone let loose in the Columbia River."

"Like I said doctor the truth will have to be told. I know it is something we have never seen before. I know you cannot capture your mistake alone doctor."

Jeff contemplated telling him the truth about Adam.

"Detective are we free to go?"

"Yes, doctor you and your colleagues can leave."

"I say take them to the precinct and hold them."

"On what Johnny? Besides I have a good hunch our doctor is up to his neck in hot water."

Johnny looked at Pete. Pete looked at him then told him there was no pun intended. Johnny smiled nodded his head several time.

"Pete," the M.E. called out to him.

Pete made his way up to her. She told him that one of the bodies did not surface and that it was still in the river.

"Get the Navy to send some seals out here. A team of scuba divers to search for the body Johnny."

"Fucking man fish," Pete said then stood at the edge of the water looking over the void of the river.

Man or beast I know you are out there. And I will terminate you "Fishman," he whispered to himself.

"Jenny get me something solid. What we need is to get a close look at this thing."

"As they say Pete. To see is to believe."

"I know you are right Jenny. I will catch you later at home."

"Want me to make some steaks and get a good bottle of cheap wine."

"Pete you need to relax a bit."

"I will see you at home meaning his apartment."

CHAPTER 46

My colleagues and I sat around the table in a daze. We looked at each other wanting for one of us to come up with a brilliant ideal. Jacob spoke up first and what he had to say was worth a million dollars. I told him to explain.

"Did either of you catch the animal channel by chance? Well if not they had sharks. I saw that they go down in the water to study these sharks in a metal constructed cages. The key word is cage.

But instead of us using it to study Adam we can reverse it. We can use it to capture Adam. There are still two bodies in the fridge haven't had a time to dispose of them."

"You are the man Jacob," I said out loud. "Well it beats the flip side Jeff."

"Flip side of what?" Mary asked.

"If it doesn't work we become food."

Later on that day Mary vanished for a while. She came down I do not know if it was stress or just excitement on her behalf. All I can say is she came down to the lab in a red dress. I looked up from the equipment on the table we would need for Adam. I felt myself swallow as I saw her. I cut the burner under the vial I was using. The liquid inside boiling slowly died out to a standstill.

"Jacob the labs is all yours tonight."

We hurried up the stairs. We forgot of this world and all our problems of Adam. We were like teenagers in love or just in that precise moment in lust. Mary fell back into the bed I followed. I kissed her softly. I unbutton her dress. I notice instantly that she was not wearing a bra. My excitement flourish like a wildfire. My hands worked like an instrument I had not known before.

She took off my shirt. I ran my hands up her thigh. I unfasten the last two buttons to the dress. Instantly I noticed she wore no panties under as well. My blood rushed through my veins with excitement. I then kissed her like never before. My hands as well as her's worked in unison unbuckling my pants and taking off my shoes. Her desire mode was out of control. She straddled me and as I like to say, "she rode the pony." Yes we were in love. This one feeling we should have used more often. There are many pleasures but none like real love.

CHAPTER 47

Five a.m., in the morning down at the Columbia River. Where the Sandy River meets up to the Columbia. Francis reached for the small foam cup of warms at his side. He placed it around a shrimp already on the hook. He secured the worm down with sewing thread then tossed it out into the river.

The five-pound weight hit the water with a plunk. Water splashed as the weight pulled the bait under. Francis sat back in his lawn chair. He caught sight of a salmon breaching for air then splashing back into the water. After a few moments suddenly the tip of his pole bent forward. It began to twitch violently. He stood quickly grabbed the pole in his hand and jerked back. He began to reel in what was on the other end. He made sure to keep tension on the line not to lose the fish. But suddenly the line went slack. He continued to reel in hope that it could just be a void moment and the fish was still on. Abruptly there was a tug on the line whatever he had shifted direction. There was something large at the other end. The bulk of its body floated on top of the water. The line became taut. It tugged on the line forcing itself backward. Francis pulled the tip of the pole up then it moved forward at a rapid speed. It flew out of the water hitting him in the chest.

"Oh shit!" He exclaimed out loud.

The thing came flying at him and scared the hell out of him. He laughed then unhooked the fish. He rebaited the hook then casted out again. He threw the fish back in the water. He saw the first of the jet skiers to arrive. They were not there to fish but to fuck around is what he thought. Unfortunately, it seemed the woman on the water ski did not care. She had noticed him and still moved in close to shore running over his line. She made a huge circle. She had stayed a little further out on the second and third run. It irked Francis it was not the fact that the woman was having the time of her life. It was the fact that she was just mean is what he thought. Common courtesy flew out of the window it appeared. His pole bent he wasted no time in grabbing it into his hands. He grabbed the pole jerked back twice as he set the hook firmly. He could see the fish head as it popped out of the water and dove back in. Yes indeed this one was a huge keeper he thought to himself. He reeled in until the fish was a few feet out. He landed the fish then picked it up by its gill. He was bewildered by what he saw. The fish was half eaten. Where is your better part his mind races? The bite seemed to be fresh for blood was still seeping from the wound. He glanced out over the river water. He caught a glimpse of something moving away. It was moving towards the woman. It looked like an otter or a seal from a distance. It couldn't be he thought. It was to big more like an alligator perhaps. Or maybe it was the sun reflection off the waves. The woman made another circle heading back in. Something hit her ski hard. She lost her balance almost falling off the ski and into the water. She looked around there was nothing she could see. She let go of the throttle. She noticed something moving next to her like a dolphin next to a boat in the ocean. She stare at it for a moment then noticed the tail of the creature as it thrash forcefully. It twisted its body then propelled out of the water at her.

Its white menacing porcelain teeth bit into her waist. It thrashed its head back and forth viciously tearing at her skin. It tore away at it as if it were soft plastic. It vanished from sight. She held tight to the handles of the ski. She felt the sting of fear and death at that moment.

She knew it was not from these waters. There has never been an attack in Portland's waters.

"What the fuck," Francis exclaimed as he dropped his pole to the ground.

Its head then its torso popped back out of the water. It moved so rapid she did not have time to move. It hit her again tearing and ripping flesh off her bones. She hit the throttle she looked over her shoulder in hope of escaping. Whatever this thing was it was gaining on her? It was at her ankle. It bit down then disappeared as if toying with her. She fell into the water. She began to swim for her life. She reached the ski climbed back on. She hit the throttle again darting off. She moved to shore where Francis stood. The creature attacked at her ankle again and again taunting her. She had one chance if she wanted to live. She needed to make it up to the man she had been so rudely to. Blood spewed from her leg staining the water like a giant ribbon in the water behind the ski. The sled hit hard on the bank of the shoreline. The sled hit toppling over and skidding on the ground. Francis grabbed her by the shoulder helped her to get up. He saw the blood and knew if he did not take her to the hospital immediately, she would surely die. He took off his belt tied it around her thigh then told her not to release the pressure but every fifteen minutes. He was about to give her his watch when he notice she wore one. Francis looked at the wound at her waist. There was no way of stopping the blood. He looked back out over the water. He noticed the creature moving towards land. It began to stand the water running off its body. The sun making its body glisten.

"Oh shit! Oh shit! We need to move like the wind now," he shouted.

He pulled and she stood. She did not question his motive. He told her if she could attempt to walk. She told him she would move no matter pain or no pain. She could see her attacker now moving in. It could not be she thought to herself as she saw the "Fishman." Francis told her not to look at the creature and to move as quick as she could.

Adam's gills moved in and out extracting the oxygen from the air. Francis opened the passenger side of the truck then help the woman in. He ran to the other side climbed in. He locked the doors. Adam hit the truck hard on the woman's side. It tore off the door at its hinges. Francis put the truck in gear then floored the pedal. But the creature was just too quick. It pulled the woman out letting her fall to the ground. Francis saw the horror of evil as Adam bite down on her thigh ripping the flesh. It was human nature to help but Francis knew if he would attempt this he would be the second course of the menu. He gunned it and spun out onto highway 40. He drove fast his horn bellowed out as he entered traffic. He swerved around a car making distance away from the monster. He drove to the precinct downtown. Fear ran ramped through him. His eyes blurred with tears for the woman he left to die. At the precinct he related the incident to the front desk. After Pete heard what had happen at the river he knew that time was of the essence. They arrived at the scene and looked down at the corpse. This creature this thing had evolved. It had stripped all the flesh off the woman only leaving her left hand intact. A skeleton with one hand. Pete mind ran thinking that it was a Jackson skeleton want a be. Pete looked at Johnny as he was about to say something.

"Don't say it Johnny just don't say it." "Fuck!!!" Johnny says in disbelief.

CHAPTER 48

Jeff listened to the news on the radio. He heard the D.J., say that there had been another attack. We could not afford to waste any more time. I rolled out of bed the next day. I looked at the alarm clock six a.m. I wiped my eyes focused them washed up and got dress. Jacob sat at the table as Silva placed a cup of coffee before him.

"Ready," I said then walked up to Silva kissed her on the forehead.

"Early bird catches the worm," Jacob said.

"Well finish the coffee then to the welding shop we go," I said.

We climbed into the van and headed out. We drove for thirty minutes or more until we had reached our destination. I looked up reading the sign above the entrance. Frank and son welding shop. At the bottom in small print read any and all jobs possible. We walked inside the building walked to the far east side of the building. We could see sparks flying as a man bent over welding something together. We walked inside and proceeded past the receptionist. I heard her calling to out to us but continued up to a man giving orders. The woman at the receptionist window watched us as we approached the man. The man put on a welding helmet then pulled down the visor. He looked at me I could see he did not care who or why I was there. The torch popped as the fire came on. He bent down the sparks flew as he began to weld. It took several minutes to finish his welding. He cut off the welding torch lifted his visor then asked.

"What do you want?"

I had to choose my words right this man was huge. I figure he played football in the past. He stood six four at three hundred or more pounds. The man welding in the east corner of the building cut his torch off then walked up to us. Except for a few differences I could tell that it was father and son.

"Can we help you?"

"I hope you can I know this is short notice but I am in dire need of something to be made quick. It is of the utmost urgency."

"My wife the one you did not give the time of day or curtesy to. You know the woman that runs the desk. She is the one that takes the orders. You know the lady you forgot to talk to first," said the father.

"I know it was rude to barge my way in. I apologize."

"Mister do not tell me tell the lady at the office. When you have done that come back and explain all that it is you need. Then tell me why I should do it in such short notice."

We walked back to the receptionist office entered the office I apologized. She was cold in her demeaner when she talked to us.

"What is it you want mister?" she asked nonchalantly.

After I explained the urgency of the matter she got up off her chair then told us to follow her.

"Listen to these men Frank," she said then handed a paper with all that I needed. He read the paper then looked at Jacob and me."

"Now let me hear why it is so important for me to do this job.

And why I would shut down the other projects to handle this. And I hope you do not waste my time mister."

Jacob reached down picked up the nozzle of the welder.

"Get your fucking dick skinners off my equipment," the man said out loud firmly.

His son smiled. Jacob put down the nozzle.

"Just looking."

"Do just that look but do not touch."

"My dad is quiet possessive of his equipment." "Now tell me why I should do this job?" Frank cuts in.

"To put it bluntly sir lives depend on it. You must have heard about the crocodile, alligator, piranhas, by now. Of the climbing death. I need this cage built to capture whatever is in the water. It must be made strong. It must not be able to bend the bars."

"You and your side kick let this thing in the water?"

The man was quick and smart. I guess not answering him gave him the answer he needed. He paused for a moment then agreed to construct the cage. He mention it was only because of the lives that depended on it. He reached out his hand. I knew it was not to give me a handshake. As I said the man was smart. I reached into my coat pocket and handed him the drawing schematics to scale of what I needed. He handed the paper to his son.

"Let me see double enforced cage this thing must be big. I say it looks good but I will need to reinforce some areas like the hinges. I have to tell you this will cost a pretty penny," said the son.

"We will push back some orders. It will take three days tops."

"I apologize again for just barging in. The cost is no concern.

Thank you."

Jacob and I headed out of the building. The sparks from the welder cracked as the little flicks of metal popped.

CHAPTER 49

The next morning in the cubical Pete says, "Johnny get O.S.U., on the phone for me. We need to find out information on all the scientist that have come from that university."

Pete believed in other life beside the ones on this planet. Still he did not believe it was an alien. Then he thought that maybe the doctor had added a few ingredients to the stew. Now he had asked himself was this thing intelligent. Or was it just a killing machine. Somehow the doctor they met had to do something with this creation. It was going to be one hell of a hunt. And in this case the hunter may become the hunted.

"Pete," Johnny says as he hands him the phone.

Pete talked to the woman on the other end. She read the names of all the doctors. After about a hundred names.

"Doctor Jeffrey Mongroll II," she said. "Thank you. I have what I need," Pete tells her and hangs up the phone.

"Did you get what you needed Pete."

"Johnny let's go and pay a visit to the genetic doctor."

Pete was certain that the doctor had a part in creating this monster. The words, "it is alive," echoed through his mind. He remembered the classic movie Frankenstein.

"Chief," Pete said then walked out of the office.

An hour later Pete and Johnny found themselves at the front of the doctor's mansion. They walked up to the door rang the bell. Nothing, he rang it two more times.

"Looks like our doctor is not home Pete."

"Looks that way Johnny but let's walk around back before we leave."

Silva opened the double doors. Pete scrutinized her Johnny looked at Pete then at Silva.

"Sorry was busy with the dishwasher. How can I help you?"

"The doctor."

"Jeff went downtown said it was urgent."

Pete and Johnny climbed into the vehicle. Back home that night Pete took several anti-acid pills. The investigation was giving him heart burn. He got out of bed went into the kitchen. He open the fridge door took out a carton of milk. He walked into the living room sat down on the sofa. It was a tan leather sofa with big cushions to soft for his needs. He always thought it was like a woman's hands. Ah, he sighed and was about to put his feet on the ottoman when Jenny called out.

"Get a glass before you put the milk carton tip to your mouth. And put the milk away."

His laughter filled the room. How did she do that? Did the woman have e.s.p.? He went back into the kitchen grabbed a glass fill it to the top. He put the milk back into the fridge. Jenny put on her robe and went into the kitchen and sat down on the recliner.

"Want some milk?"

"Did you drink out of the carton?" "No, I got a glass see."

"Yes, I would like a glass of cow."

Pete laughed again then said, "You should have let me know you were there."

"Why?"

"Well! What if I had climbed out of bed came in to sit to whack off?"

"Aren't you glad that you don't have to when I am here?"

"Baby you know that's right," Pete says then laughs.

Jenny opened up her robe. A smile appeared on his face. Pete noticed that her silk white panties fit snug to her body. He had become like a deer seeing a shining light. He was mesmerized by her beauty.

"Well, are you or do I go back to sleep?" "I am, I am," Pete exclaim.

"The creature keeps running through my mind."

"No, business talk until I am back at work.

Only play big boy," Jen said in her Marilyn Monroe impersonation.

The next day Pete parked across the street from the precinct. He looked up at the building before crossing the street. He yawned he felt tired. Hell of a night he thinks to himself. I guess one could say he was wore out. Jenny was ten years younger than he. He looked up at the window of the building. He got a slight feeling of vertical. He noticed or it seemed to him that the windows with the blinds pull halfway down where like eyelids. He could see several shadow moving about.

"Nothing like a day at the office," he whispered to himself.

Johnny was waiting in the cubical for him. Pete looked at him thinking the eager beaver.

"What another stiff?"

"Yes there is." "Where?"

"Right in front of me Pete." "Funny."

"The stiff is at the Sandy River under the bridge. I called Jenny told her you were on your way."

Well so much for the memory of the good sex he thinks to himself. He pauses for a moment.

"Now let us go to the bad crime scene."

What's next Pete thought to himself.

"Before we leave Pete the Chief wants you to hear what the victim's wife has to say. Get this she was with him of course. She was further down she states. They were just talking taking a stroll down the river bank enjoying the scenery. She was several yards away when she heard her husband crying out for help. She says our creature from the depth picked him up like a rag doll. It ripped away at him. She said then she says she ran up to the incline. She said she called out for help but to no avail. There was this thick limb as big as a baseball bat she said. It was like a club. She says she swung it at the creature but with her strength it was like a mosquito bite to it. She climbed back up the incline and yelled for help until someone stopped to help."

After hearing the old woman's testimony, they left the precinct. At the Sandy River half an hour later. Pete and Johnny made their way down the incline. The body was submerged in a foot of water. Moving back and forth on the Rocky River bed. All Pete could think of was how perfect the creature had stripped the flesh off the man's face, arms, lower limbs.

Only the intralls floated like balloons on top of the water. Most animals crush the neck at the spinal column to make sure its prey is dead. This creature was unique it ate and left the spinal column and neck intact. Perfection! Pete thought to himself. And that is exactly what it was a perfect fucking killing machine. Forensic took pictures of the body up and down the riverbank.

The M.E, tossed her gloves on top of the corpse. "Pete, Johnny," she greeted. Pete noticed that Jenny did not look tired or sleepy. I guess being young has a lot going for it his mind raced.

"Same thing?" Pete questioned.

"Almost Pete. I do have something solid this time."

"What?" Johnny said. "Follow me."

"Gary show the gentlemen what you have," Jenny says.

"Wait just a few more seconds," he said and reached down into the water at the edge of the embankment.

He grabbed the foot print he had just poured minutes ago. The water moved back and forth with life of its own. The water splashed around the small sand dam that Gary had made to keep the water out of the crevice of the footprint.

"Ah, here is the proof, detective," he handed the print to Pete.

"Take a good look detective and tell me what you see."

"I see a footprint," Johnny quipped.

"I see, one, two, three, four, digits and they all most resemble human feet," Pete tells Gary then faces towards Jenny then ads, "it as well has webbing between each of its digits."

"Looks like we have a real live fish hunt on our hands," Jenny says.

"I think it is more like Aqua man," Johnny interjects and smiles.

CHAPTER 50

Two weeks passed and Rooster Rock was reopen to the public. Jeff looked out over the river in all directions. He knew Adam was still out there. Jeff moved about on the twenty-one foot Boston Whaler. It bobbed up and down like a giant bobber in the middle of the Columbia River.

"Lower the cage down slowly Jacob." "Will do Jeff."

"Mary cut the engine off."

The motor noise died. The clank of the mechanism as the gear to the hoist moved forward resinated. The lever made its metallic sound. The chain clanked as it raised the cage out. There was a corpse in the middle of the cage. The hoist arm moved to the left side of the boat. It stopped Jacob began to lower the cage down into the depth of the river. The anxiety was eating away at Jeff. He would see Adam face to face once again. Maybe it was the fear of knowing, knowing, that the inevitable was to come and he would be face to face with his creation. His mind ran wild then suddenly the chain to the cage set firm.

"Here Jeff," Jacob called out and waited for him to turn around then tossed him the tranquilizer gun. The chain suddenly slumped. There was no way to tell if Adam had taken the bait. There was only one thing to do wait. Suddenly there was a pull on the chain as it became taut.

"Jacob bring it up slow."

The winch motor turn on. The hum of the hoist filled the air. Twenty minutes later the cage was up and on board. We were dumbfounded, bewildered, is what we were. It had not been the creature. There was a sudden relief that came to us. What was strange is that in the cage were Piranha's. We stood perplexed. The small fish flapped around on the deck of the boat. I can only come to the conclusion that these exotic fish had been with Adam. We did get an answer to the question. Do or can Piranha's live in fresh water? Mary sat down in disbelief. Jacob cradled the tranquilizer gun in his arms.

"What now?" Jacob asked.

"Want to go fishing?"

I do not know why I ask that dumb question at that moment. I guess I need a little humor.

"Want to go fishing," Mary said and shook her head.

I smiled then walked up to the steering turned the key in the ignition. We headed for shore. We would have to find another way to capture Adam. But I knew that Adam would come to us when it was time. On our way into the boat dock we could see people in the water as if nothing had happen.

After hooking the boat up to the trailer. We made our way down to the sandy beach like area. We walked down the stair I heard laughter. I could see a family on a large inner tube. I as well saw what would be imprinted in my mind until the day I die. A little boy and his sister sat on the inner tube their feet dangling in the water. Their father suddenly popped out of the water from under the tube. The boy and the girl laughed happily.

Then I saw it. I saw Adam stand up out of the water. The water streamed down its shoulder and torso. It vanished for a second back under the water. I yelled out at the top of my lungs.

Jacob, and Mary, had seen it as well. Jacob came running and yelling for them to get out of the water. They looked at us as if we were insane.

The father abruptly cried out in agonizing pain as he felt his thigh flesh being ripped apart. Blood colored the water like the ink from an octopus.

Adam pulled the man under violently. The man popped back up yelling for dear life. Adam took him under several times. The fifth time the man came up he had his throat gone. Then he felt the creature sink its teeth into his side. Its claws grabbing him in a death clutch. The man vanished from sight. The water turned red. The water churned as if boiling. I, Jacob, and Mary, ran with all we had to the children. We grabbed the children and pushed the inner tube as fast as we could. I felt something against my leg. I know it was Adam taunting me. I ignored it I knew if Adam wanted me dead he would have done so. We managed to get the children to shore. Fear and confusion covered their faces.

"Look," shouted one of the pedestrians.

Adam lay on the water like a crocodile ready to strike at any moment. Floating motionless then it moved its tail and began to move towards shore. It held onto something at first we could not see what it was. When it was close enough we saw it was two skeletons. It had eaten the flesh off the whole body. It was the second time we had seen this. I do not know why but it flung the skeletons onto the sand area. Mary took the kids into her arms turning them away from the horrible ordeal. It stopped and just glared at us.

CHAPTER 51

Pete and Johnny climbed out of the vehicle went up to the door. They rang the doorbell then knocked on the door. The door crept open on its own. They looked at each other then decided to enter. Pete looked around then back at Johnny.

"I guess he wants us to come in." "Well if he didn't it is too late." "Right you are Johnny."

Pete took out his Springfield and Johnny his colt 45. They walked in slow with their free hand under the stock of their guns.

"I'll take the stairs."

Pete searched the lower floor while Johnny went through all the upper floor. Pete noticed that the gardener and the woman they met before where not in the place. It was vacant but why. Okay, the place was vacant but there had to be something they were missing.

"I know there has to be another room or floor," Pete exclaimed aggravated to himself.

"Think movies," Johnny said. "Movies?"

"Yeah, movies as in the monster kind. In these movies there is always a hidden trap door. There over there Pete," he shouted."

Pete looked where Johnny pointed. Pete nodded his head. It was a lamp. Pete looked down smiled Johnny was right. It had to be under the rug. Johnny moved the Persian rug out of the way. There it was now to open it.

"The lamp on the wall turn it to the right or left see if that works."

Pete moved the lamp to the right. On the first try the door began to slowly creak open. Pete scrutinized the stairs leading down to the laboratory. They hit the "Jack Pot" just like in the movies. They kept their weapons pointed out in front.

"What are we looking for?" Johnny asked. "Look for anything out of the ordinary, life human, or animal," Pete says.

"Hell Pete the whole investigation is out of the ordinary."

Inside the lab they stood in silence their eyes focusing on everything inside. The first thing their eye lay eyes on was the huge tank filled with formaldehyde and the creature inside.

"Holly shit! Look at that," Johnny says astound.

Pete placed the notepad he had picked up from the computer desk back down. In a way it was funny but in another way it was scary. What kind of mind creates such an abomination? They froze their ears perked up as they heard a soft moan. Again the moaning sound reached their ears. They looked to the far corner of the room.

"What the fuck?" Johnny says.

On metal gurneys where a man and a women. These human's barely resembling humans beings.

"What makes men think they can do such things in the name of humanity or science?"

"Pete I wish I knew."

The specimens were strapped to the tables like wild animals Pete's mind ran wild.

"Jesus instead of using their knowledge to help. They waste time playing God," Johnny says out loud.

"You are just beginning to see what man is capable of Johnny."

They made their way down between the isles of shelves lined with containers filled with deformity. Deformed creatures floating bobbing up and down in the formaldehyde. Mutations from the bottom shelf to the top. Experiments gone wrong. The ungodly sight sent a nausea feeling through Pete's and Johnny's stomach. Johnny dry heaved. He could taste the bitter taste of his own bile wanting to escape. Johnny swallowed hard but still his stomach lurched in and he vomited. He slapped his weapon against the counter as he bent forward. He wiped his mouth with the sleeve of his shirt.

"What do you think Johnny out of the ordinary?" "Yes, I would have to agree Pete."

They returned to the man and woman on the gurney. They suddenly jerked then trashed in an attempt to sit up. Or to get at them. The leather straps binding them down to the tables held them. These human's had been transformed into something hideous. Their skin pale, leathery, their bodies thin like that of a starving person with jagged over size teeth. Their eyes set back deep into their sockets. They had overly large cranial. Pete noticed that there were spikes running down their spine when they lifted off the tables.

Johnny held his gun high. Pete put his back into his holster. They studied the woman at least this is what she still resembled. Though if it had not been for the breast, they would have been speechless. She spoke three word taking them by surprise. She repeated the three words.

"Please kill us."

"We can try and help you," Pete tells her. "Kill us for I will not hesitate to kill you," said the man creature on the gurney next to her.

Its green eyes pierced through Pete with a hate that he could feel. Pete's heart fell as if it had fallen to the lower part of his stomach. He knew killing them would be cold blood murder even if it was justified.

"Johnny put your gun away. Go upstairs and call for back up."

Johnny knew Pete. He knew what was on his mind.

"You nuts Pete."

"Johnny just wait for me outside."

He put his gun away into his holster walked up the stairs. Pete walked up to the shelves of containers picked up a jar that held a deform creature inside. He looked at the half dog, half pig, then walked back to them. He looked at the woman creature. He placed the container between her legs. He knew it was a dangerous thing to do but he had no choice. He began to unfasten the restraints binding her to the table. He took off the man's restraints. Pete looked at them thinking how could this benefit mankind? The mutated man growled as he sat up then got down on all fours as if to get ready to pounce on Pete. Pete knew the man was still more man than animal for he could think and speak. The woman got on all fours and in a raspy tone said.

"Please kill us. Do not let us live like this."

"I will say this. I cannot kill you in cold blood."

Pete moved taking slow steps back. Pete knew that wild animals did not wish to die. The man creature squatted down on his hands. He tilted his head to look at the woman then nodded. Their elongated arms tensed ready to uncoil and spring forward. They both growled viciously then the one nearest to him sprung off its arms and legs. Pete reached for his Springfield. He fired four rounds one of the rounds hitting the man's heart. Its body slumped over then fell off the gurney. The woman sprung off the table Pete fired the remaining two rounds hitting her direct dead center in her forehead. The second just an inch from her heart. Her body rolled to the right then fell to the floor with a heavy thump. Pete placed in another clip into the Springfield then scrutinized all the creatures in the shelves.

"God forgive me," Pete says out loud.

He then pull down the first roll of shelves then the second then the third roll. The containers fill with formaldehyde and the mutations splattered on to the floor. Pete stood in the mist of all that was unholy in the eyes of God. The doctor had no ideal he had accomplished his endeavor. He had indeed created new life.

These two would have been his accomplished dream. The perfect human specimen in the doctor's eyes. Pete took his lighter flicked it on. He looked at the creations then tossed his lighter onto the floor. Quickly the place went up in flames. Pete made his way out of the mansion quickly.

CHAPTER 52

Night came and went. The sun rose with its brilliant aura of life shinning down on the world. Down at Waterfront Park as morning crept up, birds chirped, fish jumped, in the water and people walk down the streets of the city. The hideous form of the creature slowly climbed out of the Willamette River. Water streamed off its body. The water beads seeming like small crystals falling as they reflected the suns rays. Adam's claws scraped along the concrete pavement making a wood like sound as it made its way to the center of town.

From a distance the creature's silhouette appear like that of man walking on two legs. It possessed no fear for those that saw it in the distance. From afar it looked indeed like man. In the center of downtown Portland Max was just turning the corner on its first round from Gresham Or. The conductor watched as the shadow of the man got closer. His eyes open wide as he saw what was walking towards the train. Adam continued its way awkwardly but fast. A fat man fell to the floor, a woman, dropped her bag. Adam was among them before they could run.

"My Jesus," the conductors said in disbelief.

He quickly closed the doors. Adam's eyes met the man's straight on. And in that second it ran forward and sailed through the air. It hit the windshield cracking it but not breaking it on his first attempt. Adam shook the shock off and again hit the windshield. The windshield broke scattering small fragments of glass on the floor and onto the conductor cutting him in several places. It happened so fast. Suddenly Adam jumped off the front of Max. People were dumbfounded they could not believe it was happening in today's world.

"What in God's name is it," a man shouted then began to run.

Adam anticipated the man's movement its claws struck out gouging and bring death. Adam went back to the front of Max jumped up and before the man unbuckled his belt it had him its clutches. He picked the man off the seat tearing the shoulder strap and buckle that held in the man. It hurled the man out through the open door onto the pavement outside. His body hit hard like a heavy sack of clay. The body rolled twice landing next to the department store. Blood seeped from the corner of the man's mouth. The red stain of blood from a distance looked like paint globed on the skin. The man closed his eyes as death took him. People cried out in pain and horror as Adam caught them as they ran by unaware of the creature. They died without knowing what had killed them. Kaos.

People tumbled over others but were cut down just the same. Adam was not killing for hunger but for a deep rage a hatred that it now had for humans. At the precinct just several blocks away Pete, Johnny and several of the officers rushed out of the building following Pete. Johnny jumped over several cars as they moved through the light.

"Sorry," Johnny shouted as he made his way over a third car."

"Move," Pete cried out as he shot through a crowd of pedestrians.

Like a bull in a bull ring, he plowed into several of the on comers trying to get away. Two officers on horses back made their way down the road waving cars to move aside. Adam's ears picked up the commotion and slashed out several more times at people. It took a small girl slashing her throat. It knelt down beside her and began to rip flesh from her body. It then stood after several minutes. He dress tore and only the white bones of her skeleton was left on the floor. It then began to head back to the water. Its claws scraping as it rapidly but cumbersomely made its way down the street. Horns bellowed out as Adam crashed into the moving vehicles. It remembered the alley and quickly made its way into the darkness. Pete, Johnny, and the officers followed then stopped.

They took time to look at the dead and at the conductor of Max's. At the alley the two officers on horseback stopped. They scrutinized the alley. It was dark and it gave them an eerie feeling. They saw the creature move behind a dumpster. "Did you catch a glimpse of it?"

"I did, Smith. Sure did it's a big fucker."

"Smith go around and enter through the other side. We will corner him in the middle. There is no way out for it Smith. I will stay put until you give me the sign to move in," Jones tells him.

Smith took the reins pulled back on them then galloped around the block. He reached the opening. He took his two way and gave Jones the okay to move in.

"If it starts to come at you Jones do not wait. Shoot."

Jones called for backup he knew it was a dangerous task at hand. They continue in. The horses moved slow as they kept their eyes open for the unexpected. Abruptly both horses reared up almost at the same time. They fidget as they got closer then like an apparition it was out in front of them. Adam shuffled back and forth scaring the horses. It stopped looked at them coldly. Adam then lowered onto all fours. The men knew it was about to attack. They reached for their revolvers. They fired but in one split second it moved on Smith. It leapt up Smith felt its claws dig into his throat. Smith fell to the ground when the horse reared up from fear. Adam struck again and again cutting, slashing, at

Smith. The wounds opened and blood spewed. Jones moved in with his revolver in hand. Adam squatted down on all fours then leapt at its prey. Jones fired two round missing twice. He saw his death at the hands of a creature. It struck ripping Jones throat out. It lashed out again ripping his stomach open. They both fell to the ground. Jones intestines bubbled out of the wound and laid on top of his stomach like noodles in the center of a bowl. Adam bit down on the neck savoring the blood devouring the flesh as the man gave his last look at the world.

I regret having to write this down but this is what I saw. I saw what my creation had done. My abomination and to see its evil up closed was devastating. The horror I cannot explain. I was not connected to Adam telepathically. I was just its benefactor. I caught sight of the detective. I knew he had figured different in the matter. I walked towards the courthouse. Pete stopped and said, "Doctor," as I approached Max's, then says, "good that you showed up on your own keeps me from having to arrest you at you home."

"Yes detective there will be time for that later. I have come to give you all the help that I can."

"All right. Move out of the way let see if the doctor can help these pours souls," Pete says and wave the man to go ahead.

Pete sarcastic tone cut sharply into me but as soon as I had stepped into the street the view I encountered was devastating. My heart dropped. I was supposed to have made a better being. Bodies, bodies, torn apart, degutted, and beheaded. Blood was scattered all over on the walls, sidewalk, like a splatter painting.

"Doctor I have to know is this thing is from earth?" Johnny asked.

"I would have to say a little of both. Alien and human."

"Get this place secured and barricade the streets off," Pete shouted out orders.

Pete had nothing but discontent for me. I had played God. I think deep down that if it was not for the badge he carried. He would have taken my head off that moment himself.

"Doctor follow me."

"Pete sorry to interrupt you but they have it cornered down in the alley."

"Okay officer right behind you."

They ran down the street for a block then made their way east through Lauderman's Park and in to the alley. It was the same alley where it had killed Kwok. They made their way in cautiously.

They came up on the first horse and the dead men. Pete fired to rounds off in the horse head that was bleeding and not quite dead yet. He walked to the other and fired two more rounds. It was going to cost the precinct. It would be all most impossible to replace these horse on depleted funds. Pete followed the blood trail. It lead back out of the alley. It appeared it had taken raw bleeding flesh with it. Pete faced the doctor and just stared as if staring deep into his soul.

"This thing doctor does it have a name?"

"It is Adam detective," I answered then added, "So you do not ask me why the name. I gave it the name because it is the first of its kind."

"Original, I guess that is what we will call it then. Or monster if that is okay with you."

"How are we going to profile this for the report," Johnny says.

We remained silent for quite some time. Pete broke the silence.

"Doctor have you heard the parable?" he asked and continued, "Thy son will turn on thy father and will kill his father."

I did not know of this parable from the bible but I guess he was telling me. I should say he was predicting the human half of the creature. The half that would claim me as its creator.

"Doctor I need you to come to the precinct with me. We need to figure out how to kill this thing. You know things in this world are the way they are for a reason. Call it Mother Nature, God, but you fuck around with her or God's creation and the next thing you know it happens."

"What happens detective?"

"Mother Nature gets mad and all fucking shit breaks loose and death occurs," Pete exclaims.

From all the detective had said about the parable and what it meant. I knew I would indeed fine my demise at the hands of this thing I had created. Yes, my son in away.

CHAPTER 53

At the precinct Pete and Johnny listened to Mexican channel on the radio.

"This thing vanished for several weeks and the killings just stop abruptly. Something isn't right," Pete says concerned.

"Think it left the state Pete?"

"I wish it was going to be that easy."

The D.J went on with the question. Could it be "Chupas Cabras."

"The last sighting for that creature was in Puerto Rico," Johnny interjects then ads, "it is said that it is a small, framed creature that has a tear drop head. A spike or tooth like object that projects from the creature mouth. It injects its prey right below the victim's cranium where the neck runs into the head."

"I have to say our creature is not Chupas Cabras," Pete replies.

"Maybe it is a seven-foot tall Cabras?"

Pete smile and Johnny knew he was just kidding around. Pete scanned the photographs in front of him that where on the desk. They knew it was both from earth and the heavens now. Alien lifeform intertwined with human. Fuck! Even animals that are spliced with other dogs go crazy. And these are the same animal but different species. He scratched the top of his head then took a sip of his now cold coffee. He place the cup down spilling some on the desk.

"Hand me a paper towel Johnny." "What is the plan Pete?"

"The plan is we look at these damn pictures again."

"Why not it is not like I have a life anyway."

"Good I like that," Pete smile then says, "your girl is here now yes."

"Yes, about a week now."

"You go meet up with Beverly go get a bite and something else. Don't look at me that way you know what I mean. When you are done getting caught up meet me here and we will make a plan."

"You want me to go get a bite with Bev?"

"Hell, Johnny I was young once. And if Beverly is to going to be a detective's wife? take the good with the bad. She will have to"

"I did tell you I was going to her right?" pop the question

"Why yes you did grasshopper. Do it during lunch maybe the only chance you'll have." "Oh, before I leave Jenny called."

"Oh Hell. I forgot to call her back last night."

"I guess it will be the couch for you tonight," Johnny quips.

"Laugh while you can Johnny. Things change some when you live together. I will make it good with her. It is call experience."

"Yeah, better be like Tarzan big guy."

"Hell I will swing from a tree if I have to," Pete said they both laughed.

"We can pair up and go to the Jazz festival down at Waterfront Park."

"What did you say? Just now what did you say Johnny."

"Jazz festival down at the Waterfront," Johnny tells him.

"Jesus all mighty." "What?"

"The creature it wants to be seen. It has attacked and struck out in the open. It wanted to send us a message. You know an e-mail of sorts. It wants people to fear it. It wants them to know it is stronger than man. And that it can wipe man out without batting an eyelid. No, Johnny it is no pun intended. Two plus two makes four."

"But it has not been seen for weeks."

"Spring is here and it is warm. And it is probably hungry. It will show its hideous form at the festival."

Pete stood up abruptly grabbed his coat moved out of the cubical and made his way down the corridor. Johnny followed closely behind.

"You three officers come with me," Pete told them.

"We are off duty," said an officer.

"Well you are back on duty got it," Pete said firmly then stopped and faced the men then ads, "consider it over time."

"Where to," said the same officer.

"To the festival and we need to get there quick."

The tree officers, Pete, and Johnny, rushed out of the building making their way to the Waterfront. They did not know what they were in a rush to but they figured the detective had a good reason. They arrived in the middle of the evening rush. Bands played, and the art displayed, the food trucks, gathered people. Pete looked around.

"Keep your eyes wide open. Anything that does not look human scrutinize it without prejudice. If no one is in the way shoot the thing."

Johnny nudged Pete then pointed. They could see the ripples as the top of Adam's head pushed above the water level. It walked out slowly the water rushing down its side. It made its way onto land next to the condos on the west side. The condos where a rustic red color matching the color of the Union Train Station on the other side of the river. Night was creeping in like a blanket over the city of roses. It moved towards the Fremont Bridge two flags swayed in the breeze above the bridge. The ban played people laughed and others conversed as they ate and drank a beverage of choice. Pete saw Adam drop on all fours. It began to run in a powerful gallop. Like a battering ram it charged hitting several of the pedestrians out of the way. It rammed several tables scattering drinks food into the air. One of the red and white checkerboard table cloth landed on the creature. It gave it the appearance of a checkered ghost moving forward. Adam did not have an agenda or a plan or particular person in mind. Its only gold was to kill to cause fear and chaos. The tablecloth fell exposing the horrible creature underneath. Just feet away from it paralyzed by fear a teenage boy looked on. The boy did not even have time to scream when it attacked with blinding speed. The boy's mouth gapped open but there was no scream. A gurgle is all that could be heard as its claws ripped through his flesh. Pete, Johnny, and the three officers ran with all they had.

People ran screaming for people to get out of his way. Several parents called out to their kids. Adam released its grasp on the boy's throat. The boy toppled to the ground. It then reached down grabbed him by the arm and headed back into the Willamette River. The rain began to fall it was as if a storm had passed through.

"Oh, my God what was that thing?" A plump heavy set woman says as she is holding onto her husband's arm.

Adam made his way to the embankment of the river not looking back once. He drag the boy in after it into depth of the cold water. The boy's eyes open wide his hands moving wildly for that last breath of air. But to no avail the water entered his lungs filling them with the river water. It felt as if his lungs would burst. Then the quite of death set in as it took him. Bubbles escaped from the creature's gill. It opened its mouth filled with the jagged teeth. In a swift movement it was on the boy taking quick bites ripping flesh off the bones. Its movements became faster then, faster. Blood mixed with the murky water. Even in the depth of the water aqua life stood still just looking on. Silence filled the abyss of the river. The silence on the surface when danger approaches out in the wild was deadening. Creatures of our world know when something evil is present. It is like being out in the forest and as soon as the animals sense human danger the silence comes.

"Help me someone help me," a man called out.

Johnny saw an old man crying as he held on to his wife's chest. Johnny could see the old woman's head arch back as she tried to gasp for air.

"Call and ambulance out here," Johnny says to one of the officers.

The old man held her up the best that he could but she had become too heavy. She dropped to the ground hard before anyone could do anything. Pete closed his eyes for a second then opened them. It was like seeing a movie being played out through a projector. Children cried out in fright. Parents looked for their kids several rushed off with child in hand. An officer rushes to a three year old that stood next to one of the picnic tables. He stood there alone in taking in the reality of the horror. He pick up the boy cradled him in one arm. From a distance the father saw his son. He began to run with fear relief that his son was alive.

"Oh my god Joseph," he called out. Pete had just walked up to the office.

"Thank you, thank you," the man said as he grabbed his son into his arms.

Pete walked up to the river band. He looked out over the water. His mind raced on. The thought of the doctor ran through his head. He swore he was going to make sure the quack of a doctor would spend a lot of time behind bars.

Doctor or Scientist they had no right playing God. This man had crossed over the fine line teetering on the edge. His need to play God had caused death. He wondered does the one creature out way the lives of the many. Or does the one cause man's extension? One thing was curtain and that was he was going to capture this thing and kill it. Pete cleared his thoughts then stared at the flowing water as it made its way up stream.

CHAPTER 54

The following day at the precinct in Pete's cubical Dr. Jeffery Mongroll walked up to the opening. Pete and Johnny looked at the man surprised to see him. Pete studied the man for a moment curious what the man had to say. After a moment of silence Pete spoke.

"What can I do for you doctor?"

"I need to talk to you detective."

"Sit down doctor. Take my chair I have been sitting for a while. I need to stand up."

"Detective before you say anything else I want you to listen to what I have to say first," Jeff says as he sat down behind the desk.

Pete agreed to let the doctor talk. Johnny was about to say something when Pete cut him off.

"Let the good doctor tell us why I should not just lock him up. He created this killing machine so let's hear what he has to say."

"Detective I know you have seen what was in my laboratory. You destroyed most of my work. But it is a good thing that you missed it's brother. In the far corner the big cylinder tank against the wall."

"I saw it, beautiful creature," Johnny interjected in a sarcastic tone.

"No doctor Mongroll I figured it would blow up with the fire."

"Look, I understand how you fill about me detective. This thing its sibling is the only thing at this moment that we have that can be used against Adam. It just may hold the answer to how to kill it."

Pete turned his head to the cubical opening seeing Golds standing at the opening to the cubical.

"I Heard most of what he said Pete. Three days is what you have doctor," Golds tells him then walks away.

"I will have everything set ready to go," Dr. Mongroll says.

"Good in two days you will come in and brief the S.W.A.T., Team doctor. And a hunting we will go. You do understand Dr. Mongroll. You do understand if you do not show I will come after you and your colleagues."

"I'll be here. I will have something that you can use against the creature."

"Do not show and I will hunt you down like a dog," Pete tells the doctor.

Dr. Mongroll stood and made his way out of the cubical and out of the building.

"You want me to put a tail on the guy," Johnny says.

"No. I have a feeling he will show. For now, we just wait until Tuesday morning."

"I know how to kill it," Jeff whispers to himself. I know where you are going. I will kill you Adam."

Tuesday morning came around six a.m. Jeff looked at his watch as he walked into Gold's office. Moments later they walked into the briefing room. Chief Golds introduced Jeff to the S.W.A.T, team. The swat team scrutinized the doctor. Silence filled the room.

"Okay Doc., say what is on your mind," Golds says.

Jeff stepped up to the podium and introduced himself.

"My name is Dr., Jeff Mongroll. I know that you men, and women, here can handle yourselves in combat. You can handle almost anything that comes your way. This thing you will deal with is not human or animal. It is both. It is part animal and part man."

"Then what species?" asked one of the team.

"None, but it has a name. Adam. But this Adam will not start life as we know it. It will destroy life. This is one time you will need help. So, I have asked the Navy. I have requested the help of the Navy Seal Team for phase one. You men and women will be phase two for extra protection if we do not capture or kill this creature."

"That is fucking bullshit. We do not need the help of the Navy," shouted out one of the swat team from the back roll."

"The detective will take charge of the ground maneuvers."

"It is going to be a fish hunt. All we have to do is plug this thing with a few rounds and it will cease to be," said one of the women on the team.

"I and my colleagues created this creature. I know for a fact that it will not be a fish hunt. I created this thing for acknowledgement and the right to go into a history book for prestige. But the irony of it all is I will be known one day yes. But like all the great men and women of our world. I began to laugh as the last word left my mouth. I saw the look on the team's face so I explained my outburst. I laugh for the funny thing is that I will have to die first to be recognized. Now how to avoid this. No, I think not. It is inevitable. Death will be my reward. You see I ignored this invisible blanket of death surrounding me from the time of Adam's birth. As they say we reap what we sow. I smiled then continued on. Tomorrow morning the detective and his partner, the Navy Seal Team, S.W.A.T, and a Marine Biologist, the Coast Guard, and I, and my colleagues, will aboard the ship."

Wednesday came and before we boarded the Coast Guard ship I gave the particulars before we boarded. It had been the only ship available at the time that was equipped with a crane. The Navy Seals inflated the three small inflatable rafts.

They began to load up their equipment. All three rafts where ready to go. All they need was the go sign. At the bottom of the boarding ramp Dr. Robis introduced herself and saluted. The captain of the ship saluted brought his hand down to his side.

Robis was a tall brunette, on the thin side. She wore Benjamin Franklin glasses that seemed to ride at the bridge of her nose. It was the wired rim kind. She had freckles on her face but was an attractive woman in her late thirties.

"Request permission to board."

"Request granted," replied the captain.

"Doctor Mongroll and colleagues request to board."

Detective Rodrequiz, detective Ramirez," request permission to board," Pete shouts out.

After being granted the permission to board they made their way up on deck. Johnny scanned doctor Robis legs up and down. She had well shaped legs he thought to himself. Pete turned around looked at Johnny. Johnny shrugged his shoulders then whispered.

"What? She has good looking legs?"

Pete agreed she did have shapely legs. He smiled then stood at the front of the ship watch the Navy Seal Team below. Dr. Robis walked up to the submersible on the bow of the ship. She studied it for a moment then made her way up to the captain.

"Where to Doctor?" asked the Captain.

"Here in the Willamette between the Powell Bridge and the Fremont. Directly in the center of the river."

"Captain before we move how many men aboard."

"Twenty nine including me and now thirty with you and the rest that climbed aboard."

"Before you pull away from shore, I need to give my men their final orders. I need to brief your crew as well Captain."

"Understood Detective."

Pete called for Jenkin's after the Captain granted him permission to board. Pete gave him the orders for the Team. Moments later he gave his briefing of the danger of this abomination of life of this creature called Adam.

"Okay, pull the anchor up," shouted the Captain then ordered, "five nots slow and easy."

The sound on deck as the heavy chain that held the ships anchor clanked tight. The huge chain link chain began to pull the anchor out of the water. It set tight on the bows tip. The ship squeaked as the engine pulled them forward. Soft splashing sounds as the bow cut through the water. The Seals began to push their small inflatable rafts into the water. The seven men teams climbed into the rafts and slowly pulled out into the river. The two other teams pulled out as well.

The ripples from the water caused by the ship made their inflatables rock back and forth. Even at the slow pace they had pulled out into the center of the river in minutes. We were now dead center of the river. If the rive had, had a plug and someone had pulled it. We would have been suck under as if in a tub. Pete, Johnny, Robis, Jeff, Mary, and Jacob, stood watching over the river. Pete thoughts were he just hope it would end. Johnny wanted to put a bullet in its head. Jeff wanted it dead as Mary, and Jacob. Robis wanted to catch it for study. A creature never known to man and in her hands. What could she not accomplish she thought to herself? The Seal team in their wet suits gave creed to the nick name Seal. The ship stopped and anchored. The captain came out and spoke with Dr. Robis. She nodded her head then left. She walked up to Jeff. A huge crane was on the back of the ship as well as the submersible.

They were going into the water after the creature. Not a good ideal Pete thought to himself. At this stage he could not say much it was not his expertise. The Marine biologist walked to the back with Jeff and gave the thumbs up.

"Are your assistances ready Dr. Mongroll?" "They are ready doctor."

"Good we will now climb in and take our seats in the submersible Dr. Mongroll," she then walked up to Pete, "wish us luck detective."

"I wish you look for the sooner you kill it the less I have to worry about it," Pete said.

"True, true, detective," she said and smiled for she had no intention of killing the creature.

She put on her wet suit as did the rest of the team. They were ready. Jeff, Mary, and Jacob entered the submersible. Dr. Robis looked up at the helm and gave the captain the thumbs up to start to lift the submersible up and into the water. She looked around then walked into the submersible. Moments later they felt a tug from above as the chain became tight.

"Make sure the door is secure tight Dr. Mongroll."

Pete took his two-way radio, "Jenkin's get the men stationed and ready. Any sign of the creature on land cut it down."

"Done," he replies back.

"Dr. Mongroll make sure that the four air tanks are secured at that far wall," Robis say as she points to the tanks. There was another tug as the submersible lowered hitting the surface of the water.

"Buckle up its going to be a ruff entry into the water."

Mary rushed to her seat bumping against the wall several times. She quickly buckled up.

"Tanks secure, Dr. Robis."

"Well let's enjoy the ride," Robis tells them then speaks into a microphone.

Abruptly they were jarred again. The water began to climb up slowly reaching the bottom of the viewing port window. The search lights went on instantly as they went under.

Bubbles floated up as they looked out the viewing window. The bubbles looked like bubbles in a champagne bottle except five time larger. Each bubble having life of its own. They went below the surface. The water engulfing the submersible like a vacuum causing a slight suction as the river accepted the submersible in. Mary felt queasy as they became weightless as they began to descend.

Jacob felt as if he were on a roller coaster ride as well feeling as if he would puke. Jeff felt queasy as well.

"The feeling of motion sickness will soon leave," Robis assures them.

CHAPTER 55

The Navy Seal Teams stopped the rafts in the center of the river next to the ship. The men began to fall backwards into the water as they held on to their face mask. After entering the water, they waited. The team leader from each team gave the okay. They began their descent deeper into the abyss. One man from each team stayed behind. He would tend to the motor and would recover the men back into the boat when they came out of the water. He would hold a large plastic lasso just a few inches above the water. The loop purpose was so that the Seal could grab hold of it and be slinged into the raft. One of the leaders of the Seal Team popped up in front of the view port startling Jeff. Robis faced the view port the man gave her the thumbs up. He swam away into the murky water. I felt another jerk and my stomach became queasy for a moment. Then it came back as we hit the under current making us seem weightless for a few seconds. Mary tapped me on the shoulder and pointed. It was beautiful. I was looking at an eight-foot Sturgeon. In the depth of the Willamette water. It seemed as if we were in space literally. An open wide void of space and time. Dr. Robis smiled as she saw the look of awe in our faces.

"Beautiful down here isn't it? The Willamette holds many different species. The Willamette River is a universe of its own doctor Mongroll.

"Yes, doctor Robis I can see why."

"It was amazing. I have studied these waters and that of the deep ocean. I am still overwhelmed by the creature here in these waters. Right here a challenge of life. The evolution of animal and man existence. I wonder if the depth of these waters and its inhabitance have ever been really explored in deep detail?"

She was right the Willamette has never really been studied in depth. We descended deeper into the creature's domain. We remained silent as we watched the Sturgeon, Coho, Jack, and several other breeds of fish swimming by in schools. It was amazing, tranquil, mesmerizing, then a sudden thump. A huge plum of dirt circled the submersible making the water murky. A thick cloud of silt making it hard to see. We were now on the riverbed. Robis called up on her two way. She told the Captain they were on the floor. Up on top on the Coast Guard ship the Captain called down to the submersible. His voice came out over through the overhead speakers. His voice brought us back to reality.

"Dr. Robis."

"Captain keep an eye on the sonar." "Will do. All yours Doc." "Thanks," Robis said.

The doctor switched on the engine. We rose up off the riverbed. We waited several minutes until the dirt cleared. She pushed the lever and we began to move forward. On occasions we could see a Seal member shoot by. It was amazing to see them maneuver in the water. They were equipped with harpoon's and high-tech laser guns that had just been approved by the Government. The depth and the creature made the experimental weapon a good place to see what it could do. I know what many people believe and that is that technology will be or own destruction in the future.

"Rutter thirty degrees north and hold," she said to herself. We hovered in time and space like ameba's floating as a moon to a universe.

We then move downward again. We became weightless each time the under toe to the river swept us. I could see the Seal Team fighting with the under toe to keep control not to be swept away. In a way it was like seeing a fish fighting against a current. The laser lights shone like tiny blue rods in the water. Whatever the light pointed at that is where the laser would hit. The women Seal and two others where propelled through the water by the new surfboard torpedo. They were also equipped with high density light in front of the hover boards.

It was like a circus act with all the lights and movement. It was like the lights circling around a ring master of a circus as he spoke to the audience.   Suddenly it happened our hearts dropped. They began to beat as if to explode out of our chest with the excitement and fear. We caught a glimpse of something white. I figured it was a sturgeon at first. Then I noticed it had legs. I knew what it was at that moment.

"Over there Dr. Robis," Mary says.

The sphere moved ninety degrees around then moved forward until we were close enough to see it clearly. It just swam upright remaining in the same spot. It just stayed up right like a fairy in a story book. Then a twitch of its tail and it was gone. The horror of what it wanted to communicate was before us. It had brought us to its cemetery. To its cemetery of bones. Piles and piles of bones stripped completely clean of flesh. Human bones, dogs, cats, a few sturgeons bone lay in view. A graveyard of the dead. What I remember next is etched in my memory branded into my brain. I can still see the diver next to the sphere as his eyes opened wide. I knew what he saw and what was coming his way. I just hoped that I was wrong.

But like a bad nightmare it was upon him in a matter of seconds. Before he had a chance to move Adam attacked biting down ripping the flesh from the man's ribs cage. The Seal lifted his harpoon in desperation. He squeezed the trigger the spear release. It sailed through the water then slowed then pointed down then descended to the floor bed. Funny what you see when horror is there. The trident stuck in the mud. It stayed erect for a minute then fell flat on the floor. Another trident was hurled at the creature. A jet stream of small bubbles trailed behind the harpoon. It missed Adam impaling one of the other Seal members. The creature moved quickly out of the way. The Seals blood spread mixing with the murky water quickly. Another Seal pointed his laser at the creature. It was in target range the woman fired. Adam darted away ramming into another Seal making him twirl as if to make a cartwheel. Another Seal shot the harpoon it moved again out of the way.

The harpoon lodged into another of the team. Another Seal pointed his blue laser light at the creature as he use one hand to maneuver the hover board. Adam was swift it shifted like a missile it sliced through the water and attacked the man. Adam reached out pulled off the man's mask as well as his breathing apparatus. The man began to panic air bubbles escaping rapidly. He made an attempt to keep from breathing. He could not dawn on the mask. Or take in oxygen through the breathing tube fast enough. He made a desperate gasp for air that was invisible. He felt a violent bump to his side his breath escaped. He made gurgling sounds only heard in the depth of the river. Water entered his mouth his eyes open wide. Death set in releasing him. Lasers where now coming in from all different directions pinpointing on Adam. Adam was just too fast. Adam was in his element he was superior to any other life form in his habitat. Adam cut down several other members. One of the leaders to the Seal Teams told the men to fall back. Adam stood motionless in front of the submersible. At first I did not know why then the answer came to me in a few seconds. It positioned itself in front of the generator to the submersible. I knew what its attentions were then. We felt a hard shock from the blast of one of the weapons as it hit above.

"Abort, abort, the mission," Dr. Robis pushed the button and shouted.

The hoist became taut and a forceful tug. They only had several minutes of air left. They would have to hurry. The members of the Seal Teams surfaced including the dead. The man in the inflatable circled bring one by one back on board the raft. The other two operators of the rafts circled and hauled in the dead. They moved quickly back to shore. At the the bank of the river they jumped out and began to remove their gear. Jones and the other officers were ready. Several of the cops helped the Seal's remove their gear quickly.

The officers were equipped with 9mm, mp5n, submachine guns, others were equipped with 870 Remington pump action shotguns. At close range it would be lethal. It fired a two, three quarter, and a 3 inch magnum shell. Effective range of up to fifty yards. We felt another tug suddenly we were in air moving upward onto the deck of the ship. The water streamed down the sphere falling like pebbles of glass to the deck. We now were moving left onto the stern of the ship. The crane jerked we were like goldfish in a tank being moved. We were ten feet off the deck I felt my stomach crawl up to my chest. We began to lower until we reached about a foot off the deck. The cable to the submersible snapped. It was impossible how could it have been cut through. It was steel. Had one of the laser shot, have hit it. Whatever the cause did not matter it broke. We plummeted to the deck and did a titter roll back and forth. We were thrown around like rag dolls inside the sphere. I could see the sky zigzagging back and forth through the port hole. We gradually came to a halt. We were banged up but we were safe on board the ship. I got my composer before I assisted the others.

"Mary are you all right?"

She moaned messaging her head then said, "Hell of a ride."

"Dr. Robis."

"I am all right," she brushed herself off then said, "bumpy fucking ride huh."

"Yeah I would have to say yes." "Jacob."

"I am okay Jeff."

The Captain of the Coast Guard ship opened the hatch.

"Everyone okay in there."

"Captain I could not be more happy to see or hear your voice."

"Good," he said then barked out the order, "rutter forty degrees South."

Then the second in command repeated the order then said all ahead full.

"Keep it steady for a few more minutes," he told the man standing by his side then again gave the order, "rutter forty degrees south and hold."

The ship began to make a big circle.

"Release depth charges in intervals of thirty seconds."

These depth charges were made to a smaller scale than the ones use on destroyer submarines. But they had a punch strong enough to kill anything smaller than a sub. We made our way into the ships kitchen where all the equipment had been placed to monitor the creature. We made a complete circle.

The monitors were blank no indication of life or of Adam. We waited for at least an hour give or take a few minutes. Then what we dreaded the most happen. We went from elated shouting out that we had killed it. But away from our sonar and human eyes Adam clawed at the mud layers. Its claws like a backhoe moving its hands rapidly grabbing at the dirt with the rodent like fingers. It dug inch by inch making it back to the top of the bed floor.

The mud suddenly caved in and it was free. It filled its lungs with water. But like a flash of light in one's eyes the sonar began to beep. The dot on the screen began to move upward to the surface. The fear set in. The fear of what was coming. Adam shot up to the surface like a torpedo with one thing on its mind and that was to kill.

It caught the water in the webbing of its clawed hands and feet. Its tail shifted from side to side helping it to propel upward. It stopped on the surface and became motionless just floating on top. It looked in the direction of the ship. I looked at my colleague they as I wondered what it was planning. The calm before the storm is all I could think of.

"It is there and it is just floating there like a log," the captain said over the intercom system.

Dr. Robis on the bow of the ship stared out at the creature. It vanished back into the river. The captain came down form the helm and walked up to Dr. Robis.

"Doctor what the fuck just happen and what was that thing?"

"That my dear Captain is Dr. Mongroll's creation."

On the ground Sgt. Jones told the Seal Team his patrolmen were ready for a battle.

"Get the dead out of here," shouted one of the Seal Team leader as his feet hit the water.

The water splashed rapidly away from his shoe as he rushed to shore to take off his cumbersome gear. Johnny and Pete watched as the men that had been slaughtered by Adam were dragged away to the ambulance. Jones looked into the lifeless eyes of the dead staring out into space. They had left no man behind and that was the motto of the Navy Seal.

Suddenly everything came deafening quiet. The eerie feeling of the unknown of death of evil and the danger that was coming with it. All creatures including human's know when evil lurks in the mist.

"Fuck this is not good," exclaimed Jacob.

"Creature is moving," said the captain.

"What did you say Captain?" ask Robis.

"The creature is moving our way it is moving fast."

All we could do now was wait scared like fucking rabbits at the mercy of a wolf.

"I think we have problems Captain," said the second in command then clarified, "it vanished again Captain."

"That means only one thing and that is it is right under us," said Doctor Robis.

"It will wait and attack soon," Jeff says.

"You mean a surprise attack Dr. Mongroll," Pete stated the continues, "I told everyone that maybe that it would give us enough time to devise a plan of some kind."

Adam knew no love or any ties to human beings. It was superior in the fact that it could kill like a machine without any remorse. It need to be destroyed and not given the chance to breed. But the question I ask myself now is how many of us must die at its hands. We did not kill Adam but we did kill many fish of all kinds now floating on top of the surface of the water with their guts hanging out. My thoughts ran the scenario in my head then I got my answer. The answer to our problem was its sibling.

"Captain head for Salvie Island," I said.

I explained my theory with my colleagues and Dr. Robis. The anchor moved up and we were on our way. The wind rushed by us caressing our bodies. The clouds moved in which meant that rain would soon come.

CHAPTER 56

Twenty minutes later we arrived at our destination. We anchor at the base of the shoreline at Salvie Island. Adam's sibling was at the high priority list. We left the ship. Dr. Robis, Mary, Jacob, and I were now on the expedition to find this alien life form the third life form that escaped in the water. What it looked like we did not know. I hoped that this one was not a killer. It was getting dark. All creature scurrying about and to the eyesight a blur more of shadows moving about. We searched about four hours. We were ready to head back to the ship. It was cold and hunger had set in. It had been by luck that Dr.

Robis had looked down at that moment. She knew what it was instantly. She smiled then pointed as she spoke.

"Stop Jacob do not move. Look down by your left foot."

It was the small vial at the tip of his shoe. The small container had not opened or broken. This sperm like creature moved inside. But how? How could it live without air? She grabbed it then put it in a small brief case she was carrying. We wrap things up and quickly headed for the ship. I asked the captain if we could use the kitchen galley to construct a cage. I explained to the Captain the purpose of the cage. He agreed he knew we needed some kind of plan. We boarded the ship then returned to the Willamette. Jacob and I left the ship and returned later with the material and equipment we needed to build the cage. I requested the use of the crane to lift the material up onto the ship. Everything was ready. We took the tubes of metal into the kitchen. We waste no time in beginning the construct of the cage. After its completion I placed the organism in a small Petri dish in the center of the cage. I hoped my plan worked. I took an earthworm placed it next to its moving lips. It sucked away at the earthworm taking in its DNA. I knew it would grow at an unbelievable rate once it began to eat. I asked the detective to get one of his men to go and by manure. It was food for worms. It was like fertilizer to a plant. I locked the cage door behind me. No, sign of Adam yet. Two days passed. This thing grew rapidly its appetite was insatiable. It now stood taller than most men. It seemed to be a docile creature as of now. It did not attack. It just ate and slept. From within it began to make a high pitching sound indicating it was still hungry. We brought more manure and some ground up meat. It refused the meat. It was now about seven feet long. Its bulk was massive in diameter. We had to find out if it would attack.

Jacob said he would go inside the cage. Jacob hesitated then took in a deep breath then walked into the cage. He closed the door behind him. The creature opened its mouth wide. Jacob jumped back then just stood still. Jacob slowly raised the harpoon in his hand. He pointed the tip at the creature's head. It began to make a noise like that of a cow that had just been caught up in bob wire. And the terror setting in as the wire tighten around its neck. The sound made him feel a tingling sensation.

"Fuck these things are getting worst each time you decide to create something new Dr. Mongroll," Pete says.

Jacob made his way around then attempted to pet the creature. It seemed to calm down.

"Captain can I get your best high tech man up here. We are going to have a light show."

"Yes, doctor I will get him for you."

The captain walked away later he returned with high tech mechanic. He was a Navy Seal explosive expert.

"I figured you want more than a light show doctor?" says the Navy Seal.

"Doctor, you and your crew take a nap I will help this man. We will rig up this monster up with electricity. Electric show like ten time than that, that could kill it. The man looked too young to be an explosive expert Pete thought to himself. Still no sign of Adam. Why? What was it up too Pete's mind raced. Suddenly the Captain's voice came over the intercom.

"Dr. Mongroll, Dr. Robis, the sonar is picking something up."

Pete and the rest of the crew looked out over the bow of the boat. It was Adam and it was moving in fast. The creature reached the anchors chain. It began to climb up it. It was climbing up like a fly onto a wall.

"Get into position," the Captain told his crew.

"All hell is about to break out," Johnny said out loud.

The Navy Seal tech., walked up to the bow he told Jeff that it had been taken care of and handed him the detonator. Jeff nodded his head.

Abruptly the sound of the laser guns blasting away filled the air. The blast hit the helm then the side of the ship's bulkhead. We scrambled like damn zombies in the night. In this case not the living dead but the dead living. As I continue on with this story you will understand the analogy behind what I have said.

"Get to the kitchen," Pete shouted.

The blast where sporadic with the illumination of the lasers. We were able to find our way back into the ship. Adam screeched out. Men fell at it and side sliced open like loaf of spam.

"Mary," I called out.

"We are ready Jeff. Jacob is at the switch."

Jacob held the detonator that would allow thousands of volts to surge through the cage. The fight was stupendous a light show to remember. But it was a losing battle. Out of the twenty-four men maybe five remained alive.

"Get into the kitchen," the Captain ordered.

The creature followed. It entered the kitchen galley stopped staring at its sibling. We looked on. It made a gurgling sound as if to communicate with it. It stepped forward to the door. It scanned us but it knew we would not attack. It grabbed the cage door.

"Now, I shouted.

Mary blessed herself then crossed her fingers. Jacob moved the lever down. Sparks shot out. The lights flickered on and off. With each flash of light, you could see the face of someone staring in awe of what was occurring. It was like a strobe light. Still the charge did not stop Adam. It pulled the door off its hinges. It walked into the cage and up to the creature. It dropped something into its mouth. It looked dark so I have to say it was blood. That is what we thought. The blue blinding electric light moved up and down Adam. It leaned back screeched out loudly. It then turned and left. Pete and Johnny fired their weapons as they ran after Adam. At that moment the firing of weapons seemed like a free for all. Blast of fire hit everywhere. It jumped and splashed into the water. Rippled moved out as it went under. I ask myself? Why had it gone through all that trouble? What was it up to? I knew something was up. I just could not figure it out. Jacob pulled the lever up just a few small flashes of electricity ran down the creature and the bars to the cage. In the next couple of hours, it had grown bigger. We waited before entering the cage to examine the creature. This is when I noticed there had been a new addition to its makeup. It now had razor sharp teeth like Adam. Teeth that could slice with ease. I told the Captain I needed his tech again. I need a collar like device like a huge dog collar to put around this creature's neck. I told the tech to put high charge explosive and to attach it to the collar. After the collar had been made. We put it on the next day. I would have to enter the cage to get tissue samples. Everything seemed to be going well. Mary bent down to open its eyes. And what happen next happen so quickly. We did not have time to react to call out. I will never forget as long as I am alive. The screams the horrible screams that echoed out. Like a whip it reached out and had grabbed Mary's arm into its mouth. I cried out as if someone had pulled my heart out.

No. No. It ripped her arm right off. It ripped it off as if it were just a twig. It then pulled her up close to it. It bent down and began to eat the flesh off her back. Mary turned her head letting out a fainting sound. A soft moan and then her body went limp. In a matter of seconds, it was at her face ripping flesh off devouring her right before my eyes.

"Move back," shout the Captain.

I felt someone pull me away to safety. There was a loud blast. I became deaf. I felt as if I had an out of body experience. The blood and flesh of the abomination splattered on me. We reentered the cage I put out the remainder of the fire with the extinguishers. I scanned the area for Mary. I then saw her roll off one of the counters as she hit the floor. Her eyes wide open looking back at me. I felt as if she were say that it was my fault. But where was the rest of Mary's body? I had some of her blood, and flesh on me. I realized that she was next to this thing when the blast went off.

"God no, God no," I sorrowfully cried out.

I was going to stop it. I had always know what I had to do and now was the time. My creation my son the hideous creature I made. I was bound to it now in death.

"Captain I need your tech., man again."

I then ordered my colleague and Dr. Robis to cut the creature into small chunks. I told her to place then in the middle of the deck. I told the Captain he could tell the five remaining crew members that they could get to a safe place. He told his men but the men replied back that they would go down with the ship in a figure of speaking. The Captain nodded his head then told them to take their positions and to be ready. It would be a battle that they knew they could not win. I explained to the tech., what I wanted done once more. He acknowledged and left.

"Johnny take the boarding ramp. I will take point at the bow at the anchor. There will be no surprise this time." Pete says.

Adam would soon come. It felt that its sibling was no more. I hope that it would maybe give us that one chance we needed. I hope its human part would grieve. Then maybe it would know the same hate that I felt for it. It was the witching hour. I looked at my watch. Seven p.m. Now the gates of hell would open.

"I will be the last line of defense detective. I will be in the kitchen galley with the dead creature."

"I hope you know what you are doing Dr. Mongroll."

"It is poetic justice detective. I thy father. The son will kill thy father and thy father the son."

Pete knew what the doctor meant he knew he understood what he had told him.

"It is coming get ready. It is coming," shouted the Captain then he ran down to the quarter deck.

CHAPTER 57

Patrolmen, five of the ship's crew, seals, Pete, and Johnny fired as if a war had just broke out.

Though cumbersome on land in water it could move rapidly and with ease. Adam had one intent that was to kill. Its claws raked against one officer's face. Blood spilled out instantly. The man cradled his face in his hands. Blood seeped out between his fingers. Red droplets fell on to the ground. Adam took that moment to slash at the man's throat. The gash opened up wide letting his head rolled back. For a moment it was suspended in time as it hung by a strand of flesh from his body. The skin pulled stretching from the heads weight then gave way. The head hit with a thump then rolled twice and stopped. The man's eyes open staring towards the sky. Weapons cried out they prayed that they could hit that one vital area behind the creature's ear. But what they did not know was that in battle an extra bone grew over that one area keeping it from been hurt or killed. It grabbed another officer clawed his stomach spilling his intestines. It grabbed the man by an arm it took him into the water. It lashed out again cutting the man's artery. The water even though murky stained like a dull rusted color of red. The water churned as if boiling as Adam devoured the man before their eyes. Pete knew if this thing procreated fishing would not be the same as we know it. The though ran wild in his head. A rush of fear at the thought entered him. He looked at Adam it had reach the shoreline.

"Sgt. Jones get the man out of there move back," Pete shouted.

"You heard now move back," Jones shouts out to the men.

Night came now Adam was cloaked almost invisible to the human eye. Gun fire echoed out cries of dead filled the air. By the time we knew it Adam was on the ship. I remember this for I had just walked on to the deck. Again an onslaught of bullets echoed out. The ringing in my ears made it hard to hear. My eyes focused on the horror. It clawed, ripped, gouged, and decapitated, the crew. It gutted several men like a man would a fish.

Guns fired but it was a futile attack. I gazed at the heavens. The heavens held a vault of knowledge like no other. Men and women alike search and research for answers but for what real reason I ask? Is it to full fill a void in one self? Or is it the fact that what comes from the sky is mysterious and majestic. I had done a heinous crime again it was that I played God. We seem like Gods walking this planet at one time or another.

But if we look closely we cannot even began to compare to the great creator, God. His is pure a beauty and power like no other. It is his alone. Creation from his hand is call humanity, a miracle of life. Creation from man or woman hands that play God is called death. We dream of finding intelligent life that we may encounter out in space. We forget to ask the one question. That one question? What did advance life do to their world? I should have taken time to read and study the words on the vials. I should say I should have deciphered the lettering sooner. The alien language was not much different than ours. The linguistics was the same except for the vowels.

Here is the alien writing on the vials. DNGRS LF FRM DSTRY. Meaning, "Dangerous life form destroy." What had the aliens high tech., advancement cost them in their world. Had technology, knowledge, and Mother Nature rebel against them. Had genetic structuring been their only way to survive their world. Had they gone mad? I wonder how close I am to the real truth about their planet. Had their own species began to kill like rabid animals? All my life I have read of some kind of creation by man's brain. I hate to write this, but the fact is that man has created. But most of his creations have helped to kill man not cure. The only thing for certain in this life is death. I should have destroyed it when we had found the alien lifeform. I hear more gun fire. I looked up I saw the creature picked up a harpoon on the deck floor. It flung it at the man hitting him in the heart next to Johnny. The harpoon penetrated the man's heart and went out his back. His laser gun dropped out of his hands. He dropped hard on his knees. The man slumped over and was held up by the harpoon.

Johnny picked up the man's laser he pointed the gun then pulled the trigger. He dove making himself into a ball then rolled. He stood up fired but nothing came out of the gun.

"Fuck," Johnny exclaimed as he saw the creature moving his way.

"Push the red button down," one of the Navy Seal shouted out as he moved out of the way.

Johnny pushed down on the button the gun zapped on.

"Now come get some you ugly son of a bitch," Johnny says out loud.

He fired laser blast after laser blast but the creature proved to be too strong and too fast. It reached Johnny. Pete fired his revolver. Johnny dove out of the way of Adam's razor-sharp claws swept by. It screeched out in pain as one of Pete's bullets penetrated a soft spot.

"Move back into the ships quarters," Pete shouted.

They moved back down below deck closed the hatch behind them. There were loud thumps on the door. The metal door bent in the center. Another thump came soon the door would open. We all moved to the kitchen galley. Adam hit the door again and it was in. In moved in it now stood in front of the Captain. Adam slashed out blood gushed out of the Captain carotid artery. The Captain's head rolled slowly to the left then dropped to the floor. It bounced twice. Johnny caught a glimpse of the creature.

"Dr. Robis this way," Pete shouted.

You could see the fear in her eyes as she moved incoherently to our words. We moved in a rapid pace through the ship finding a safe place to hide. They entered into one of the sleeping quarters.

"Lock the hatch Johnny," Pete shouted. There was a moment of silence.

"We are getting out of here alive Dr., "Pete assured her.

We search the quarters for an escape route. "There Johnny," Pete said as he pointed to the porthole.

Johnny nodded his head then fired at the window. The window broke. At that instant it rammed the door. The laser gun dropped out of Johnny hand. Hitting the floor it went off shooting lasers blast as if someone were squeezing the trigger. It seemed as if the laser had bounced and hit all four walls. Another hard thump at the door and it gave.

"The chair place it next to the wall so we can climb out of the porthole," Pete says then grabs her by the hand and ads, "Dr. Robis look at me. Listen you will be alright. Just close your eyes pretend you are diving."

Dr. Robis went out of the porthole splashed into the water below. Frighten but she managed to start to swim for shore.

"Big guy," Johnny says.

Pete stepped on the chair then looked at the porthole. He grabbed his stomach the ten pounds he gained might be detrimental to their health he thought amused. Pete pushed forcing himself out. He was stuck at the waist.

"To many doughnuts partner," Johnny says. "Quit with the quips and fucking push." "A little goose will help you out."

"Funny Johnny fucking funny. This is no time for quips."

Johnny smiled then placed his shoulder at Pete's feet and pushed. Johnny grunted making it seem as if he were pushing something heavy as a car. Another loud thump the door almost gave way. Johnny jumped on the chair. He began to push himself out the porthole.

"Quit wasting time and jump Johnny," Pete shouted from below as he threaded water.

Another loud thump the metal door flew open. Johnny pushed and was about to make it out the porthole window. Suddenly he felt the razor-sharp claws sink into his Soleus and Tibialis posterior muscle. At the porthole half of him was hanging out. He suspended in air by the creature grasp.

His chin bones resting on the porthole window cause him severe pain. He moaned out loud but suppressed the screen of pain. He felt as if his legs would snap in half. In a way it was a good thing that the creature's claws where razor sharp. Johnny flesh opened and he was released. He fell to the water below half unconscious hitting the water hard. Pete grabbed him then began to swim holding on to Johnny making his way to shore.

"I just hope that the detective and his partner made it to safety. I knew it would not leave without coming to do what it had to. And that was to come to see me. These are the last words I will write down for I am reaching for the detonator.

The rest will be recorded by the overhead video camera. I will place the detonator on the desk away from its eyes. I cannot for see if I can detonate the explosives if I am attacked. Adam has entered the room now. It is standing before me. It suddenly lets out a screeching pitch. I stand here as it gives me a cold and deadly stare.

"Well my son do as you will it is time that we end all of this."

It stopped and just stood scrutinizing me then it came. Its lips snarled upward without a hint of warning. It did what I knew it would. It leaped forward all I could see were its jagged teeth. I held on to the detonator placed it next to my tail bone. I sat down as I felt its hands grab me. Its claws penetrate my skin. I had planned it to a T. There are no regrets. Finally, I released myself from the grasp of hell. The echo of the blast filled the air. Jeff had known that it would be him that would end Adam. In a way with all his love ones gone he did not mind. It was poetic justice of the most pure kind.